CROCODILE TRAPP

Also by Brian Callison

BRIAN CALLISON

Crocodile Trapp

HarperCollins*Publishers*

05712909

HarperCollins*Publishers*
77-85 Fulham Palace Road,
Hammersmith, London W6 8JB

Published by HarperCollins*Publishers* 1993
1   3   5   7   9   10   8   6   4   2

© Brian Callison 1993

Brian Callison asserts the moral right to
be identified as the author of this work

A catalogue record for this book
is available from the British Library

ISBN 0 00 223805 5

Set in Trump Mediaeval

Typeset by Harper Phototypesetters Limited
Northampton, England
Printed in Great Britain by
HarperCollinsManufacturing Glasgow

Autobiographical Note

There have been happy periods in my life.

And then there have been my voyages with Trapp.

Not that I wish to convey the impression that having sailed as Trapp's Chief Officer, no matter how deviously – to say nothing of repetitively – he's manipulated me into so doing has fuelled any resentment within me.

Please – no. No, I beg you not to assume that at all.

No more than I would have you conclude, simply because such craven duplicity on Trapp's part has invariably resulted in my playing surrogate *paterfamilias* to his whole degenerate menagerie of ocean-going psychotics as WELL as second fiddle to that pugnacious, dogmatic, utterly irresponsible tyrant of a captain – and all *that*, I might add, despite my being a fully certificated master mariner in my OWN right – that those vile experiences have . . . well, left me ill-tempered or embittered or spiteful or anything.

I mean, have I ever claimed that Trapp MEANT to cause World War Three to break out during our last voyage . . . ? That he *deliberately* manoeuvred the Superpowers as they were then to the very brink of scrapping *glasnost*, forgetting the whole idea of a Russian Commonwealth, and settling for thermo-nuclear Armageddon instead?

No, I haven't. Not once. Because I fully accept that, like the rest of Edward Trapp's monumental screw-ups, all those British and American and Soviet warships sinking each other had simply been one more accidental consequence of the bloody man's obsessive pursuit of profit.

So I bear him no malice whatsoever. I wasn't even surprised things turned out that way. I've always known that Trapp possessed a . . . well, a sort of *affinity* for upsetting the status quo. That conflict and mayhem and intrigue will trail as surely in the wake of the Captain's avaracious passage through life as vultures will home on a soon-to-be cadaver.

I don't even argue that Trapp is unique. Genseric the Vandal had much the same predilection for mass destruction. So did Ivan the Terrible . . . Genghis Khan . . . Hitler.

Though there is one significant difference, I grant you. Those other megalomaniacs had help - Chiefs of Staff and armies and Hordes and things - whereas Trapp never needed any. Trapp's ego has always afforded compensation enough for such personnel shortfalls. The Captain's conceit, his bloody-minded obstinacy; his cupidity; his ill-humoured talent for overlooking the obvious and ignoring sensible advice from me have invariably proved more than adequate to escalate any perfectly ordinary crisis to catastrophic proportions.

But I must repeat: I harbour no malice towards him.

I mean, it wasn't of *my* choosing, was it . . . ? That one of my happiest of happy times just happened to coincide with the conviction on my part that Trapp had . . . well, had finally got himself killed at last?

I first became aware of that - ah - intensely saddening possibility in the days immediately following his Libyan Bomb fiasco.

The one I've briefly touched upon already. When he set out aboard his mouldering hulk the *Charon II* - or was she the *Charon III* . . . ? I tend to lose count of how many ships Trapp's managed to get sunk under him. *And* under ME! Anyway, that last voyage in which Trapp - according to *his* appreciation of the master plan - set out with some very strange passengers to rob a small desert branch of The Bank of The Socialist People's Libyan Arab *Jamahiriyah* . . . yet somehow finished up carrying a cargo of deep-frozen dead men; being chased by a thinking torpedo twice as clever as Trapp could ever hope to be, and completely shattering Colonel Brother Mu'ammar al-Qaddafi's ambition of becoming the sole proprietor of an Arab nuclear capability.

Oh, and like I've already mentioned - causing World War Three to break out between the Superpowers as they were then, for an encore.

A happily brief conflict, I have to concede. With only a few warships sinking each other but, nevertheless, one which had the end result of making them – the Superpowers as well as the Libyan High Command – extremely disgruntled with Trapp.

. . . But to engage in too specific recollection yet again and so soon after the event would be unbearable. *Trapp and World War III* is a nightmare already recorded, and one upon which the doctor in Djibouti said I should not dwell. Another of those tales by which I've tried, in a desperate attempt to exorcize the stress-fiends within me, to relate the bizarre events of all my previous voyages under Trapp's erratic command.

Like our first. When I was given the choice by a quite unreasonable Admiral of either being shot or sailing as First Lieutenant to Trapp's original and thankfully long-drowned Q-ship *Charon*. The one I later referred to in *Trapp's War*: a euphemism, really, to describe the horrendous special operation in which Lieutenant Commander Edward Trapp, Royal Navy, not only commandeered a critical part of His Britannic Majesty's desperately needed firepower to deploy as a tool of piracy, but also did a deal with an equally squalid element of Hitler's *Kriegsmarine* to further his madcap determination that, if the Second World War had to be fought at all, then it should be fought along strict commercial lines.

And then came our second voyage. Embodying what *Trapp* considered his Machiavellian strategy to make a killing from the Peace which followed. Which, to give him his due, he did. Only it wasn't quite the kind of killing he'd intended. A lot of would-be criminal entrepreneurs of Middle Eastern origin discovered too late that Peace, when Trapp organized it, was anything but peaceful.

As did quite a few Chinese gentlemen of the Hong Kong Tong persuasion who found themselves abruptly and unpleasantly deceased.

And a few multi-national corporations specializing in marine INSURANCE . . . !

I'm sorry. It's just that I get carried away sometimes. I know I'm supposed to be recording only the more recent past. Starting from the aftermath of Trapp's Libyan shambles.

So, without intending to further confuse – I finally managed to convince the submarine captain who rescued us that, really, the whole embarrassing affair had been nothing whatsoever to do with me: that I'd just been Trapp's Chief Officer and bound by the Merchant Service Act to carry out his orders, so he let me stay aboard while – acting, he told me somewhat waspishly I thought upon a unanimous decision taken by the United Nations Security Council – the Royal Navy did its duty and got rid of Trapp as ordered.

By landing him ashore in Beirut. In the precise dead centre of the killing ground between two opposing militias.

The irregulars were engaging in their routine dawn hate at the time: their pre-morning-prayer artillery barrage. It was then that I felt a first tentative surge of optimism. It hadn't escaped me that Trapp's commercial acumen had, over the years, earned him more than a few disenchanted ex-business associates in the Lebanon. I felt quietly confident that, if the Beirut Boys even suspected it was him out there in no-man's-land, they'd've cheerfully depressed their gun barrels and joined in common purpose for the first time in twenty bloody years.

But there was no way I could tip them off openly. Not with the submarine's officers so tight-lipped and jumpy; all anxious to dive before Trapp talked his way back aboard . . . and even with the aid of binoculars it had proved quite impossible to make out the confirmation I craved. Not through all that smoke and exploding sand.

It meant my being plagued with concern for Trapp's safety over the succeeding weeks. About whether or not he'd managed to survive.

I just *knew* the bloody man possessed the innate ability of a trapdoor spider to disappear from ground zero when the going got tough.

But despite that niggling uncertainty my health started to improve from then on. Months passed without word from Trapp. Either the separated parts of him really *had* gone to walk that great ship's bridge in the sky, or he'd at last learned enough sense to adopt a low international profile.

Even my nervous tic, a legacy of the Trapp years, began to subside, now betraying itself only in the face of extreme trauma . . . the sort triggered by overhearing a chance Glasgow accent in some waterfront bar which, until I became adept at controlling an unreasoning panic, recalled awful memories of yet another noisome, insanitary creature called Gorbals Wullie who simply had to be the most bizarre of all the Captain's flotsam companions – a fawning, cowardly, moronic scarecrow of a mini-Scotsman who Trapp kept as an alternative, albeit a rather less intelligent alternative, to a pet goldfish.

Mind you, on second thoughts I don't know about Wullie being the most bizarre. Certainly he was the dirtiest . . . but then again, Blind Spew – Trapp's hulking, disarticulated Second Officer – now HE took a bit of beating when it came to weird.

Oh, admittedly Mister Spew had been the most amiable of all Trapp's ocean-going psychopaths, and he did try very hard to please . . . but what d'you do with a navigator who can't even find his mouth when he's eating? Keeps throwing most of his dinner over his left shoulder 'cause his co-ordination's shot to hell . . . ? And, while I'm on the subject – I frequently had to call into question Spew's academic ability. For one thing, I'd always clung strongly to the old-fashioned conviction that a ship's navigating officer wasn't *supposed* to need a postal correspondence course in ship navigation while he was actually navigating a ship . . . and secondly – it hadn't helped Spew all that much even when the mail did catch up with him. Seeing he couldn't bloody well read anyway.

While as far as Spew's being a WATCHkeeper . . . ? The guy only HAD one eye, and that wasn't exactly eagle sharp – even in broad *daylight* he kept bumping into things like masts and deckhouses and lifeboats an' stuff.

Or would have done.

Had Trapp ever owned a vessel that actually CARRIED any lifeboats.

. . . And then there was Trapp's new Chief Engineer – the one who'd replaced Maabud Something-or-other after Trapp got the little Egyptian killed by Zarafique the Iceman. At least Maabud Whatsit had been experienced: been Chief of the *Cairo Flyer* for years before he signed on with Trapp, which would've made him a good man to have as senior engineering officer, except the *Cairo Flyer* turned out to have been a bloody RAILWAY engine . . . !

Anyway, getting back to his successor: Trapp's current Chief was a blob of muscular grease on bandy legs called Popeye Bucalosie: ex-Cosa Nostra *Contrabandieri*, professional assassin and mechanical genius. Trouble was, Bucalosie's genius extended no further than to repairing Fiat getaway cars and the working parts of flick-knives. Mind you, he had hidden depths: I soon discovered, when the water started coming in, that Chief Engineer Bucalosie could've also gained a Doctorate in Panicking. I used to think the chap had *some* merit: had at least tried to learn to love someone other than himself . . . until I discovered the only reason Popeye Bucalosie had 'POPE . . !' tattooed on one arm was because he ran out of lire before the tattooist had quite finished . . .

And then there was the last of Trapp's key seagoing executives . . . Bosun Bligh. Well, I mean – what *can* I tell you about Bosun Bligh? Except that he was a certificated homicidal maniac; spent most of his time aboard trying to kill me, and conversed only in four-letter words at the top of his voice.

But I'm wandering off course again. Even the thought of a Glasgow accent does that to me . . .

Then I would remember with exquisite relief that they'd frogmarched Gorbals Wullie into the exploding sand along with Trapp: protesting every inch of the way, as was Wullie's wont, about his being protected by *thon Geneva Convent* in between screaming and grovelling and embarrassing everybody – not, I hasten to emphasize, that I disliked Wullie. It's just that getting blown up by a few artillery shells wouldn't've made *that* much difference to the normal state of the scruffy little turd anyway.

I'd actually got to the stage of sleeping again through part of each night.

I'd even got myself a seagoing job. Almost as soon as I changed my name yet again from Miller to Smith . . .

Okay, so I concede it wasn't much of a job: not exactly captain of the Queens. Not sailing as replacement master of a clapped-out nineteen-thirties three island trampship called the *Bar Abir* after even her previous old man had deserted; jumped his own command in Djibouti to enlist in the Foreign Legion in search of a better quality of life.

But frankly, after Trapp I didn't care.

It didn't matter to me that the *Bar Abir* was owned by an Afro-Cuban syndicate who ran refresher courses for Mafia hit men, and who operated out of Aden or Port Sudan or somewhere else not exactly uppermost in Interpol's minds.

It didn't matter when I discovered my employers had a way of moulding the opinions of previously incorruptible marine surveyors sent from Lloyds to assess the *Abir's* seaworthiness by offering them alternative modes of returning to their loved ones. Either they travelled home in an aircraft seat dressed in an expensive suit on the house, or in the baggage hold wrapped in a greaseproof parcel.

Wrapped, in fact, in several greaseproof parcels . . .

It didn't matter that I drew certain less-than-subtle conclusions from discovering that the only creditors, including her crew, who'd been paid for the preceding seven months had been her Insurers. Quite specifically, the premiums they demanded to ensure full cover in respect of her total loss.

It didn't even matter when, having tentatively prodded the eggshell thickness of hull plating not yet dissolved by rust, I confirmed the *Bar Abir* for what she was – a coffin ship. That it was a racing certainty she was scheduled to founder in the middle of some not-too-distant night without my realizing it until I began to float gently out of my bunk. Or maybe go with a little more flair: hit a five foot high wave and break in two.

Or simply blow up in deep water when her boilers decided to empty into her fireboxes. With or without the bomb that was probably hidden aboard to help them.

None of those trivialities mattered. Like I said, the *Bar Abir* afforded me anonymity. A refuge. A whole new dimension of peace. Pneumonia, drowning, high flying dismemberment – any one of those likely options was still infinitely preferable to

11

getting involved yet again with Trapp and that collection of sub-human flotsam he had the absolute gall to call a crew.

But fate was to decree that happiness – true Trapp-free happiness – was merely a fleeting wisp; a cruel illusion . . .

You see, my trapdoor spider theory had been right.

All that Beirut high explosive. Bloody well wasted.

My biggest mistake had, of course, been in assuming that *Trapp's* idea of maintaining a low international profile would've been the same as any normal person's.

Which meant that while I, happy in my false sense of security, was commanding my own coffin ship instead of being chief dogsbody aboard one of *his*, Trapp, on the other hand, was preparing the ground for . . . well . . . making himself a thoroughly undesirable hostage in the Lebanon; getting himself hijacked in an aeroplane; meeting a highly suspect ghost and, as a consequence of those perfectly routine Trapp-type events, planning a new career path for himself . . . by deciding to become a great white CROCODILE hunter!

Not that I meant a hunter of great white *crocodiles*, by the way. No . . . No, I mean that he – Trapp – was deciding to become a great white hunter OF crocodi – !

In Papua New *Guinea*, f'r Chrissakes . . . ?

Chapter One

Apparently it all started with Trapp conducting his daily interrogation.

Which, in Trapp's case, meant lounging comfortably on a lice-infested straw mat, very much in command of the makeshift cell despite his manacles, and glowering at his Palestinian jailer.

'What d'yer mean mister – NO-one *nowhere* won't pay no ransom?'

The Beirut Commander of the People's Front for the Liberation of Somewhere-or-other looked blank. He didn't think he'd said it quite like that. Surreptitiously he attempted to conceal his Iraqi-made machine pistol behind his back to avoid appearing more contentious than neccessary. Ever since they'd sent him into the Lebanon to negotiate an exchange deal in an already totally-collapsed hostage market he'd learned to dread these meetings with his fractious charges.

The Chief Fractious Hostage especially: the Zionist-Imperialist lackey called Trapp. The one he couldn't get rid of even when the kidnap business had been at its peak. The thoroughly unhelpful Englishman who persisted in wearing a blanket quality brass-bound seaman's reefer jacket in uncompromising defiance of the 120° heat: exploded-toed rubber things that may have begun life as vaguely white tennis shoes back in World War II, and a British Merchant Navy officer's cap which, because its partly severed lid bobbed up and down each time its owner moved, did tend to look rather more like a half opened tin of dog food.

'Christ, it wus a simple enough question, wusn't it?' Trapp appealed irritably to the blast-fractured ceiling. 'Can't *none* o' these bloody Ayrabs understand plain English?'

Gorbals Wullie, who was chained to the opposite wall, sniggered intimately. 'Nae educashun, Captin. They cannae talk proper: no' like us.'

But then Gorbals Wullie, himself commanding a turn of phrase slightly less comprehensible than that of a mentally retarded parrot - to say nothing of the tactful discretion of your average Victorian-era British seaman when engaging in loud verbal intercourse within earshot of frogs, wogs, micks, spicks or dagoes - Wullie always had felt most at ease when Trapp's venom was directed towards someone else.

He'd miscalculated. Trapp fixed his co-hostage with an equally malevolent glare.

'Talk proper - YOU? I've had philosophical discussions with dried-out *barnacles* more intelligible than you . . . an' it's all your fault anyway'.

'Whit is?'

'Us bein' stuck here.'

'No it's no'.'

'Yes it is!'

'No it's . . .'

'LISSEN!' Trapp exploded. 'We 'ad a nice comfortable hole out there when the shells was fallin', din't we? And we could've easy sat it out 'til they got fed up an' went back to shootin' the shit out've each other, couldn't we . . .? Except that YOU wouldn't stop bloody screamin' an' grovellin' an' attracting everyone's attention - WOULD yer?'

'There wis a horrible big crawly insect in thon hole,' Wullie protested defensively.

'I *know* there WUS!' Trapp roared, positively clanking with frustration. 'I'm bloody TALKIN' to it . . . !'

'Excuse me pleese,' the Palestinian broke in timidly. 'Can we concentrate on the problem of your release?'

'No we can't because it's not MY problem, Ali Baba,' Trapp snarled. 'I din't take myself hostage, did I? I din't ask to be bloody chained up an' starved f'r months on end . . .'

'You keep Choker *Bligh* chained up f'r months on end,' Wullie interjected spitefully; it still rankled that he'd been classed as an insect. Which he most emphatically wasn't. He didn't have enough legs to qualify.

'I keeps the *Bosun* chained up because he has a habit of tryin' to assassinate Mister Miller the Mate if I don't,' Trapp, mercurial as ever, pointed out perfectly reasonably.

'Well then, I still dinnae agree aboot the grub. It's no' too bad,' Wullie persisted, secure in the knowledge that not only might he curry himself a little favour with his captors, but also that Trapp's chain was just too short to reach him. 'Come tae that, Captin, they've gi'ed you much the same rations you've always given us lads in the foc'sle. Except the Arab stuff's been better cooked.'

'There's gratitude for you,' Trapp complained to the Commander, suddenly morose. 'I feed my crew like kings, I do, and that's all the thanks I get.'

'I understand only too well, *effendi*!' the Palestinian agreed sympathetically. 'I do my best in these difficult times to feed my liberation fighters, my brother *fellaheen* ... yet still they complain – "*This* soup is sheet: that mutton is crap . . ." '

'D'you know, mister,' Trapp gloomed, by then totally preoccupied with his own injustices, 'that I once give 'em solid protein: prunes and stewed kidney an' custard an' pilchards in tomato sauce, f'r weeks on end?'

'Aye! Usually all together,' Wullie muttered, concerned he was losing the debating edge. 'He picked up a load o' water-damaged cargo cheap 'cause all the labels had soaked aff the tins . . . Ah'm telling you, Abdul: for months after, eatin' oor dinners wis like sitting down to a game o' Russian roulette.'

Bored Christian militiaman firing from somewhere hopelessly out of range began directing random bursts towards the Muslim positions. A line of M16-calibre holes stitched the already perforated wall above Gorbals Wullie whereupon Wullie, who'd always tended to make an absolute fetish of self-preservation, promptly curled into a much-practised ball and hit the debris-strewn deck, scrabbling and shoving to take cover behind his captor.

Trapp, black-furious once more, clanked ponderously to the barred window. 'Blind as bats, aren't yer? How often do I have to tell yer – he's only little . . . aim LOWER!'

'Sorry about that. Ignore them for the dungs of camel that they are. Infidel tools of the Anglo-Israeli-American dogs,' the Palestinian spat routinely. '. . . But to return to more pressing matters. I have good news for you, sir. My superiors have decided that this situation cannot continue: that the hostage market has totally caved in since the good old days when a Holy Jihad really *was* a Holy Jihad . . . and that you and the Grovelling One are therefore free to go.'

Wullie stopped grovelling momentarily, outraged. 'Whit d'ye mean . . . *grovelling*?'

Trapp stopped clanking. Outraged. 'What d'yer *mean*: FREE?'

'If you an' the Ayatollahs think you're going tae get the Captin tae do onything for free, pal,' Wullie predicted delightedly from the floor, 'then youse has another think comin', so youse have.'

'I have tried vairy hard to exchange you,' their jailer ventured. He'd feared it would end up like this: unpleasant and acrimonious. 'First I try the British Ambassador. Then the United States Ambassador. Then the French, then the Italian, then the Swiss . . . they all slam their gate in my faces: tell me, 'No deal. Piss off!'

'The British *Ambassador* said that?' Wullie looked impressed.

'You should've tried the Turks,' Trapp growled airily, then looked pompous. 'It so happens I got important connections in Istanbul. A long-time financial associate. Distinguished business gentleman: name of Korkut Tokoglu the Fifteenth.'

'Not any more you don't,' Wullie reminded him. 'Korky's called Tokoglu the Deceased now – you got his throat cut for him by accident last time we wis doing business doon the Grand Bazaar. Anyroad, Captin, did you no' say he wis jist a robbin' old Turkoman coot?'

Trapp ignored his co-restrainee loftily. 'Well?'

'Piss off!' the Commander shrugged. Then added hastily, 'Their words, sair; not mine.'

'Then what about the Sudanese? The . . !' Trapp struggled to overcome his aversion, '. . . even the *Australians*?'

'Piss . . !'

' . . . off?' Wullie hazarded. Certainly the phraseology held the ring of authenticity with the latter.

Trapp made a valiant attempt to rally.

'Course if you'd done some proper market research, put any thought at all into it, yould've gone straight to one o' the new Russian republics,' he said deprecatingly. 'Seeing I'm just the kind o' new blood the Ivan economy needs. Noted expert in the field o' internashnul maritime commerce? Champion o' free enterpri -'

'I did. They mentioned something about the old Soviet Navy losing their top gun *Spetsnaz* - their best Special Service team - because of you. And a . . . brand new submarine?'

'Piss off again?' Wullie hazarded sympathetically.

'I theenk so,' the Arab confirmed. 'My Russian is not so good but I do know an AK-47 gun barrel when I see one.'

'Greeks . . . Chinks? The *Liberians*?' Trapp muttered desperately, really starting to grasp at straws.

'Piss OFF?' Gorbals Wullie anticipated ecstatically.

' "Diplomats" they call themselves.' The Arab shuddered reflectively. 'You wouldn't believe how crudely picturesque the Afghans can be when they want to underline a point.'

Trapp retreated into sulking non-cooperation. 'Well, like I said - me bein' your hostage ain't my problem . . . apart from which, Ali Baba, it's about time your galley came up with some lunch. It's past eight bells an' me stummick's rumbling.'

'Soon, pleese.' The Commander drew a deep breath and pressed on. 'But after that I am ordered to escort you to the Syrian border and there, sair, to release you and the rest of your crew . . .'

' 'Ang on a minute. Here I am, thinking 'ow important it was to maintain a basis of mutual trust between us, an' I catch you out in a lie,' Trapp broke his sulk to look as irritatingly virtuous as he always did when it wasn't one of *his* being exposed. 'I distinctly remember you sayin' you'd exchanged my crew six weeks ago f'r artillery shells from the Christians 'cause they were too abusive an' noisy - my lads, that was: not the Christians.'

'I am not . . . what you say - a twister, mister?' their host responded stiffly. 'The infidel dogs sent them back. They hinted we were conducting biological warfare: that your men were a public health risk.'

'Oh, aye? So what aboot the ammo you conned?' Wullie countered, making it very clear that, in his view, the whole tawdry arrangement smacked of sharp Middle Eastern practice.

'We sent every round back,' the Palestinian assured him - and smiled for the very first time.

'Well, I'm still not GOIN' and that's flat.' Trapp sat down again and folded his arms firmly. 'Not into a dump like Syria. Even a

17

sandfly with half a thought in its head wouldn't go to *Syria!*

'Syria's all right,' Wullie argued on principle.

'See what I mean?' Trapp said.

'. . . There's no *way* we can afford to send you to Macao, sair,' the Commander pleaded wearily two hours later. 'Since his Excellency Sadaam Hussein went down the tubes credibility-wise, we're fighting this Holy War on a shoestring already.'

'YOU'RE onna shoestring?' Trapp retorted furiously, the negotiating bit firmly between his teeth now. 'So what about me an' MY lads, eh? A whole ship's crew kept sat sittin' about, denied the chance to get back aboard an' earn a livin' wage plus a bit o' miserable profit for their Owner – who's gonna pay f'r *that*, then?'

'But I understood you don't have a ship anymore, sair. That you sank yourself in the Gulf of Sirte.'

'Little misunderstanding over a bomb,' Trapp dismissed airily. 'It's not a precise science, seamanship.'

'And you don't pay the crew either, Captin – they pays you,' Gorbals Wullie pointed out, switching loyalties chameleon-like in the interest of fair play. 'You sign on lads that's on the run frae Interpol an' desperate f'r a berth onywhere outward bound, then charge 'em hush money . . .' He turned to the jailer, preening himself. 'All except me, o' course, Alladin. Ah'm Key Personnel. Salaried staff. I get mah own mug, one square meal most days an' a pot of jam every Christmas.'

'You may be interested to *learn*,' Trapp informed his Key Personnel tartly, 'that your nex' season's festive pot o' jam has just gone right down the same tubes as Hussein . . . so how about sending me an' my lads to Karachi, then? That's not so far. While Paki Immigration don't have no hang-ups about entry visas an' stuff once they see a few rupee notes stuffed inside a passport.'

The Palestinian shifted guiltily. 'They will in your case, sair.'

'Oh, you DI'N'T go and *ask*, did you?' Trapp grumbled, then glared at Gorbals Wullie whose lips were already forming the anticipatory letter 'P'. '. . . An' don't you DARE say it!'

'There's always Ethiopia,' the Commander mused. 'We work vair close with the counter-counter revolutionary forces over there. I might manage to swing a few airplane tickets to Addis

Ababa on something they don't plan to hijack!'

'Now that might bear a bit o' consid'ration,' Trapp conceded doubtfully. 'But then again, as a ship's master I got certain standards to maintain. They'll need ter be top seats, Aladdin: promenade deck accommodation? I ain't flying zoo class in no Air Ethiopia stringbag!'

But Trapp never had been capable of differentiating between chancing his arm and committing outright suicide. Wearily the Palestinian unslung his machinegun and laid the muzzle alongside his tormentor's starboard temple with the air of a man about to terminate negotiations.

'Pleese, I wish you to know, *effendi*, how much I admire your courage. Your willingness to die rather than compromise on standards!'

Wullie stuck his fingers in his ears. 'Jist remember, General: Syria wis perfectly OK by me!'

'O.K. - so we settle f'r Business Class . . . split the difference?' Trapp suggested, reasonable to a fault.

'I still say they got no sense of humour, them Ayrabs,' Trapp grumbled, craning round for the fiftieth time to survey the crammed after end of the fuselage balefully. 'When I said "zoo" I *meant* it more jocular than bloody prophetic!'

They'd been flying for nearly an hour. The aircraft was full and the Captain was in his usual foul mood. Which was appropriate really, seeing there were quite a few of them aboard - fowls, that was.

Plus ducks, a sheep's carcass being fondly transported on its final approach to some eagerly awaiting Ethiopian stockpot, and a tethered goat. A very alive goat. A goat that, from the evil glint in its eye, appeared no more enchanted with the aviator life than was Trapp.

There was Trapp's crew as well, of course, sprawled untidily in the forward section. All except the Bosun, Choker Bligh, who - just because he'd tried to bite the head off a duck which had given him a provocative sideways glance - had been stuffed back in his straightjacket and propped against the galley.

And then there were the human passengers: mostly Arabs with

19

a sprinkling of Japanese. Co-traveller-wise, from their point of view the goat must've seemed infinitely more appealing than Trapp's mob.

So, come to that, must the dead sheep.

'Mind when you was rude aboot Air Ethiopia, Captin?' Gorbals Wullie, never one to miss an opportunity for snide comment, sniggered from the bucket seat beside him. 'You wis jist bein' your usual optimistic self, was you . . . ? *Fly Abdul's Pan Eritrean* the brochure said. *The happy traveller's dream*. And ah thought Dakotas went oot wi' the last tea clipper.'

The aeronautical equivalent of an Arabian coffin ship lumbered into an air pocket and simply stopped flying for two thousand feet pretending it was a lump of rock. Terrified shrieks from the less resolute of Trapp's crowd – which meant most of them – filled the compartment along with a pillow fight of displaced feathers from the aircraft's winged complement. Bosun Bligh, on the other hand, started to cackle in manic delight at the prospect o' all them greasy bastids bein' sick at the same f*$%*&! time while Trapp's Key Personnel promptly stopped being a smart arse and took refuge in his standard foetal cringe.

The Captain himself lashed out irritably to remove a by-then totally disoriented duck which had force-landed on his lap.

' '*Scuse* me, Cap'n?' Mister Spew called amiably from the row behind. But Blind Spew was never phased by crises: in fact Spew, being a bit of a slow thinker, never actually got round to realizing a crisis was happening until it was history.

'WOT?' Trapp snapped, trying to land a last vindictive punch at the fleeing duck.

'I, er . . . I dunno now.' Mister Spew's eyebrows collided in the middle. 'I fink I forgot.'

'Jesus,' Trapp gloomed.

'Never mind, couldn't've been important . . . By the way, would yer like to say 'allo to my new friend?' Spew, always the social animal, persisted. 'Quiet as a lamb, 'e is. Good company without bein' too conversationally demanding.'

Trapp gave up and squirmed awkwardly round, only to meet the glazed accusation of the sheep cadaver strapped in beside his Second Officer.

'Sometimes,' Trapp muttered, 'I think 'e should see about that last good eye o' hi – !'

. . . But then Trapp's own became diverted by a fleeting sparkle from the body of the aircraft – an all-too-brief but unmistakable incandescence, as if from a finger ring. Instantly the Captain froze, entranced. Possessed in equal measure of an uncanny ability to home both on the often elusive lights of maritime navigational aids and the magnetic glint of superior quality diamonds, the mega-carat lure of that most unexpected sighting revised even Edward Trapp's jaundiced assessment of the class of person who flew Abdul's Eritrean.

Not that it came as too great a surprise. Evacuees from Beirut would cheerfully sit on the nose cone of a Scud missile to get out of that permanently unhappy city during those periods when the ambient hostility gets too physical.

'Oh, *I* remember wot it was now,' Spew frowned, suddenly beginning to wiggle strangely. 'I'd got the call to perform a . . . well, a natural *function*, Cap'n. C'n you oblige me with a passage plan ter the nearest toilet?'

But then, being not only an instant-replay amnesiac but thick as mince as well, Mister Spew always had tended to be a bit tardy at interpreting signals from his various internal parts.

Trapp ignored him. Just sat staring hypnotically astern with bull neck contorted and the lid of his cap bouncing erratically in time to the swooping passage of the aircraft.

Gorbals Wullie removed a gnawed thumb from his mouth and levered himself confidently upright again. 'Ah wisnae scared, by the way. Ah wis jist looking for something I dropped doon the back o' the seat.'

'*Cap'n?*' the forgotten Spew appealed with dawning urgency, beginning to go blue in the face.

'It's . . . it's simply *beautiful!*' Trapp whispered, still locked-on to the diamond aft.

'Ye mean the sheep?' Wullie, who'd been a long time in jail as well, determined suspiciously while easing to starboard to open a bit more space between them, 'or the Second Mate?'

'PLEESE, CAP'N?' Mister Spew hissed, eyes by then bulging more prominently than his mutton-flavoured companion's

21

while, at the same time, slowly starting to slide from view. '*Pleese* will yer tell me where the lickle BOYS' room is?'

The Dakota rocked violently as it hurled itself into yet another bank of storm clouds with kamikaze determination. It was enough to cause Trapp's stalwart complement to crack up completely.

Which meant that Popeye Bucalosie the Chief, corncob pipe clenched cartoon-like between Italian marble teeth, began beating the head of the sailor in front with enormous tattooed fists, sobbing, 'We're-a gonna die! We're-a alla gonna die THISSA time f'r sure . . . !' while Fred – alias Lucille – Grubb, Trapp's . . . well, Trapp's unorthodoxly-inclined engineroom greaser commenced shrieking in a high-pitched falsetto which tallied very well with the guy's floral print dress but struck a slight note of incongruity emitting, as it did, through a ten-day growth of beard.

Gorbals Wullie just went back to looking for something under the seat again.

'Oh – STARB'D side forr'ard if you *reely* must!' Trapp grumbled absently, indicating the furiously vibrating bulkhead separating them from the flight deck . . . always assuming the flight deck was still functioning as a flight deck, of course: that the pilots themselves hadn't baled out in panic.

Clawing erect with unaccustomed alacrity, his Second Officer shaped a gingerly course for the bows while Trapp went back to full-time coveting. Not without effort he broadened his horizon just enough to encompass the prospective target wearing the ring.

The white-bearded Arab projected a quiet dignity in contrast to those about him. Hawk-nosed and aloof he gazed placidly from the window with a fatalism born of great age. Beside him sat a nervous dark-eyed child. Occasionally the old man patted the boy's knee with gentle reassurance.

The observation came as a crushing disappointment to the Captain; for Edward Trapp had been afflicted throughout his buccaneering life by one major imperfection. Trapp had always been burdened by 'Principles'.

Not many principles, admittedly, and even those – most of which concerned the contractual responsibilities Trapp considered binding on any party enjoined with him in what he tended to describe somewhat euphemistically as *internashnul commerce* but which police forces across the globe filed more specifically under headings as wide-ranging as *maritime fraud, barratry, arms dealing, sanctions-breaching, piracy* and *illegal immigration*; to say nothing of good old fashioned *smuggling: dutiable items, various* - even those few principles which HAD survived were prone to compromise at the end of the day by either the Captain's tendency to misinterpretation, or - much the same thing - the Captain's total bloody *incompetence* in any endeavour outwith seamanship!

. . . It was at that point in the flight that a distraction occurred - a trivial incident, one which diverted Trapp only briefly from contemplation of the inconvenience imposed by Good versus the commercial advantages promised by Uninhibited Evil - but an incident which was, nevertheless, to prove of considerable significance later.

It began when Gorbals Wullie frowned, captivated by something happening up front.

'Captin?'

'Shuttup,' Trapp proposed morosely. 'I gotter crisis of conscience.'

A minute passed. Gorbals Wullie frowned even more curiously.

'Cap –'

'Shut UP.'

Yet a further two minutes dragged by.

'It's jist that – '

'SHUDDUP!' Trapp bellowed, black determined not to be drawn into social intercourse, not even with Key Personnel.

'All right – ah'll *shut* up! You jist SEE if I care,' the Key Person yelled back, dead miffed.

There came an even longer, by-then thoroughly embittered, silence.

Until, eventually: '. . . it's jist that ah wis *wondering*,' Gorbals Wullie observed heavily to no one in particular, 'why the Second Mate's TRYING tae jump out of the fucking AEROPLANE?'

Trapp swivelled, finally defeated, to observe Mister Spew jousting desperately with the various wheels and levers and things that locked the Dakota's forward door. A skin of battered aluminium beyond Spew beckoned a ten-thousand foot drop into oblivion.

Which didn't, admittedly, threaten any major departure from Mister Spew's normal day-to-day operational status, but it got bloody cold at ten thousand feet while, once caught in the slipstream, the door would've been impossible to shut behind him.

'I TOLD 'im', Trapp snarled, routinely implying it was all Wullie's fault, 'the heads wus on the *starboard* side . . . Go ON then, seein' you're so clever – go an' steer 'im on the right course before 'e steps out thinkin' it's a bloody BIG toilet f'r such a small aeroplane!'

. . . Whereupon Trapp divested himself of all further responsibility in the matter and about-faced to resume perusal of the magnetic sparkler astern while railing once more against the frustrations associated with having to observe Principles.

But some of them really were quite inflexible. For one thing he'd always been very hot on honour among thieves, had Edward Trapp. While he may have interpreted some conditions and sub-paras a little loosely, he never actually *broke* his word on a contract . . . a somewhat eccentric virtue in the circumstances and one which – because Trapp *did* tend to go over the top in reacting to provocations like being blown up or shot at – had led to abrupt shortfalls in the life span of more than a few one-time partners tempted into unilateral treachery.

Trapp didn't touch drug running either; no more than he countenanced procuring women for immoral acts. What was more, Trapp could also reveal an unexpected depth of compassion. He could become quite maudlin at the death of a goldfish, for instance; while topping people outside of a proper war, even for a guaranteed king's ransom, was emphatically out – apart from squaring accounts with such aforementioned global business associates who nurtured secret intentions of firing first. Or of murdering Gorbals Wullie, of course. Most days. But that was more of a pipe dream . . .

One thing Trapp did *not* do was take advantage of gentle old men and children. In fact, had they but known it, that elderly Arab and the boy in his care were a sight safer being envied by

Trapp than in the hands of whoever was supposedly flying the bloody aeroplane.

So eventually the Captain dragged his gaze from the rock which, to a less complicated adventurer, could have offered a passport to gaining another ship; could even have opened a whole new vista of potential maritime skullduggery; and just resigned himself to staring wistfully into space.

Meanwhile the Dakota trundled on leaden wings towards Addis Ababa or thereabouts . . .

Second Officer Spew trundled cheerfully back from the correct toilet door looking forward to renewing an animated conversation with his friend the passed-away sheep . . .

Greaser Grubb overcame her girlish vapours sufficiently to produce an electric razor as a prelude to repairing his make-up . . .

Bosun Bligh got tired of being propped against a wall modelling a rigid canvas suit, and preoccupied himself instead with challenging the goat to a f*$%*&! butting contest . . .

Gorbals Wullie rose from his seat and - being so much more intelligent than Spew in that he could recognize a toilet door just so long as it had a little man painted on it - announced to his indifferent mentor, 'Jist away tae pump bilges, Captin . . .'

He put on his best Humphrey Bogart tough-guy swagger. 'Course, if we gets hijacked while ah'm in there, gie me a bell, kid - ah'll sort them oot.'

'That's a *very* good imitation,' Mister Spew beamed, dead impressed. 'Jus' like James Cagney.'

'Hijacked - THIS lot . . . ?' Trapp jeered scathingly at the closing toilet door. '*Don't* be so bloody daft!'

Two minutes later a dark-skinned lunatic wearing a combat jacket and a Zapata moustache came rushing down the aisle, snatched the little Arab boy from the seat beside his aged mentor, dragged him unresistingly to the front of the plane, then brutally held a revolver two sizes larger than a field gun against the terrified child's head.

Screaming: 'This issa hijack! Don't nobody MOVE or the kid gets it . . . !'

Chapter Two

I received the letter a few days later when my ship sailed - well, got herself towed, actually - into Singapore.

Though it wasn't so much a letter as an early warning: the unsubtle hand of Trapp betraying its grubby self in every lugubriously forged line despite being barely decipherable through the sticky patina of a second-rate airline plastic dinner.

It said:

deer mister miller if you reely
want to make a lot o money
ring singapore 7389...

I smiled softly. Wistfully. Cleverly. Trapp was running out of devious ploys - he'd already tried sending me a bait as naive as that once before.

As if I would *ever* be stupid enough to fall for such a pathetically transparent device.

Again!

I threw it carelessly into a chartroom drawer; politely excused myself to the pilot controlling the tugs from the *Bar Abir's* bridge; and set a dignified course for the cupboard which, even in 1931, had been somewhat exaggeratedly described on her general arrangement plans as the 'Master's Bathroom'.

. . . and was violently sick in the basin.

I awakened sobbing uncontrollably several times during that night. Once I jerked bolt upright, sweating, staring blindly at the deckhead thinking I'd heard someone screaming: 'No they couldn't've missed him: not ALL those soldiers with all those guns! No . . . *no* . . . NOooo . . . !'

Then I remembered there wasn't anybody left aboard the *Bar Abir*, largely on account of my whole crew having deserted *en masse*: scurvy dogs all of them – clawing and trampling over each other the way they did to get ashore the moment her gangway went down. And simply because one of my Filipino stokers had been about to swing another shovelful of coal into the firebox when he'd happened to notice he'd also picked up a tubular thing with wires sticking out of it.

I mean, I *told* them it was hardly likely the Owners would've hidden TWO bombs in our bunkers. Not when one would have proved more than adequate for insurance purposes . . .

I divided the whole of the following morning between convulsively emptying my bowels, catching up on my Bible, and resolutely ignoring Trapp's letter.

The voice on the telephone answered, 'Jewel of Malaysia Chinese Lestaurant, Accommodation Addless Servlice and Massage Parrour . . . which you want?'

'Tlapp!' I snarled in faultless pidgin. 'I want you give message to Captain Tlapp, savvy?'

A cautious hesitation.

'Who calling?'

'Cap'n Smith . . . *Miller*! Look, you just get TLAPP, pal: plenty quick chop chop!'

'Captain Trapp no here', the voice retorted. 'Anyway, you Engrish . . . why you no can say "Trapp" proper, huh?'

'The British *Army*, sir, may have left Singapore', I warned stiffly, 'but it can always return. Get Trapp!'

'He no good. He sheepskate. He and sneaky Scottish turd with him done moonlight frit. Maybe you pay bill instead, huh?'

'For which *service*?' I said acidly, then realized I was wasting my gunpowder in pointless insults. Even if Gorbals Wullie *was* still sailing in wretched convoy with Trapp and not sub-divided all over a shell hole in Beirut as my informant's reference to ethnic excreta seemingly implied, it was highly unlikely they'd've had ten-foot barge poles handy in the Jewel of Malaysia's Massage

Parlour Division, anyway.

There came a loud knock on my cabin door.

'ENTER!' I bellowed irritably.

Hobnail boots entered. And the squeak of tennis shoes on the worn rubberoid decking. Probably belonging to more of the inevitable brotherhood of debt collectors who trailed trans-globally and persistently in the *Bar Abir's* faltering wake in pursuance of my low-profile Owners.

I ignored them with lofty indifference, being more preoccupied with dominating the Oriental Connection.

The door creaked shut and there followed the careless scratching of chair legs as my visitors sat down. Without even so much as a 'by your leave'.

'*Lissen*, Chop Suey or whatever your bloody name is,' I yelled at the phone. 'You speaky him from me – forGET it! You tell him go jump in LAKE! You bloody TELL him Mister Miller say no *way* never AGAI – !'

'Piss off, Engrishman,' the telephone retorted matter-of-factly.

I gaped at it, utterly shocked. I was a British shipmaster, dammit! More: I was still an officer of her Britannic Majesty's Royal Naval Reserve . . . Good grief – *I'd* been at sea in The War. In the days when the Red Ensign had been proudly evident in every port in the world. In the days when the United Kingdom *had* a bloody merchant fleet . . . ! In those heady, nostalgic days when we'd carried so many hardcases in our foc's'les the colonials hadn't *dared* tell us British how much they hated our guts . . .

'Whaddyou MEAN – piss *OFF*?' I bellowed as the telephone went dead.

'That wouldnae be the British Ambassador on the phone by ony chance, Mister Miller, sir?' a vaguely familiar whine enquired with enormous interest.

'An' YOU can piss off as well!' I snarled in the general direction of the interruption, utterly furious.

'Wrong, stupid,' a second vaguely familiar voice jeered at the first voice. 'Language like that – 'e thinks 'e *is* the British Ambassador.'

. . . I remember clear as day my immediate response at that juncture. After all I *had* been through it all before; had already endured the sub-zero onset of a not-dissimilar sense of *déjà vu*; experienced an almost identical daytime nightmare triggered – until I could bring myself to open tightly closed eyes and verify the unthinkable – by those same still-mercifully disembodied interlopers.

Trouble was, on that previous occasion I'd become aware of them while in a much more resilient frame of mind; languidly sipping a glass of chilled beer amid the carefree hubbub of a sun-washed Italian piazza.

I'd only managed to get a grip on myself and stop one scream short of a nervous breakdown *then*. Just before I'd found myself embarking upon a certain voyage to war-torn Libya.

Not that Libya had actually been war-torn at the time. Not 'til HE got there . . .

'I *know* you must still BE here in Singapore because you've never possessed enough money to buy an aeroplane ticket to move you from anywhere to anywhere else . . . but please go away before I wake up, Trapp – *please* . . . ? And take your troglodyte Familiar with you?'

I became aware of an abrupt *snap* while simultaneously feeling a sharp pain in my hand; then Gorbals Wullie asked curiously, 'Why's Mister Miller broke his telephone in half, Captin?'

'Because 'e's all tense an' overcome with excitement, that's why. Jus' so pleased ter see us,' Trapp explained with enormous understanding.

And quite breathtaking misinterpretation.

Cautiously I opened one eye to check I wasn't bleeding to death. Not that the prospect didn't afford *some* positive aspects under the circumstances.

Trapp leaned forward with the solicitous concern of a weasel about to make friends with a rabbit, and proffered something all sort of scrubbled up into a cauliflower-shaped ball, streaky black with engine oil.

I opened the other eye.

'What's *that* supposed to be?'

'My hankie, Mister. First aid!' He sighed dramatically. 'Greatest

29

burden I carries through life, as you well know, is concern f'r the well-being of my crew.'

'*Is* it?' Wullie queried, mystified.

'You've never given a fig for the well-being of your crew, Trapp,' I informed him coldly. 'Otherwise you wouldn't starve them, exploit them, and keep trying to drown them like you do. Apart from which - I wouldn't dab any wound of mine with *that* if I found it floating in a bath of antiseptic.'

I paused to glower for a moment, aware that venom had diverted me from the principal thrust of my thesis. 'And, most importantly - I am NOT one of "your crew" any longer, d'you hear? I say again, Trapp: I . . . am . . . NOT . . . one . . . of . . !'

He smiled at that. One of his infuriating *I know somethin' you don't* smiles. It worried me a lot.

'You 'aven't changed, Mister,' he said appreciatively. 'Still the same calm, unruffled Number One I 'ad under me command during the war.'

He hadn't bloody changed either. The barbed emphasis on 'under *my* command' hardly failed to escape me.

'And don't try THAT on,' I yelled. 'That was a long time ago and you've milked it to the full.'

'I'm still tallied on the Royal Navy Reserve List as a full three-ring Commander.' Trapp fixed me with a supercilious eye. 'Same as you are. Except, o' course, you only got two-an'-a-half - *Lootenant*-Commander!'

'And *I'm* still down as an Ordinary Seaman,' Wullie reminded us proudly.

'True,' Trapp agreed. 'In fact I'd say you're a *very* ordinary seaman.'

I decided polite but withering self-control was my best form of defence.

'You only stayed on the List through an administrative oversight,' I reminded Trapp as icily as I could. 'Because after the War, Winston Churchill was so ashamed of how you'd conducted your bit of it he ordered the Admiralty to expunge all records of your operations. They simply forgot to obliterate your name from the nominal roll.'

'They still pay us, too,' Trapp leered triumphantly. And

forgetfully. 'Me an' him – we gets our Navy wages through the post every month.'

'We gets *what*?' Wullie interrupted, suddenly alert. What with his thinning hair and stringy neck, he looked a bit like a somnolent vulture that's just discovered its cadaver's been stolen.

'Er . . . nuthin'!' Trapp muttered hurriedly.

'He says HE still gets *your* Naval PAY each month,' I volunteered helpfully.

'And here's me tryin' ter be nice to a . . . a junior *officer*,' Trapp shouted, bitterly resentful at being caught out. 'I could've come in 'ere all rude and tactless an' *made* you SALUTE me!'

I stared at him disbelievingly – he had the outright nerve to say he *could* have been tactless . . . ? TRAPP? – whose level of tact was roughly on a par with Hitler's when he invaded POLAND . . . ? '*Screw* self-bloody-control . . .' I decided.

'I've not the slightest bloody INTENTION of saluting you: I do not *want* you to be NICE – an' DON'T you call me a junior bloody officer!' I catalogued at the top of my voice.

'I save you frae a *hijack*, Captin,' Gorbals Wullie was screaming, trying to get a whinge in edgeways, 'an' that's what ye do tae me – steal mah WAGIS?'

'YOU . . . ? You ain't *worth* no wages,' Trapp bellowed back, grateful for any excuse to redeploy his fire against an easier target. 'I've paid wages to SEA SLUGS got more life innem than you. And you didn't save me from no hijack. YOU coul'n't save yer own bloody BREATH, you couldn't . . . YOU coul'n't save TIME if they give you a free *grandfather* clock . . .'

'Yes ah did!' Wullie shrieked back. 'I saved you frae a *hijack*!'

'NO you di'n't!'

'YES ah DID!'

'No you DI'N'T . . .'

'Tell me about the hijack,' I said.

Resignedly.

According to Wullie's expurgated version, it appeared that Trapp – being one who blithely accepted accident and disaster as being the norm largely on account of his invariably turning out to have been the catalyst anyway – was caught totally unawares by that particular emergency.

Or, more succinctly: 'Banjoed wi' his bluidy pants doon as usual . . .' as Wullie's bitter allegation had it.

According to Trapp, on the other hand, *he'd* been on full harbour stations stand-by even before the gunman made his move; alert to every contingency. 'I got a sixth sense f'r these things see? Like a coiled spring I wus, Mister, but smart enough to let 'im think I wus just ordinary: not letting 'im see I wus only waiting for the right moment.'

Which, interpreted again but *sans* Trapp's modest embellishment, meant he – same as everybody else – didn't have a *clue* how to react.

In the end I deferred to Wullie's version, having the advantage of knowing Trapp better than a chart of the English Channel.

Being both complacent and tunnel-visioned, he'd relied on his contract, you see? With the Beirut Hostage Corporation? It had never occurred to him that anyone might be so unscrupulous as to act as an independent heisting contractor outwith the control of the Sudanese Liberation Whatever-they-were and completely in breach of Clauses 48a, 48b, and Sub-para 74g of the aforementioned solemn and binding agreement guaranteeing a hijack-free flight.

So Trapp, who never had learned to be wise before the event – or even after it, for that matter – just sat thinking furiously in his seat while the screams and disconcertion of the other passengers swelled astern of him.

But it is at this point in my chronicle that I have, albeit grudgingly, to afford Edward Trapp his due.

For, while he knew better than most what that weapon could do to him if turned in his direction, and that the one thing you *don't* do in a hijack situation is to attract attention to yourself, the Captain stared straight and determined nonetheless into the wild eyes of a man who was base enough to hold a gun to a little boy's head.

'Let the youngster go, Mister,' he advised. Ever so quietly.

It was that uncharacteristic mildness, that undeviating gaze which would have alerted anyone unhappily familiar with the Captain's moods. Trapp Bombastic was a routine pain in the neck:

Trapp Expressionless betokened a terrible forewarning. But when Trapp spoke softly *and* looked at a person like that, the icy-fingered weathercock of Death had already begun to swing in the recipient's direction.

And, just for a moment, a shadow *did* seem to pass over the hijacker's face. But being, as it turned out, quite mad as well as callous, Zapata Man dismissed it.

'You some kinda smart guy, huh, or jus' tired of life? So maybe you wanna be spokesman, eh?'

Trapp swivelled, and bleakly surveyed the after end of the swaying Dakota. Ducks, geese, even the goat had been silenced by the initial fear. People hunched themselves to look smaller, less significant. Only the old Arab still sat erect, but his previously proud eyes were watery, vacant now with shock, one gnarled, uncertain hand reached without full realization to comfort the empty place where the child had been.

Predictably, there wasn't an unkempt head to be seen projecting above those seats where the Captain's gallant band had been lounging a minute before. Apart from Mister Spew's, that was. Who still hadn't noticed anything amiss.

And the sheep's. Who didn't care.

Trapp turned back and sniffed. 'I don't exac'ly see no queue of volunteers.'

'So tell the pilots - take this plane to Addis Ababa,' the gunman snarled.

Trapp blinked, all set for every eventuality including a voyage to Hades. Except that one.

'This plane IS goin' to Addis Ababa, you asshole,' he growled.

But I've already dwelt at some length upon the extent to which Trapp's tact had formed the keystone of his survival to date . . .

Zapata Man fixed him with a crazy-clever stare and shrugged philosophically.

'OK: so get me a million dollar US and a parachute. I jump instead.'

'Watch a lot of movies, do yer?' Trapp asked understandingly.

It was then that the Second Mate, reflexes honed razor sharp by his previous voyage forward, decided to make his play. He rose awesomely, threateningly; a lethal weapon in humanoid form, from his seat.

'I fink I'll nip along ter the little boy's room again, Cap'n,' Mister Spew said, concerned, as a responsible ship's officer, to keep the Master fully informed of his movements.

In, it seemed, every sense of the word.

' 'Scuse me, old son: back in a minnit,' Spew apologized, squeezing considerately past the sheep.

' *Allo* there: stretchin' our legs a bit, are we?' he greeted affably while circumnavigating the stunned gunman before heading onwards, brow creased in furious concentration on the job in hand.

'Don't mind him,' Trapp called urgently, suddenly frightened for Spew: focussing Zapata Man's attention back on himself as the gun wavered. 'He can't do more'n one thing at once an' believe me, Mister, you ain't top of 'is emergency list right now.'

'You get me a million *dollar*, shitface,' the lunatic screamed, just about at the end of his own all-too-fragile tether. 'Anna PARAchute!'

Trapp made a great play of patting his pockets, then frowned and looked up. It seemed to him the only course left was to play the psychological pressure game: find out just how loony tunes the guy *really* was, then exploit the knowledge.

'Look, how d'yer feel about jumpin' with a letter o' credit?' he experimented tentatively. 'Negative the parachute?'

The gunman felt bad about it. Without further warning he shifted his grip to the little boy's hair, grinding the gun cruelly into a shock-white cheek. The child began to cry.

. . . Knowing Trapp, Zapata Man - whether simply vicious or irredeemably insane - had gone quite beyond the pale by that callous action: had assured his own dying in that fearful moment. He simply wasn't aware of it right then.

But suddenly, dreadfully, from aft and before even Trapp could act, there arose a keening wail as if from an animal in pain. The Captain, shaken to the core himself, whirled to catch sight of the child's venerable guardian, spindlestick arms extended, hobbling on faltering legs down the aircraft aisle.

'NO! Please - I implore you for the love of *Allahhhhh* . . . !'

The gunman smiled a crazed smile and shifted the weapon from grandson to grandfather . . .

Too late Trapp erupted from his seat; lunged, hopeless in the certainty that he himself would die and possibly half a hundred more with him.

'. . . BELAY THAT YOU BASTARD!' he roared in a whiplash bellow that had flayed a thousand sea-storms; penetrated a shrieking frenzy of typhoons.

The gun hesitated, swung searchingly again. Steadied.

This time on Trapp.

The blued and rifled hole which was the barrel must have looked *very* big indeed . . .

'. . . Then what happened?' I whispered, fascinated despite myself.

Trapp sighed heavily, and looked sad.

'For Heaven's sake, Trapp - what *happened*?' I persisted, filled by then with concern for a child I'd never seen.

' 'E shot me, Mister.'

I blinked. To me he looked depressingly healthy.

'Where?'

'Clean through the 'eart,' Trapp specified solemnly.

Then grinned, all pleased with himself.

God, but how I hated Trapp's invariably mistimed attempts at humour.

'Then he made a cardinal ERROR, didn't he?' I snarled, provoked straight back into being bloody furious. 'He should've used a SILVER bullet!'

'Thought that wis what they use on vampires?' Wullie queried uncertainly.

'*You* catch on quick,' I grated.

Trapp promptly went into the huff. 'It wus a joke.'

'So's HE!' I indicated Gorbals Wullie distastefully. 'I just don't happen to think *he's* funny either.'

'Ah'm too busy bein' a killing machine tae be a full-time comedian,' Wullie claimed defensively. 'Ah'm jist a Tiger, me . . . I saved the Captin, mind?'

'NO you di'n't,' Trapp bellowed predictably.

'Aye, ah DID!'

'NO YOU DIDN - !'

'I know it's unusual but, in this case, one of you *has* to be telling the truth,' I said encouragingly.

According to Trapp, he'd stared into that gun barrel for what seemed a very long time.

I believed that part.

'. . . not that it *bothered* me partic'larly, of course,' Trapp, always image-conscious, qualified hastily in case either of us thought he'd been concerned at the imminent prospect of being shot to death.

Odd as it may seem, I believed that part too.

I'd observed, on all too many occasions, how Trapp cherished an absolute belief in his own immortality. I'd seen him display an ill-humoured insensitivity to even the less subtle nuances of impending hazard - like guns being pointed at him by half of Rommel's *Afrika Korps* or, more recently, by most of the Libyan Army. To say nothing of the late Soviet Navy and odd task elements of the US Sixth Fleet.

In my view, such crass disregard for one's own safety simply *had* to be founded upon more than blind faith and so, in the course of many hours spent taking cover alongside Gorbals Wullie while people shot at us collectively, I'd formed my supernatural theory . . . that almost certainly Trapp, indubitably the quintessential survivor, had done some kind of Faustian deal way back when merely an apprentice skulldugger and negotiated himself some form of demonaic patronage. Managed to wangle himself the protection of some . . . well, of some Black *Force* dedicated to destroying the world while making it look like an accident.

So I wasn't being entirely waspish when referring to the need for a silver bullet, don't you see . . . ? Trapp had managed to survive and bounce back grumbling and picking fault for far too long otherwise. Even ignoring the failure of his enemies to terminate him - who were legion, persistent, and virtually all expert-homicidal to trade - it had to be the only explanation for why at least one of his former *friends*, one with more facility for that sort of thing than I, hadn't succumbed to the impulse to blow the Captain away years ago.

Even one who'd appeared perfectly rational in other ways. Though mind you, reflecting again upon Trapp's immediate social circle, such a qualification *would* tend to restrict that particular field of likely candidates.

The alternative, of course, lay not so much in Diabolical Deliverance as in the bloody man's being an egotistical, overbearing idiot who kept getting lucky.

Which he was, irrespective.

Anyway . . .

Trapp, discomfited or not, actually *saw* the hijacker's finger whitening; taking up first pressure on that massive cannon – knew he couldn't possibly close to grapple before . . .

. . . before the toilet DOOR immediately to starboard of Zapata Man was flung open with careless abandon, whereupon Lethal Weapon *Wullie* – quite unaware of the drama developing since he'd disappeared to pump bilges – hobbled out, furiously resentful, with ragged trousers still at half mast and waving an empty brown cardboard tube.

Complaining vociferously: 'Lissen, will wan of youse tell they pilots there's nae bluidy TOILET PAPER in this airborne soddin' . . .'

In pseudo-scientific terms, Gorbals Wullie's action then triggered a phenomenon known as the Domino Effect – in this event meaning that, because hijacking space is severely restricted in Dakotas, Wullie's door cannoned violently into Zapata Man, causing HIM not only to lose his grip on the child but also to stagger uncomprehendingly to port.

All of which happened to coincide with the precise moment when Mister *Spew* – who, after ten minutes, had quite forgotten which door should've had a little man painted on it anyway, and had consequently been struggling to open the port EXIT door as before only, this time, without let or hindrance on account of nobody having given a shit for Spew's current suicide bid due to their own ongoing internal crisis . . . well, even Mister SPEW had to succeed in accomplishing something sometime.

And had apparently managed to pull the right lever.

The overall result being that Spew's door cracked ajar and was immediately snatched by the wind of the Dakota's passage, erupting wide open and taking Second Officer Spew with it.

Mister Spew clung like a battered leech to the last handle, eyes half closed against the gale, legs flailing and entwining, trousers flapping in the slipstream.

'By *golly*,' the suddenly aerobatic Spew said, filling his lungs appreciatively, 'but a bit o' fresh air DOES do yer good.'

The knock-on effect continued with the aircraft's instantly filling with fluttering birds and screams yet again, while previously inanimate objects - excluding, regrettably, Trapp's crew - adopted a life of their own and began to hurtle in column through the gaping doorframe, sucked out by the roaring wind.

Trapp, meanwhile, had hurled himself full length to make a desperate grab for the little Arab boy who was *also* beginning to slide helplessly to his death.

'GETTIM - GET THE GUY WITH THE *GUN* . . .' he bellowed at a suddenly transfixed Gorbals Wullie, by then looking not so much like a lethal weapon as a man caught with his strides down: trying vainly to come to terms with just how much of a stir a simple event like a roll of *toilet* paper running out could cause.

Until he finally registered the 'gun' bit of Trapp's message: instituted a quick visual appreciation of its calibre; went an even pastier shade of hostage white . . . and instantly made to reoccupy the toilet with the practised facility of a tortoise withdrawing its head into its shell.

'Ohhhhh - 'ANG ON TO THE LITTLE *LAD* THEN . . . !' Trapp snarled in disgust.

'Dinnae shoot in THIS direction, mister - ah'm *nuthing* tae dae wi' THEM,' Wullie screamed at the still-disoriented gunman, then grudgingly scooped the child up, whirled about and hobble-galloped back to cover.

The toilet door slammed shut; there sounded a frantic rattle from inside, and the little red disc flicked to *Engaged*.

'With *your* reactions to stress, at least you're in the right PLACE!' Trapp hurled vituperatively after his disappeared Key Person while reaching up desperately for the gun.

. . . which, in *its* turn, went off as Zapata Man squeezed the trigger before it was knocked from his grasp.

The shot scorched yet another ragged hole through the wildly bobbing lid of Trapp's cap which, fanned by the gale from the door, promptly began to glow and smoke round the edges while the bullet *itself* ricocheted astern; neatly parted the plaited grass rope tethering the goat: sheared the most critical buckle clean off Bosun Bligh's straightjacket, and finally exited through the tailplane via two ducks, an Arab urn and the viewfinder of a Nikkon camera.

As well as through the Japanese tourist who owned it.

. . . who'd been taking a picture to show the boys back at the Datsun factory at the time.

Meanwhile the Domino Effect - the Gorbals Wullie Phenomenon - continued to gather momentum . . .

Choker Bligh, long noted in Interpol files as being the Houdini of the maritime underworld, immediately shrugged free of the constraints of his travelling suit, lowered a head which roughly matched the shape of the departing bullet but had a harder, more bristly casing, and took on the goat - Bosun Bligh never having been one to go back on a threat.

The goat, surprised to find itself supersonically released, took one look at Choker and decided to shop around for less formidable adversaries; caught sight of Trapp and Zapata Man down the front end, both scrabbling frantically on hands and knees by then for possession of the gun . . .

And took off in their direction like a cruise missile!

Trapp registered the thunder of approaching malice even above the roar of the wind; screwed round hurriedly; caught the red glint of hatred in maddened eyes - then saw the goat as *well* as Bligh . . . and threw himself flat just in time to experience the staccato punch of cloven hooves careering up, then overshooting his spine.

'Watch OUT!' Trapp shouted in automatic warning to the still crouched Zapata Man. ' 'E's going ter . . .'

There came an uncomfortably fleshy thump! Followed by a long fading scream.

A millisecond later the clatter of hooves on aluminium cut dead as well, converting instead to a long, fading, rather surprised bleat . . .

'. . . butt yer,' Trapp finished.

Always one to insist on having the last word.

★

39

The Dakota's intercom wheezed and crackled, then the pilot – who, to his eternal credit had stuck the trip out after all – said: 'We vill be landing mos' probably in Addis Ababa in ten minnits. On be'alf of Pan Eritrean Air Services, pleese we hope you found your flight of great comfortings . . .'

Gorbals Wullie stretched contentedly before rising, hunched against the still howling gale from the open door, to retrieve his colour-coordinated Gucci-style plastic bag from the madly vibrating, airscrew-coordinated luggage rack.

He swaggered ostentatiously back and sat down, suave and tough again like Humphrey Bogart.

'It comes natural tae me, of course – bein' a Tiger and saving people,' he said.

Then waited for Trapp to retort with something appreciative.

Trapp didn't.

'It's, ah . . . jist as well I wis handy to deal with that nutter, eh, Captin?' Wullie prompted eventually.

'YOU? *You* di'n't save nuthin'!' Trapp snarled, exploring the charred hole in his cap with an ill-tempered finger. 'You coul'n't save a . . .'

'Aye ah DID!' Wullie pouted. Then settled for a compromise. 'Okay – but I def'nately saved the wee lad.'

'Helped to,' Trapp conceded grudgingly.

'. . . *and* you,' Wullie slipped in slyly.

'Oh, no you bloody DI'N'T!'

'Och yes ah bluidy DI –'

'Excuse me, *effendi* – please may I speak with you?' a gentle voice cut in.

'Shove OFF, I'm busy arguing!' Trapp yelled.

Then swallowed. The elderly Arab stood before him. To Trapp, the diamond on the old man's finger seemed to light the whole aeroplane.

Hurriedly he booted Gorbals Wullie back into the aisle and dusted the vacated cushion with his cauliflower black-ball.

'Do take a seat, Sheik,' he encouraged. 'Gratitude wus it – that you wanted to chat about?'

'Here, what aboot ME?' Wullie demanded, dead peeved.

'You're busy. *Ord'nary* Seaman!'

40

'Doing what?'

'You being a Tiger who risks 'is life to save people an' everything, I know you'll *reelly* enjoy climbin' out there carryin' a rope!'

Trapp pointed triumphantly to the gaping, tornado-racked opening in the fuselage.

'. . : or had you forgotten our Second Officer's still with us? Clingin' like a sucker fly to the 'andle?'

'. . . Well, it was very nice of you to come all this way just to brief me on your adventures - to say nothing of warning me of your return to a still-largely unsuspecting world,' I said, squinting pointedly at the bulkhead clock. '. . . so goodbye again. I'm sure if you both leave now you'll easily thumb a lift downtown to wherever you propose to hide from the Jewel of Malaysia's debt collectors this evening?'

'That's all right, Mister,' Trapp shrugged generously. We're in no 'urry.'

I covered my disappointment well.

'Then, if you really do feel compelled to stay a few minutes - a *very* few minutes - longer, I'd rather you didn't keep on calling me "Mister",' I admonished politely. ' "Mister", as you may recall, Trapp, is the conventional form of address used by a ship's master to his Chief Officer . . . ? Whereas I am not, thank God, *your* Chief Officer any longer. AM I?'

Trapp didn't answer. Just avoided my eyes and started examining his fingernails intently. I understood perfectly. It must have been hard for him to come to terms with me being my own man. Crisp, perfectly composed now I'd grown to accept he still existed, and quite clearly beyond his further Machiavellian control.

I leaned back expansively in my chair. In the Master's chair. In the Master's cabin. In *my* cabin. Aboard MY command.

Where *I - CAPTAIN S. Miller* like it said on the little brass plate on my door - reigned supreme.

'Jist like old times, eh?' Gorbals Wullie ventured appreciatively, spoiling the ensuing silence. 'Naebody speakin' tae onybody?'

'Even if I *could* understand what you have just said,' I retorted

41

coldly, 'I suspect I wouldn't wish to respond.'

. . . I think it was about then that Trapp rose and began sticking the point of his sheath knife into the wood panelling around the door.

'Why's he doing that?' I asked Wullie uneasily, forgetting I'd just broken off diplomatic relations with Scotland.

'If *I* wis a Captin, Captin - then I'D be expecting *me* to know without askin',' Wullie sniffed, back in his childish huff.

Trapp shaped a pensive course for one of the iron deadlights used to cover the portholes in heavy weather, and tugged at it. Fifty years of corrosion, lack of maintenance and Trapp's genius for destruction working in concert proved too much for the hinge pin. The deadlight came adrift in his hands. He sucked a tooth disapprovingly and laid it on the deck with a tight expression.

. . . the deadlight, I mean. Not the tooth.

I'd observed the same sort of overly-critical attitude to structural collapse before. Particularly since I'd joined the *Bar Abir*. To my mind, Trapp looked for all the world like a marine surveyor surveying a ship, and not overly impressed by what he saw.

I swallowed nervously. His expression was even sourer than that.

In fact, he looked for all the world like a man who'd just BOUGHT one.

. . . with funds provided by - say - an elderly Arab?

Grateful for deliverance from . . . a *hijack*?

'Trapp?' I muttered, already feeling a sense of impermanence in my Master's chair. 'Is there something you haven't quite got round to telling me yet?'

He turned then, and looked at me.

All puzzled. Innocent. Beatific, almost.

'Now whatever could THAT be, I wonder?' he asked. '. . . Mister?'

Chapter Three

Second Officer Spew laboriously finished painting our new name below the overhang of the ex-*Bar Abir's* bow then peered myopically skywards, inviting appreciation from us voyeurs – including me, the ex-*Bar Abir's* ex-captain – lounging silently over her bridge front.

Well, still numbed as I was by a gloom-laden sense of *déjà vu* I didn't appreciate re-enacting that depressingly familiar ceremony, so I wasn't going to applaud. In my view, for Trapp to have christened even the first of his appalling ships after a mythical ferryman, who'd transported the souls of the dead across the River Styx to Hades, was not only bad taste and typical, but had a rather too prophetic ring to it. *Charon II* had proved an equally predictive renaming, seeing she'd been ringed with floating corpses when she went down . . . and he now expected me to sail aboard his *CHARON III* . . .?

No one else clapped either, of course. Like common sense and the work ethic, generosity had never become exactly obsessive aboard Trapp's commands. Not even on account of the Second Mate's managing to get the spelling right for once, which had been quite an achievement for a bloke who couldn't read, write, or see what he was doing.

Though possibly my having cut a stencil to guide Spew in such academic endeavour had helped a bit.

'He's maybe no' too good at feeding hisself, but he *is* a dab hand wi' a stubbly brush,' Gorbals Wullie conceded, draped scarecrow-like over the rail beside us as usual. 'Youse have tae gie him that.'

'DON'T . . !' Trapp began to caution in a voice of mild urgency as Spew began to betray worrying signs of ringing down for half astern with the legs to admire his handiwork.

'Begging your pard – ?' Mister Spew started to query, thrilled to bits at actually having accomplished something.

. . . Just before he stepped backwards into space – the painter's batten suspended dangerously from the foc'sle had only been a few inches wide, lethal even to an intelligent humanoid – and plummeted with little grace but impressive dignity into the Singapore Port Authority's water.

'. . . step back to admire it,' Trapp finished.

Down on the welldeck Bosun Bligh joyously began rushing about, pathetically grateful for any excuse to hit people with his belaying pin now they'd let him loose again, and bellowing, 'Emergency lifeboat AWAY, yer scurvy dogs! BOAT'S CREW ter the boat deck at the f*$%*&! DOUBLE . . . !'

'We 'aven't GOT a bloody lifeboat!' Trapp roared back irritably. 'An' besides, we're alongside anyway. Throw 'im a rope.'

'Gosh, you mean we've still got a *rope*?' I muttered, simmering not only over the injustice Fate had dealt me but also the awareness that, in an attempt to generate enough cash flow to bribe and corrupt anyone who might come up with suitably devious employment for his latest vessel, Trapp had begun to sell off every single item of surplus ship's gear like boats, lifebelts, emergency flares – essentially everything that wasn't screwed, bolted or welded down – as soon as he'd formally taken command.

Which, in his case had meant announcing diplomatically, 'You're demoted. She's mine now 'cause I owns 'er, Mister, so kindly remove yer stuff from the *Master's* cabin to the Mate's cuddy. An' remember ter take that poofter kit you stowed in me bathroom with yer.'

'Just because I happen to possess my own toothbrush,' I'd retorted stiffly as I'd trailed disconsolately down the alleyway, 'doesn't mean I'm exactly decadent, you know.'

'No? Well, I still reckons it's an odd thing f'r a *proper* seaman to own!' he'd shouted after me. 'Toothbrushes is passenger ship stuff. A fancy f'r soft livin', Mister – that's always been your weak spot.'

I'd ignored him.

'Bet you gotta poofy sponge bag with poofy soap innit too,' he'd screamed, goaded by my supreme self-control.

'Don't be ridICulous,' I'd yelled back, hurriedly covering it with my spare cap . . .

Anyway . . . we fished Mister Spew out and pumped him dry. Trapp, meanwhile, stamped off to sulk in my – *his* cabin – just because the last leg of the 'N' in *Charon* had extended to a high-speed vertical white smear which, on account of our not having any black paint to correct it with, threatened to leave his newly aquired vessel with an eccentric look for ever, seeing Spew hadn't had the forethought to lift his stencil brush clear of the hull plates on his way down . . .

And then, that very same night, it happened.

As 'It' invariably did, with Edward Trapp.

. . . The catalyst for his next disaster reared its head.

Only Trapp of course – being Trapp – elected to misread it as 'opportunity'.

The berth the Authority had directed us to in the hope of losing us was both derelict and quiet, almost eerily quiet, for Singapore. Well away from the Eastern Anchorage with its massive and, to certain unspecified maritime criminal elements, highly tempting container complex; far enough from Kusu Island and its sacred temple so's Trapp wasn't likely to start another holy *jihad* by accident; sensibly distant from Chinatown to avoid any urge our crew might've cherished to sabotage the spirit of *Wak Hai Cheng Bio* – the Guangdong People's pagoda-decorated Temple of The Calm Sea – on Phillip Street . . .

Though on second thoughts, a nostalgic stroll along Boat Quay and the original Singaporean waterfront with its weathered Chinese shophouses and old trading company offices might just have proved salutary for the profit-obsessed Edward Trapp. Sandwiched between the smoke-wreathed gables of Telok Ayer Street I could have shown him a Shenist religious place called *Fuk Tak Ch'i*.

Where the God of Wealth stands as a lesson to all. Humbled, in a mourner's sackcloth.

It began as one of those very few evenings when our vagrant world seemed at peace with itself. When sanity briefly regained a foothold on the born-again *Charon's* decks and her complement ceased, for one magical sliver of time, to be pariahs and underdogs and became sailors once more. When a mouth organ and a balalaika and a battered concertina came to life in the hands of those who had nothing else to their names, to extemporize the kind of sad, haunting sea music that no land-bound virtuoso could ever hope to emulate.

When even Edward Trapp emerged finally from his cabin and his sulk, and came to lean quietly over the bridge front beside Wullie and me, to listen and reflect in the jasmine-scented night and, perhaps – just perhaps – feel even a little sense of regret for what might have been.

And when it was over, when the last of the *Charons* had trailed below to endure sweating in the dank steel coffin of her foc'sle, not one of us broke the ensuing silence for quite a long time.

'They're good lads, Mister Miller sir,' Wullie sniffed eventually, dabbing a wee tear from the corner of his eye. 'Hearts of gold, so they huv. Hearts o' pure gold.'

'I know,' I said, feeling a catch in my own throat. 'It's a pity about the rapes and the murders and the muggings and stuff they keep on committing.'

'Nobody's perfec–' Trapp stopped in mid pre-argument and frowned suspiciously down along the wharf. 'What's that there?'

'Where?'

'Hid in the jungle stuff abeam o' the foremast. A black figure, Mister. Just stood standin' . . . no – stood *watching* us.'

I felt an inexplicable prickle at the back of my neck before dismissing it, annoyed with Trapp for disturbing my previously relaxed mood.

'This *is* Singapore, you know. Full of Chinamen and Malaysians. People stand everywhere.'

'Not so still as that one. I got a sense f'r them that's watching me – and he's carryin' something . . . see it glinting? Looks like . . .' Trapp's brows met in the middle. 'Damme,' he muttered, 'if it don't look like a *cutlass*.'

'What d'you mean – a cutlass?' I jeered uncertainly.

Trapp got all irritated again. 'Ow many kinds o' cutlass ARE there? I mean a . . . well, a *sword* kind of cutlass. A cutlass like you cut peoples' throats with. A swarm-aboard-an' spittem kind o' cutlass!'

'I've never swarmed aboard and spit anybody in my LIFE!' I snapped, still quick to take umbrage. 'That's more your line of work, not mine.'

Gorbals Wullie moved nervously. Whit's all yon aboot cutting people's throats?'

'Shut up,' Trapp invited absently, moving out to the bridge wing just as . . .

'Edwaaaard?' a voice called. A keening, most unsettling voice.

'Di'n't I tell you to shut UP?' Trapp snarled over his shoulder at his shambling Familiar. 'An' don't you never call me "Edward" neither.'

'I did – an' I didnae,' Wullie protested uneasily. 'Ah huvnae said a word since – '

'EDWAAAARD *TRAPP*.'

This time I really did feel my hackles rise. Maybe it was a trick of the dim light; maybe it was only the fact that I was already emotionally drained, but I swear I sensed a physical chill descend over the *Charon's* bridge deck. A . . . an *unearthly* ambience.

'It's that bloody Chief Bucalosie taking the Mickey,' Trapp muttered, searching for conviction. 'Jus 'cause I poured a can of engine oil over 'is spaghetti – *Bolognese alla Arabian Crudeo* I told 'im it wus – to prove 'e was a liar an' that food could taste worse than Cookie usually fixes it.'

'No – no, he enjoyed it that way,' I countered, trying to keep my composure. 'Told me it was a definite improveme –'

'The light!' Wullie stammered, eyes suddenly beginning to protrude like those of an apprehensive hermit crab. 'Och Jeeze, Captin. Look at yon *light.*'

'Bloody hell,' I exclaimed.

It spawned first as a greenish aura, drawing our ever-widening eyes; touching and reflecting from the lush tropical undergrowth still concealing the watching figure. Gradually the green turned to purple and then to an incandescent, almost an ethereal blue.

'Edwaaard, where ARE ye?' the voice insisted once more. 'EDWaaaard, me lad?'

'Lad?' Trapp appealed gruffly. 'What's he mean: "My *lad*"? Who's 'e talkin' to?'

'You - Edward,' I volunteered gratefully. 'It's you he wants, apparently.'

'Och well, I'll just away to my bed then,' Wullie the Crab announced with elaborate care, already sidling on an emergency heading for some safer haven on the opposite side of the ship. 'Gie me a shout if ye cannae handle thon nutter wi' the cutlass, Capti -'

It was at that moment that the so-far disembodied voice stepped forward into the light, and we first caught sight of the long black beard all plaited with ribbons and so abundant that strings of it were carried back and looped above ears already heavy with golden rings . . .

'Ohhhhh JEEZE,' Wullie added. 'It'ssaGHOST . . . !'

And promptly fainted.

I myself blinked, swallowed . . . took in the wide-brimmed tricorn hat; the powdered wig; the long, silver-embroidered frock coat with Belgian lace cuffs . . . the single white stocking and elaborately buckled shoe supporting that most hirsute of apparitions' starboard side counterbalanced by - I rubbed my eyes and blinked again - counterbalanced by a crudely fashioned stump of a WOODEN LEG to port . . . ? And all *that* circumnavigated by a broad leather belt a-sag with powder horn and flintlock pistol; boarding axe; silver hafted dagger . . .

. . . and cutlass!

That PIRATE's cutlass . . . !

. . . that 18th CENTURY pirate's cutlass . . . ?

'It *could* be a ghost, I suppose,' I conceded doubtfully.

Wondering precisely which place of refuge the dormant Wullie'd had in mind.

'Fear me not, lad,' the Awful Being called, timeously reassuring for my part, from its terrible pool of light. 'I make this, me very last earthly passage, bearin' only a cargo o' generous proportion.'

None of us aboard the *Charon* said a lot.

The Spectre tried again.

'I comes to set you a-sailin' on course towards thy Rightful Destiny, Edward boy . . . To bring thee thy INHERITANCE.'

That triggered a response.

'Did 'e say inheritance, Mister?' Trapp double-checked faintly, instantly focusing on the potential implications of such dialogue despite our eldritch circumstance.

'A bequest, lad. A dying vow. A promise made on the gallows by none less than meself, your greatest ancestor of all.'

'You're my ancestor?' Trapp echoed numbly.

'Aye, THAT I be. Edward Teach Trapp at yer service . . . *Cap'n* Edward Teach Trapp.' The Apparition deliberated a moment. 'Mind you, that wus jus' me Sunday name: Blackbeard Trapp wus wot they called me most times.'

'BLACKbeard Trapp?' The Trapp of the moment's usually less than discreet voice found bottom in an ecstatic whisper. "They" called you *that*, did they?'

'Who's "They"?' I muttered uneasily.

The Spectre was obviously pyschic.

'Ayyyye, *They* did an' all! All them screamin', tortured souls as wus me *victims*, lad . . . All o' Them 'oo 'ad the dread misfortune to fall into me bloodstained 'ands. All o' Them 'oo stared into the eyes o' Blackbeard Trapp as They breathed their very last,' it explained with, I felt, somewhat tasteless gusto.

As well as with a measure of glib self-satisfaction which, carrying as it did the all-too-familiar ring of genetic authenticity, went part way towards persuading me we could indeed be talking pure bloodline heredity here.

'Ayyyye, a black *beard*, and an even blacker 'EART I 'ad,' came the Spectral claim. 'In fact I wus the mos' fearsomest; the mos' buccaneerin'; the mos' terrible . . .'

'Most unassuming?' a little voice inside me giggled on the verge of hysteria.

'. . . mos' diabolickle, most *cruellest* cut-throat ever ter sail out o' the Port o' Nassau, boy. The greatest scourge ever ter put to sea in pursuit o' plate and plunder among the Polynesias. The maddest DOG ter pillage an' burn the treasure galleons off Madagascar . . .'

'You were a pirate, then?' Trapp, always sharp as a razor, hazarded tentatively.

I shot a sideways look of disgust but saw I'd already lost him. He

49

was entranced; utterly seduced by what - if appearances *were*, so to speak, to be believed - was fast establishing itself as some kind of Trapp family role model.

'The very worstest there ever wus,' the Spirit assured him firmly. 'I wus the mos' - '

'Ask how many galleons he got blown from under him while he was plundering,' I interjected hastily.

'That's got nothin' to DO wi' it. Bein' a pirate ain't exac'ly a precise SCIENCE yer knows!' the Ghost yelled back, possessing, apparently, a facility for supernatural hearing as well.

'He got sunk a lot. He's definitely a Trapp,' I nodded, finally satisfied.

'You . . . er, mentioned a *bequest*?' Trapp, never having been one to allow a natural awe of ectoplasm to interfere with avarice for long, reminded the Spectre. 'A dying vow, did you say? Made on the . . . ah, gallows, wus it?'

'Before they 'anged me in the King's name - aye! In the year o' Our Lord sixteen ninety-two that wus, lad. Off of the ramparts o' Fort Charles in the Guinea Gulf the dire deed took place . . . the *'anging* o' Cap'n Edward Teach Trapp,' came the Spirit's masochistic response - once again delivered, I thought, with a thoroughly unhealthy relish considering the circumstances.

Ohhh, *Jesus* - what was THAT . . . ?

A macabre black shape rose from the bridge deck behind us as I whirled, nerves shot to ribbons, to find myself confronted by yet another dreadful, goblinesque creature of the night.

'Has yon Spook Thing gone yet, Mister Miller, sir?' the resurrected Gorbals Wullie asked hopefully.

'Negative!' I snarled *sotto voce*. 'Piss OFF!'

'. . . then they chained me 'anged corpse to a post, they did,' the garrulous Ghost on the wharf persisted in its voice of gravel. 'Then they let the tide wash over me, lad. In and out, it washed - in an' out; in an' out f'r three 'ole days accordin' to British Admiralty Law . . .'

'Go on?' Trapp encouraged, deeply interested.

'THEN they 'auled me ashore an' dipped me in tar,' the Vision obliged without the slightest trace of resentment. 'And *then* they bound me 'andsome body tight in chains, they did. An' set me

HEAD inna metal cage so's the bones of me skull would stay in place when me tissues rotted.'

' 'Scuse me,' Wullie muttered faintly and lay down again, reaching for a bucket.

'THEN they 'ung me poor carcass from the gibbet on Dead Man's Point. *As a great Terrour to all Persons from Committing ye like Crimes for all time to come*, the sign around me neck said it wus . . . and so the long months dragged by, Edward lad. Tick, tock: tickey tock tock . . . An', as them months passed, the 'ot SUN slowly dried me flesh like crusty bread . . .'

I gulped convulsively and spared a covetous glance for Wullie's bucket.

'. . . an' the winds an' the rains prized me PARTS apart. An' the black seabirds peck, peck, pecker-peck-*pecked* at me 'orrible starin' EYES . . .'

'*Black*? I thought seagulls wis white?' Wullie debated in between retches.

'Go on - go ON!' Trapp prompted ecstatically, even he so diverted by such explicit pathology as to lose sight of what I could only presume had been the main point of his antecedent's Second Coming. Sourly I nudged him back on course.

'Never mind the family nostalgia - what about the dying vow, Trapp? You pick up that inheritance, maybe some of us'll get paid.'

. . . it began to switch off and on again then: the light. While at the same time curious white flashes which looked, to me anyway, more Singapore Power and Light Company than divine started popping and spluttering from somewhere deep in the undergrowth.

'Awwww SHIT!' the suddenly strobe-like Spectre of Cap'n Edward Teach Trapp, the worstest pirate of all, bellowed before hauling what looked like a rolled-up paper from his frock coat and waving it towards us with an urgency at some odds with what I, albeit a non-ecclesiastic, would have expected from your average Lost Soul on earthly walkabout.

Well I mean, apart from the embarrassment of abruptly finding itself looking more like a flickering image in some old Charlie Chaplin bioscope than a Denizen of Hell, why the tearing hurry to get back down to Davy Jones's Locker for any truly buccaneering doppelganger anticipating the drudge of serving a few more millenia in the Abyss once his interim run ashore was complete?

Apart from which: 'Did pirates actually *use* oaths like "shit" in sixteen ninety-two?' I asked Trapp suspiciously.

'Keep yer VOICE down, Mister,' he snarled at the top of his. 'You'll scare 'im *OFF*, dammit! Ghosts don't 'ave nothin' to do with unbelievers.'

'True. And I think I know why, now,' I said, turning for the bridge ladder.

'And where are YOU going?' he yelled.

'To poke him with a boathook,' I retorted confidently.

'WHO?' Trapp screamed, appalled.

'Your great, great, great,' I tried working it back to 1692, '. . . great, great, *great*-grandfather.'

'We huvnae *got* a boathook, Mister Miller sir,' Wullie - always prepared to afford spite priority over nausea - reminded the bucket. 'HE sold it. Along wi' oor lifejackets.'

'Don't yer DARE come near, yer scurvy dog,' the Phantom roared nervously from the wharf, 'or me ectoplasm might explode an' tear the livin' flesh from yer BONES!'

'An oar'll do nicely,' I said firmly. 'Anything. As long as it reaches further than a fake cutlass . . .'

Of course there was nothing to be seen by the time I'd clattered down the ladders to the centrecastle deck then made my final descent to the darkened wharf with the caution, to say nothing of the kamikaze philosophy, demanded from all who risked negotiating the *Charon III's* rickety accommodation ladder.

I poked tentatively at the tangled jasmine with the oar, but nothing moved. Not a splutter of ectoplasm to be seen. Never having been too keen on the idea of precipitating night actions with snakes and other horrid tropical creatures, I didn't chance pushing my luck by a deeper exploration of the undergrowth.

'All right, but don't blame *me* if 'e puts a CURSE on yer, Mister.' Trapp was clutching at vituperative straws from the bridge wing in the meantime. 'Don't you blame ME if yer wakes up a droolin' *idiot* one mornin' to find you gone all black an' MOULDY!'

I ignored him completely. The Awful Curse of The Family Trapp had already been deployed to maximum effect: had plagued me since the very first day I'd met him. Finishing up as a cretin with a bit of black mould on me promised to be neither here nor there by comparison. And anyway, Gorbals Wullie had been like that for years and nobody cared.

Pensively I studied the ground where the outrageously over-the-top caricature claiming to be Trapp's turbo-tongued ancestor had allegedly manifested himself. Unfortunately dockside dynasties of coolie squatters snatching a quick smoke, to say nothing of other even more insanitary forms of relief between cargoes, had long ago compressed the arid earth to the consistency of concrete. Try as I might I could identify no traces, paranormal or human-contrived, of recent footprints.

It was frustrating. Like everything else involving a Trapp. Had the ground been a little softer or the scattering of dust a little thicker, I might just have been able to convince myself beyond doubt that those circular indentations I imagined I could see really *were* circular indentations and not simply tricks of the wind. About stump size, they appeared to be. About stump-of-a-wooden-leg size . . . ?

There were other faint scrapings in the dust which gave me cause to purse my lips, too. Sinuous trailing marks which may or may not have been left by, say, an electricity cable? The kind which could have powered some kind of ultra-violet lamp for instance? Which, in turn, might well have cast an unworldly light on a certain hammed-up theatrical performance?

. . . though then again, the trails could equally have indicated the recent passage of some particularly lethal hunter-cruiser variety of the suborder *Serpentes*. Which brought me back to nervously imagining snakes in the grass again without, for once, making an automatic association with Gorbals Wullie.

Anyway, I followed that slender thread of conjecture with extreme caution, steadfastly holding myself aloof from the by-then bellowed conversation in full spate above me.

Which, for what it was worth, had consisted essentially of Trapp's ordering foul-temperedly: 'Go ON then! You get down ter the wharf an' see if the Mate's gone an' got hisself ectoplasmed yet.' To which Wullie's caring response had been an inflexible, 'Ah'm no' going near yon hairy spook an' that's fur sure. He's YOUR great, great somethin' grandfaether so he is, Captin - *you* go an' get all black mouldy if ye want to . . .'

My quest ended at the gable of a derelict transit shed. High up on the wall I could see a rusted electrical junction box with its cover hinged open and drooping. It was difficult to tell whether the black stains emanating from it represented the ravages of time, or scorch marks caused by a very recent short circuit - the sort that made lights flicker, and ghosts assume a sense of frantic urgency.

Thwarted, I turned for the ship, bracing myself to dice with her predatory accommodation ladder once more until suddenly - lying in the shadow cast by the jasmine - I caught sight of something white and seemingly tubular. Retrieving it gingerly I found myself holding a tightly rolled paper. Turning back one corner I could just make out, in the pre-dawn gloom, the beginnings of some spidery legend on its inner face. It all suggested I was holding a chart of sorts, though not the kind I was familiar with. More a scroll of parchment rather than conventional heavy cartridge paper.

I began to smile, vindicated. The self-proclaimed spectre of Blackbeard Trapp, the mos' terrible pirate there ever wus, had begun waving just such a rolled up phantasma in the moment when the plug was pulled on his grand *finale*. Yet what I held in my hand was perfectly tangible.

About as ectoplasmic as yesterday's copy of the *Straits Times*.

'*Well*?' Trapp demanded, hardly able to conceal his avarice as he waylaid me at the head of the bridge ladder.

'Yes I am, thank you,' I confirmed. 'Not a trace of mould on me.'

'I din't mean THAT, Mister,' Trapp growled, the state of his Chief Officer's mental, spiritual or physical well-being an irrelevance at any time. 'I meant more sort of: "Well, wot's that in your hand?"'

'Ohhh, you mean *this*?'

'COURSE I bloody do!'

'It's an oar,' I said.

54

'Good. So all we need now's a lifeboat – tae make up the set,' Gorbals Wullie muttered. 'We'd've had wan too, if you hadnae gone an' sol–'

Trapp lashed out with his foot and Wullie retired injured from the conversation.

'I *meant* . . .' Trapp started to specify laboriously again.

'Far as I can make out it's a chart,' I surrendered, hastily turning away.

'NOW where are you going?'

'Would you believe: to look at it in the *chart*room?' I asked. Wearily.

It was either Tanglin Road antique bazaar genuine or faked with considerable artistry. To my inexpert eye even the parchment itself appeared suitably aged, the land masses etched in convincingly faded browns lapped by seas of cobalt blue which were in turn inhabited by sketches of every bizarre sea creature a seventeenth-century mariner's nightmare might have been expected to conceive. According to the cartographer each and every voyage must have entailed a harrowing prospect: navigating between all those fanged and rearing serpents, giant squid, breaching whales and mermaids with breasts so overly developed they must surely have represented dangers to navigation in themselves.

'Seems to be centred around New Guinea,' I said, trying to decipher the unfamiliar scripted captions. 'From the Spice Islands west to Tagula. There's the Torres Strait and what we now know as Cape York at the northern tip of Australia.'

'I CAN read, Mister,' Trapp growled, patently still annoyed by my earlier avowed intention of poking his Grandpa to the power of five or thereabouts with a boathook.

'Just as well,' I retorted, determined to enjoy the satisfaction of puncturing at least one Trapp, even if only metaphorically, before the night was out. 'Because tomorrow, right after *I've* jumped ship on the perfectly legitimate grounds of my fast-approaching malnutrition, your contempt for basic human rights, and her Owner's – which means you again – imminent bankruptcy, then *you* can start reading the situations vacant columns for megalomaniac seamen wanted seeing you've no hope, no prospects . . .'

I made great play of rolling the chart up again dismissively. His brows collided in outrage.

'NOW what're you doing?'

'Going to ditch it. Which is what you should be doing with the rest of the useless rubbish you've collected aboard what used to be MY ship. Like your crew f'r a start, Trapp - particularly that *Wullie* person still clutching his private parts and screaming so childishly out there.'

The mistake I made was in using the description 'childish'. It was enough to trigger a self-fulfilling prophecy in itself. I saw his bottom lip beginning to project and felt a first twinge of unease. Invariably such a phenomenon signalled the onset of a major Trapp Tunnel Vision attack. It was time to retrench: deploy reason as opposed to malice.

'You're not getting any more delusions than normal, are you?' I asked anxiously. 'You aren't beginning to hallucinate again - fantasize that this clap-trap Trapp crap, Trapp . . .' I hesitated, trying to work that one out myself, then pressed on doggedly, '. . . might offer some last-ditch prospect of financial salvation or something? I mean, you aren't taking that charade on the wharf seriously? Not, well - not *seriously*?'

'Me inheritance, he said it wus,' Trapp muttered. 'A bequest, 'e said. The Legacy o' Blackbeard Trapp.'

'Looking at it objectively,' I pointed out, with little hope that he would on account of Trapp's having elevated his lack of objectivity to the status of an art form years ago, 'the only legacy Blackbeard Trapp's left you so far boils down to a blown junction box; what looks suspiciously like the stump holes left by a theatrical property department peg leg, and an obviously unrehearsed - to say nothing of uncommonly hasty - retiral from what I suspect was never a very convincing acting career in the first place.'

'And *that*,' he nodded petulantly at the chart I'd been too tardy in trying to conceal behind me. 'He left that too, remember? The secret's gotter be on there somewhere.'

I sighed and unrolled it again. Trapp dabbed a stubby, triumphant finger. 'Look, Mister.'

I blinked. *That* was odd – the fact that I hadn't noticed the hatched area the first time. The one squaring off the approximate centre of the chart and encompassing several rivers in latitudes to the order of nine degrees south and longitudes extending from one-thirty-eight to one-forty-four east – essentially the land mass forming the southwesterly coast of New Guinea to the Gulf of Papua.

Marked well inland alongside the tributary of one river was a crudely depicted cross of what presumably, judging by Trapp Ethereal's earlier preoccupation with the minutiae of necrology, could only represent human bones.

And an equally crudely scrawled caption. Complete with an authentically forged Trapp ink blot:

Here be buried Ye Bountiful Treasures of the mos'. admirable Pyrate, Captain Edward Teach Trapp

Right next to it there was another drawing: this time of a sickly green crocodile which, if scale had anything to do with it, must've been roughly twice the size of Mount Everest! Its jaws, dripping an ominously lurid crimson, appeared to be about to clamp on the graveyard marked 'X'.

It might as well have been labelled straight out:

Ye Irresistible Invitation to Ye mos' wurstest EYER. Trapp Adventure of All Time...

'. . . not again. Please – not AGAIN!' I heard someone – I can't think who – sobbing from a very long way away.

Chapter Four

On closer inspection with the chartroom magnifying glass - which, judging by Trapp's expression of chagrin, had merely been overlooked during his earlier forays in search of ship's assets to convert to cash - the gory embellishments did indeed seem to have been drawn by a rougher, less artistic hand affording, I concede, a neat touch of piratical authenticity. The colours, however, appeared suspiciously fresh, which didn't surprise me at all. Come to that, I wouldn't have evinced the slightest astonishment had we discovered the bloody *ink* was still wet! But then again, I wasn't Trapp.

Nor could I begin to conceive of why anyone should even wish to perpetrate what could only be an elaborate hoax on such a gullible target in the first place. It seemed to me that trying Trapp's credulity could, at best, only afford the would-be trickster much the same level of winner satisfaction as would my challenging Second Officer Spew to a game of *I spy*.

'Not much to go on. How does Grandpa Blackbeard expect me ter find treasure on a chart coverin' an area that big?' Trapp gloomed, confirming (a) that he *had* swallowed the ploy, hook, line and sinker, and (b), by definition, my gullibility theory. In fact his disappointment was so intense it took him well over a minute to remember to pocket the magnifying glass with the dexterity of a professional shoplifter.

Deploying two distastefully extended fingers I recovered it, now covered in bits of sticky fluff, and pointedly hung it back in the otherwise denuded navigating instrument rack which he'd also forgotten to sell.

'Just as well, seeing you've absolutely NO chance of going to Papua New Guinea anyway because, even if Bucalosie could get the engine started and we did have enough coal aboard to steam more than a hundred yards off the berth before having to send out an SOS, only a lunatic would go to New Guinea on the strength of *this* ludicrous forgery. In fact only a lunatic would go to a place like New Guinea for any reason.'

'Oh, I see. So as usual, you knows all the answers before the questions is even asked,' he challenged grumpily. 'You been there personally 'ave you, Mister?'

'No. But I've seen the size of that bloody crocodile.'

'It's only three inches tall,' Trapp said.

Gorbals Wullie limped in, still with tears in his eyes, and squeezed between us, gazing down in awe. 'Jeeeeze, would ye look at the size of that *crockledile!*'

'Bugger off!' Trapp suggested.

I clung to the bright side. 'Anyway, as you say, this chart's useless for all practical purposes. Nowhere near enough detail to work on - so goodnight: I'm off to bed.'

'Maybe there's a bigger map on the back?' Wullie had to go and theorize helpfully before I could make my escape.

Trapp turned it over and looked beatific.

I blinked for a second time. The green crocodile had grown eighteen inches in the split second it took to reverse the chart. And now there was only one very large-scale river, with leading marks and channels and magnetic compass courses; all in bizarre company with drawings of what seemed to be fast becoming the mandatory charnel ground of Trapp skeletons and skulls punctuating a trail through thatched huts and tufts of grass in areas marked ominously: *Ye Impassable Swampes ande Bogges . . .*

'Dunno aboot a pirate's chart. Mair like a map o' Custer's last stand,' Wullie commented, looking at the skeletons.

I suddenly felt aware of an odd sensation. Something I couldn't explain began to niggle me about the alleged treasure map of Blackbeard Trapp from that moment: something to do with the fact that I could've *sworn* it had been blank on the back when I first found it. But last-ditch defence was all about priorities - and something else was worrying me even more.

'Hang on a minute,' I muttered. 'Those impassable swamps - they're situated right between the so-called navigable channel and the so-called treasure!'

'Trust you to nit-pick,' Trapp disparaged sourly. 'Anyroad, we c'n always bypass 'em: go another route once we gets that far. See - round that way there, to starboard?'

He let his fingers do the walking. Confidently through one cadaver-strewn area warning *Beware ye Miasmas, Feveres ande Plagues*, suicidally skirting a patch labelled *Where Be Lurking ye Mos' Hugest ande Orrendous Crocodyle*, and encroaching well into a particularly clean-picked bones bit marked *Cannibale Kingdome* . . .

'It's not exactly the Yellow bloody PAGES you're looking at - that's genuine unexplored jungle,' I snarled. 'And anyway, you just said: "*We* can go . . ".'. What's with all this WE stuff, Trapp?'

'I'm nothin' if not over-generous,' he retorted with a sincerity which made me want to find Wullie's sick-bucket again. 'You been reasonably competent as a junior officer through the good times . . .' He misinterpreted the apoplectic flush rising in my cheeks and shrugged in good-natured condescension. 'All right, all right, I admit it - even through the odd *bad* time past as well, Mister. Either way I ain't the sort of shipmate to cut you out now me fortune's good as made.'

'Excuse me, but we haven't *had* any good times, Trapp: they've ALL been bad,' I pointed out with enormous care. 'And your fortune is a delusion; a con trick; a *Boy's Own Bumper Book of Silly Adventures to Get Involved In* fantasy. Your granting it any credibility at all is, of course, explained by the clinical certainty that you are a lunatic.'

I included helpful bloody Wullie in my thesis with one withering glance. 'The fact that *he* is Olympic competition-standard whacky has never been a matter for dispute - whereas *I*, Trapp, have NOT quite achieved such depths of sociopathic irresponsibility - yet - so . . .'

'First thing we gotter find is a charter: somethin' with enough profit to finance our way out there,' Trapp mused, allocating me to his *Minor irritants to be ignored* file.

'I am *trying* to make an extremely important point,' I interjected stiffly.

'Wonder if there's a market demand f'r gun-runnin' into Papua

New Guinea?' he speculated. 'Or 'ow about illegal immigration? A spot o' blackbirding . . ! ?'

'Judgin' by the jaws on thon greeny crockledile,' Gorbals Wullie opined, 'ah'd say there wis mair a rush of people tryin' tae get OOT the place, Captin.'

There's nothing more demoralizing than simply being ignored: being made to feel like an invisible rat caught in a . . . well, a *Trapp*. I flapped my arms vaguely to attract at least some flicker of awareness on their part.

'This *is* a cargo ship. You *could* try something legal. Like carrying cargo?' I suggested.

Trapp proved, as usual, magnanimous in victory.

'Jus' because you resent my charity in givin' you yet *another* chance of a berth in an employer's market, Mister,' he cautioned sourly, 'there's no need to be bloody offensive.'

There wasn't any night left, but I certainly worried for most of that morning while I sweated and turned in my microscopic cabin, trying desperately to achieve the sort of merciless unconsciousness people who haven't met Trapp describe as sleep.

I never made it.

It was that odd experience with the chart that continued to plague me. I really had been certain at first sight that its obverse side had been perfectly plain and unmarked. No greeny crockledi . . . *croco*-bloody-DILE! NO skeletons; no swamps, no detailed river passage surrounded by primeval no-go areas . . . which was totally ridiculous because obviously there must have been, only I just hadn't noticed them in the half light. It was merely a symptom of the strain I'd been under since he – they – since the whole bloody LOT of his old *Charon* crowd had reappeared to plague even my waking hours as all-singing, dancing, continually bickering three-dimensional nightmares.

Which was okay. That I could live with – a mere trick of the eyesight which meant, at absolute worst, I was only going blind rather than becoming embroiled in yet another Trapp adventure. But what really gave me cause to sweat, above and beyond the Singaporean humidity, was my absolute *certainty* that the dotted INSET hadn't been on the chart the first time we'd examined it.

That crudely outlined square embracing south-west PNG, its several rivers, and what now seemed - at least in retrospect, having looked at the bloody back - the comparatively innocuous Son of Monster Crocodile . . . and all baited with that positively Machiavellian *coup de grace* - that one phrase so blatantly emotive as to guarantee Trapp's undivided avarice.

Ye Bountiful Treassures . . .

I say again - and bear in mind I had even scanned it closely through a magnifying glass . . . I *swear* that dotted box had NOT existed on Blackbeard Trapp's ridiculous chart previously.

Not when I'd first carried it up to the bridge!

I found Trapp still poring over the chart table when, wearying of sleepless and solitary torment, I trailed in eventual search of someone to fall out with.

He'd managed to lay his acquisitive hands on some back-up navigating instruments in the interim. I didn't ask, but had a feeling that the master of some unwitting ship berthed nearby was going to be awfully put out when he reached automatically for dividers and roller rule to lay off his next critical course - and grabbed air.

My sense of futility was doubly reinforced on discovering Trapp had also done a cut-price deal with Albert Fuk Yew, his officially appointed local purveyor of marine chandlery and receiver of stolen property, on a slightly used British Admiralty chart folio covering the passage from Singapore to Papua New Guinea.

I mention cut-price because, apart from Trapp's deals never having been anything else, the most recent chart in that well-thumbed set was dated 1938 and every single one had been stamped with a large red warning: *Condemned - Not To Be Used For Navigation* - probably around the year 1942. Which was, I ungrudgingly conceded, neither here nor there in Trapp's case so long as the main land masses were still legible, seeing he'd always possessed the directional sense of a frigate bird linked with a natural ability to feel his way through the most hazardous of close waters with only eyes, ears and nose to guide him. Whatever my view of Edward Trapp's shortcomings as a world citizen, on a purely professional level I was prepared to bow unreservedly to his superlative qualities as a seaman.

'Hard to read the names on these rivers. Seems Grandpa Blackbeard weren't too good at the handwriting,' Trapp announced fondly.

I reflected briefly on *his* appallingly crafted and – as he persisted in deluding himself – anonymous letters to me with their atrocious spelling and ink blots and jam smears: as incontrovertibly Trapp as any signature.

'Not too good at the acting either,' I said. 'Still, now at least we know who you've inherited your superbly honed skills in illiteracy from.'

He didn't rise to the bait which unsettled me even further because it meant he was in a good mood. The one adversary more insulated from objective discussion than Trapp Aggressive was Trapp Amiable.

'Yeah, well, you'll be glad ter know I've figured out which one we got to take the ship into to find the treasure.'

'Delirious,' I muttered. 'Jolly super news like that makes my not having had any breakfast because there isn't anything to eat on board seem thoroughly worthwhile.'

'They're everywhere on that coast – rivers,' he continued, conveniently stricken with a sudden hearing disability. 'Not that it helps. F'rinstance, checking this,' he tapped Blackbeard's chart, 'against a modern chart . . .'

I sighed and let it go.

'. . . it seems most of 'em in the Gulf of Papua aren't navigable to big ships more'n a few miles inland. Too shallow once you're inside the estuary.'

I frowned at it. Son of Monster Croc gazed balefully back at me with a malevolence that seemed far more real than any painted fantasy. Or was it? I mean . . . well, there wasn't the slightest chance the drawing had been done from *life*, was there . . . ? That area of Trapp's Yellow Pages trek warning the gullible – or the arrogant disbeliever – of some place *Where Be Lurking ye Mos' Hugest ande Orrendous Crocodyle . . .?*

I shivered again, my previous strange unease sending a further trickle of cold water down my spine. Yet there *wasn't* any logical justification for such apprehension. Ghosts – particularly very solid-looking ghosts – did NOT exist. Ergo, neither did the legacies of ghosts! Therefore, by the simple process of elimination, neither could the luridly sketched *fantasies* of ghosts.

'Which one's supposed to be Blackbeard's river, then?' I heard myself ask. Purely to appear sociable, of course. Not because I took any of it seriously.

'That one. He calls it the Beetel.'

I frowned. The others I'd heard of – the Kikori and Turama to the east of the crocodile-guarded box; the Rivers Aramia and Bamu and, of course, the greatest of *all* New Guinea's malarial-swamp-logged, malignant-insect-and-poisonous-reptile-infested bloody inaccessible geographic highlights – the River Fly.

But I'd never, ever, heard of the River Beetel.

Which wasn't, perhaps, surprising.

Because, according to Trapp's 'modern' chart, it seemed that neither had the British Admiralty.

Okay, I'll grant you that maybe *some* members of the Royal Navy had heard of it. I mean, they were bound to have found and surveyed it at some time since Blackbeard Trapp allegedly sailed into it in 1689 or whenever.

Trouble was, they probably never returned alive from the many hazards Blackbeard had enumerated to *tell* the bloody Admiralty to add a River Beetel to their *Coral Sea (Northern Section)* chart.

'Mind you, that *is* goin' back to nineteen thirty eight, Mister,' Trapp defended when I politely drew his attention to the apparent discrepancy. 'That part of New Guinea wus mos'ly unexplored in nineteen thirt–'

'*That* part of New Guinea's mostly bloody unexplored TODAY!' I yelled, snapping for once and for all, '. . . and I'll tell you *another* thing while we're on it. THAT part – where you say your River Beetel lies – THAT part is just about smack dead centre of what is now the dividing line between Papua New

Guinea and West Irian . . . and when I *say* dead centre, Trapp, I MEAN dead centre!'

'Why?' he muttered, finally noticing I was a bit irritated.

'Because West Irian is Indonesian territory – Irian Jaya they call it. And there's a dispute been going on for years between PNG and Indonesia about who owns what on the border – though Christ knows why *either* of 'em should want to bloody own ANY of it . . . and people get killed for even being there, Trapp. Shot – shelled – bombed . . . eaten up by CROCKLEdiles!'

'Shot an' shelled? Here, youse two aren't thinkin' of going back tae Beirut, ah hope?' Gorbals Wullie was triggered into protesting as he shambled through the wheelhouse door eating a banana, which was enough to make me loathe him in itself.

'PISS OFF!' we both screamed in unison.

'. . . but, well . . . before you *do* go, old man – you, er, don't happen to know if there are any more bananas around, do you?' I added, hating myself.

'This one wis the breakfast ration f'r the whole foc'sle, Mister Miller sir,' Wullie whined, hastily cramming the last three inches of it into cheeks already bulging like a puffer fish. 'Today's jist my lucky day – ah won the raffle.'

'If you're still a bit peckish by tomorrow, Mister,' Trapp tempted, trying to worm his way back into favour so's he could exploit it, 'I'll make sure you gets a ticket.'

It may have been the innovative way I wielded the dividers, or the homicidal glint in my red-rimmed eye, but he changed tack from ingratiation to his version of reasoned argument very quickly. 'Look, all I needs is a *charter* an' . . .'

'Traaapp. . ?' a distant voice from outboard called. 'Captain Edwaaaard TRAPP?'

You could have cut the silence of the chartroom with a knife.

'It's 'IM!' Trapp finally whispered, eyes protruding on stalks. 'It's Grandpa Blackbeard again. Come ter put us on course for the treasure.'

The still unmasticated lump of banana bulged its way down Wullie's scrawny neck like a goat gulped too hastily by a boa constrictor. 'Anyone . . . ah, seen thon bucket?' he enquired, withdrawing discreetly into the shadows.

'Captain Edward TRAAAAPP?'

Trapp passed me running on his way to the starboard wing and craned over, scanning the wharf frantically.

'Where is 'e? Where IS 'E?'

'This side,' I called from the port wing. And smiled a secret smile.

Trapp hurtled back through the wheelhouse; leaned dangerously far out; looked down - went black-faced furious with disappointment - and bawled with customary hospitality, 'So wot the 'ell do YOU want, then?'

'Good morning, Captain,' the visitor, arms akimbo, boomed from the sampan lying off the ship.

'No it's NOT - it's too bloody *hot*,' Trapp shouted. 'And I'M busy workin' up a passage plan so you c'n jus' . . .'

'Excuse me.' I injected a note of anxious caution. 'He might be from the Missions to Seamen, or even the Salvation Army famine relief people.'

Though, if the truth were told, our current apparition *did* give rather more the impression of being someone on his way TO such a charitable institution.

He was a man in, perhaps, his early sixties: immensely tall but of lean and angular proportion.

The other feature which struck me immediately and most forcibly were his eyes - they burned like fire from beneath hugely bushy eyebrows. He *did* have a beard, but not a black beard. In his case it was more unkempt-goatee and yellowed with cheroot smoke. He wore a crumpled khaki bush shirt with colour co-ordinated tobacco stains and a jungle slouch hat, bearing what looked like a reptile-skin band, from below which a mane of shoulder-length white hair sprouted and struggled to escape. A worn leather ammunition belt set off flared knee breeches encased in calf-length boots reminiscent of a Twenties Hollywood film mogul. A bandolero studded with brass cartridge cases added a final flourish of eccentric panache to this, the most recent of Trapp-seeking bizarreries to hail the *Charon*.

'Now *thon*,' Gorbals Wullie breathed ecstatically between us, having first ascertained we weren't back in ethereal confrontation mode, 'is reel elegance, Captin. Pure dead magic gear. There, you have tae admit, is a man whit *knows* how tae dress wi' style.'

Wullie was, as ever, being less than diplomatic. If there was one thing Trapp hated more than losing money, it was losing sartorial centre stage.

'NO, 'e doesn't - he's got no idea of 'ow to dress proper like me,' he disputed so vehemently his open-toed WWII tennis shoes flapped and his dog-tin-lid cap waggled in jealousy. 'An' anyroad, there's nothing clever about dressin' different to us normal people.'

'Aye there *is*,' Wullie insisted sullenly.

'NO, there isn - '

'Permit me to introduce myself.' The visitor bowed quaintly albeit slightly erratically because, apart from our being thirty feet above him, sampans do tend to be a bit unstable. 'My name, gentlemen, is Smith. Walter Beedham-Smith . . . emeritus *Professor* Walter Beedham-Smith.'

Trapp went even blacker jealous.

'Ah, well o' course, tarted up like that an' with a double-hyphenated *name* like that, it has ter be PROFESSOR, don't it? And I suppose that bein' a *professor* means you thinks simple seamen like these two . . .'

'Steady *on*,' I protested.

'. . . oughter be impressed by fancy rig an' bookworm titles? I s'ppose *you* thinks educashun gives you the right to - '

'Oh, do shut up long enough to at least find out what he wants.' I levered him aside and made play of appearing irritatingly servile. 'Perhaps we can be of some assistance, sir?'

'Stop ENCOURAGING 'im, Mister: I can't afford to be diverted from me vital train of thought,' Trapp grumbled, squirming with impatience. 'I gotter concentrate on 'ow to get a *charter*.'

'I wish to enquire, sir, if your Owner may be interested in negotiating a charter?'

'. . . to Papua New Guinea an' *nowhere* else!' Trapp, always one to look gift horses squarely in the mouth, qualified quick as a flash, then leaned over again and bawled, 'I TOLD yer: I'm too busy. An' apart from havin' a full order book, this ain't no common tramp ship . . .'

'Yes it is,' I said. 'It's *full* of common tramps.'

'. . . available to jus' anybody to hire f'r money . . .'

I couldn't stand it any longer.

'That's *it*. That's IT, dammit . . . ! Until last night – before you met Grandpa bloody Trapp, Trapp – you'd've hired out your own SKIN for money; never mind your ship . . . *and* you'd've been only too happy to have thrown HIS into the deal on a permanent, non-return basis . . .' I included the appreciatively bystanding Gorbals Wullie in my tirade. 'Always supposing, that is, it wasn't so wrinkly an' dirty anyone'd bloody WANT it!'

'I had a bath, Mister Miller sir,' Wullie demurred cautiously. 'Once.'

'You'll have ANOTHER in a minnit if you don't shut UP!' I screamed, staring wildly over the side. Trapp opened his mouth, took note of the foam flecks beginning to dribble from the corners of mine, and shut it again conceding, for one of the very few times in our relationship, discretion as being the better part of suicide.

'What is more,' I roared, by then in full spate. 'What is MORE, Trapp, I am hungry. I am *very* hungry. I am, in fact, SO hungry that I am verging on the stage of being prepared to spit-roast a baby so long as it's left unattended, plump and eatable . . . therefore you will accept ANY business that will place food on our table, no matter how mundane: no matter how boring; no matter how *legal* it happens to be – and THAT, Trapp, means you will forget treasure hunting; you will *forget* Blackbeard Trapp and, above *all*, you will forget all thoughts you ever harboured of going to Papua New God-forsaken bloody GUINEA!'

Trapp shuffled uneasily, marshalling his last defences, prepared even to stoop to caution.

'Shouldn't we . . ?'

'Shouldn't we WHAT?'

'Shouldn't we, well . . . before rushin' into a firm commitment,' he counselled meekly, 'wouldn't it at least be prudent to ask where it is he wants to charter us *for*?'

I stared disbelievingly. Him . . . *him* advocating reason?

Him - TRAPP? Who usually displayed all the prudence of a lemming tipped off to the existence of a cliff ahead . . . ?

'Lissen, I don't care WHERE he . . !'

Recklessly I swung, determined once and for all to torpedo Trapp's ludicrous obsession with heading for that same jungle graveyard into which, legend had it, a whole Imperial Japanese Army division had disappeared without trace during World War II.

On that occasion *without,* as it happened, Trapp's help!

'Climb aboard - we'll take it!' I yelled to the blessed catalyst of my salvation in the sampan below.

'I should add that there will be a requirement to accommodate my personal staff, sir. Three research associates of mine . . . brilliant minds - quite brilliant.'

'So long as you pay cash up front for vittles an' fuel, she's yours. No *ifs*, Professor: no *buts* - jus' tell me where you wanna go, an' I'll get the charts out.'

'Splendid; absolutely splendid, my dear fellow. Then might I suggest you select those most appropriate for . . '

It was a bit late by then to suddenly become aware of how the eyes under the bushy brows locked on me, glittering strangely as our new employer raised a cadaverous face to mine.

'. . . a voyage to Papua New Guinea?'

'SAURIANS?' I exploded again in the *Charon's* mouldering saloon a few minutes later, after Trapp, suddenly nauseatingly hospitable, had invited what was so transparently some kind of academic lunatic aboard to firm up on detail.

'Whadd'you mean, Professor - you intend to charter this ship to study *saurians?*'

'Correction: he don't *intend* to - 'e has chartered it, Mister. And being the Owner I has to be bound by yer word, acting as me legal agent,' Trapp reminded me with cherubic satisfaction. 'You cut the deal yourself against my advice, remember? No *ifs* you said; no *buts*. Jus' . . '

'Do you have the remotest idea of what he wants this ship *for*, Trapp?' I snarled. 'DO you, f'r that matter, even know what a saurian *IS*?'

'*Course* I do,' Trapp retorted hotly. Then fell uncharacteristically quiet and examined a stubby fingernail closely.

'I can assure you, sir, that the specimens our expedition will seek out are the most exquisite and scientifically important examples of the *poikilothermic* order still surviving in the world today,' Professor Beedham-Smith interjected solemnly.

'I don't care HOW exquis - '

'All right, ah give up - whit *is* a dyo . . . doykill . . . a saureyanne, Mister Miller sir?' the least exquisite and scientifically fascinating member of our crew conceded, admitting, at least, to an honest ignorance utterly alien to Trapp.

'They're bloody CROCODILES - *that's* what saurians are,' I shouted, already terrified for the future. 'And he jus' said "our" expedition. That means he expects *us* to go poking under bushes LOOKING for 'em!'

Wullie's cheeks went a predictable shade of paste.

'CROCKLEdiles?'

'Yes - snap-crackle *crocodiles*. And, to save you the trouble of asking, you'll find your plastic bucket on the bridge,' I informed him cruelly.

'Crocodiles, eh?' Trapp mused, then remembered he was supposed to have known that already, and looked cool.

'Grocklediles?' Mister Spew, who'd been brought into the discussion because he was an officer, though only God and Trapp knew why on either count, breathed tenderly, his single eye going all dewy with emotion, 'I jus' *luv* grocklediles, Cap'n. They're cute, they are. All cuddly and furry.'

'Crocodiles, Spew,' I explained carefully, breaking the silence which ensued, 'are pure killing machines. They are neither cute nor furry - they are evolutionary triumphs of survival in that they are not edible in themselves; they can live equally well on land or in water; they have an upper jaw like a spiked manhole cover and can eat virtually anything or any *one* they fancy. They can also renew their teeth whenever necessary, Mister Spew, which is just as well because they do tend to use them a lot and are, in fact, the only babies in the world which can rip a man's finger off soon as they poke their little snouts out of the bloody EGG!'

'Pr'aps the Cap'n'll let me keep one f'r a pet?' Mister Spew persisted happily, impervious to the less attractive facets of undomesticated wildlife in his own little world. 'I could play games wiv it, an' take it walks along the deck, an' . . . an' I could *feed* it . . '

I appraised Gorbals Wullie with renewed interest. 'Who with?' I asked hopefully.

'You said "scientific", Prof?' Trapp probed, looking as if he suspected something I hadn't got round to being suspicious of. 'Jus' how "scientific" wus you and your eggheads planning to be when we've caught these . . . ah, syrians?'

'Our specialist field of research into the reptilian order *Crocodilia*,' the *Charon*'s new patron boomed, 'will be primarily concerned with a meticulous anatomical study of the genera *porosus*, *johnstoni* and - naturally - of *Crocodylus novaeguineae* itself!'

'Naturally,' Trapp nodded with complete understanding. 'Meaning you got to chop 'em up to study 'em proper?'

'Regrettably, sir, any fundamental investigation into animal aestivation, reproduction and longevity such as we propose does necessarily call for an element of . . . ah, dissection - yes.'

'Meaning you chops 'em *up*. After relieving them of their shiny little suits, o' course,' Trapp reiterated cheerfully. 'Incidentally, Prof, what *is* the current blackmarket rate f'r smuggled croc skins on the Aussie coast?'

'First quality ones? Roughly ninety dollars Australian per . . ' Professor Beedham-Smith raised a wintry smile. 'Naturally, Captain, as our expedition proceeds to amass species it may well find itself encumbered with a considerable quantity of, ah . . . scientifically valueless detritus. The saurian epidermi you refer to . . . ? Yes. Yes, If I interpret your meaning correctly, then I do concede we may be able to defray certain research costs were we to identify a suitable antipodean market for such salvage.'

'Excuse me . . . ?' I tried to butt in, finding myself somewhat at a loss.

'Seventy per cent o' gross scientific detritus sales to me . . . I mean, to the ship - thirty to yerself an' your associates.' Trapp ignored me, watching the Professor calculatingly. 'An' you pay

71

all passage costs to PNG up front, like the Mate said.'

'Fifty-fifty: net costs excluding overheads, Captain,' Beedham-Smith's beard projected challengingly.

'*Excuse* me,' I snapped. Much more firmly.

'Sixty-forty – gross, allowin' f'r capital depreciation! You retain the franchise on scientific paper publishing and tooth necklaces?' Trapp countered.

'Done!'

'WHAT'S done?' I demanded in mounting panic, already suspecting the answer was bound to be me.

'The deal you wasn't smart enough to make. I jus' fixed you up a partnership, Mister. As a . . .' Trapp read the wild light in my eye again, and ground to a tactical halt, moving in behind the wall-to-wall protection of Second Officer Spew.

'As a *what*?'

'I 'opes you appreciate you're *very* lucky indeed? I could easy've got a hundred unemployed run-of-the-mill seamen ter . . .'

'As a WHAT, Trapp?' I screamed.

'Oh, nuthin' – just as an industrial tycoon, that's all,' his disembodied voice specified, falling back on truculence. 'Jus' as a . . . well, a low-profile executive in an internashnul *fashion* accessories enterprise!'

'Low profile execut . . .?' I worked it out then, and felt threadlike veins in my eyes pop. 'YOU mean I'm gonna be a crocodile POACHER, *don't* you? You mean you just sucked me in again – stuck me this time with sailing Mate onna bloody HANDBAG FACTORY SHIP . . .'

I could have embarked upon more specific criticism of his proposal for my new career path than that, but I didn't. Because I caught one fleeting sight of the expression on the bewhiskered, skull-like countenance of emeritus Professor Walter Beedham-Smith when he thought Trapp wasn't looking, and broke off abruptly.

There was a madness there. An evil . . . a terrible, chilling insanity of purpose and I knew . . . I just *knew* that, whatever Trapp believed were the Professor's declared reasons for going to Papua New Guinea, the self-proclaimed man of letters had some far more complex motive in mind than simply penetrating a few disease-ridden primeval swamps to confront several hundred kilos of fast-moving prehistoric Armageddon machine with a view to rending it – or more probably, *them* in abundant quantities – apart for the supposed biological secrets they held.

Oh, I didn't doubt there was still a scientific bent to his craziness: that the poaching element was merely a pragmatic, albeit arguably a conservationist-unfriendly way for a naturalist to fund his researches. But I suspected that bit, the easy catch a crocodile-by-the-tail bit, would only be for starters. Before the going got *really* bizarre . . .

I got a grip on myself: forced myself to think positive. For one thing there was always the chance we wouldn't even make it as far as PNG, especially with Trapp's proclivity for getting himself and the rest of us sunk. Our ancient ship, my ex-*Bar Abir*, was still, as I knew better than anybody, a maritime death trap. More promisingly, she'd even been renamed *Charon*, which was as good as signing a suicide note on her behalf – I simply had to cling to that flicker of hope. With luck and a semi-moderate sea state she might even founder before we cleared Singapore Roads. Either way, and speaking from bitter experience, abandoning ship into an open lifeboat wasn't too bad in decent weather.

As long as you *had* one . . .

I even began to feel quite optimistic. No question that the Prof deal had its plus side. Maybe I had lost a battle but I'd still won my war over The Phantom Treasure of The Trapps. Dogmatic as he was, Trapp usually stuck to his word other than where I was concerned. There was no way the Captain's warped commercial values would permit him to divert from New Guinea's traditional crocodile hunting grounds up the Sepik or the Fly or wherever it was we were headed, in order to pursue his own search for some obviously mythical River Beetel. Not now I'd subtly contrived to bind him to what, according to his lights, was an inviolable contrac'shul agreement . . . albeit between lunatics.

Unless, of course, Smith was even more mad than I was beginning to figure and blew the ethics bit first. Deviated from his declared purpose of studying saurian longevity at the expense of ensuring his own.

'Okay, so we're going croc poaching – so what?' I shrugged

toughly, enjoying, at least, Trapp's disconcertion. 'So which part of PNG d'you want me to lay our course for, Professor?'

'A hazardous and largely uncharted area I must caution you, Chief Officer. Very little pilotage data available. Hard to pinpoint without local knowledge: tricky to make a landfall.'

I smiled deprecatingly. 'I *am* a Member of the Royal Institute of Navigation, sir.'

'Splendid, absolutely splendid. Then once my preparations have been completed we sail, dear fellow, for the approaches to the River Beetel.'

Chapter Five

We got our first chance to appraise the Professor's personal staff early next morning: the ones he'd referred to. The ones with the brilliant minds - quite brilliant?

'Well, they don't look a lot like scientists to me,' I said moodily, eyeing our three new passengers from the safe height of the bridge.

'You're always pickin' fault, ain't you, Mister?' Trapp grunted. 'Jus' because they ain't wearin' white coats an' bottlestop specs you get some daft notion they're hard men.'

'No. No, it's more the guns and knives they're wearing make me consider that as a possibility,' I defended. 'The big academic especially: the one with the bristle hair, cauliflower ear and slashed cheekbone? That's a pretty high-powered microscope he's carrying - along with enough ammo to take out half the Chinese Army.'

'Sturm-Ruger M77 high velocity: probably bored f'r three-fifty calibre Remington Magnum.' Trapp, who knew all about guns, having smuggled enough, chose his next words carefully in view of my accelerating tendency towards hysteria. 'Anyway, bear in mind we ain't exac'ly going bird-watching. The Prof's branch of natchral history c'n get a bit, well - *exciting*, you might say. Some crocs may, ah, express irritation at bein' asked to donate their skins f'r scientific research? Should you happen to come, well . . . face to snout with one, so ter speak, you'll probably feel easier with a bit of intellectual backup - like a rifle that c'n shoot the shit out've an elephant's big brother at five 'undred paces.'

'Face to snout with a crocodile, Trapp, I wouldn't feel easier with a bloody *field* gun behind me.'

He evinced close professional interest as emeritus Professor Beedham-Smith's other two already-lethal-weapons-hung assistants hoisted a long khaki-painted box from a cargo sling and carried it towards the strongroom for which they'd already appropriated the only key.

'Then 'ow would you feel about a shoulder-launched anti-tank missile?'

He asked.

But I should have *known* it wasn't going to turn out to be a simple straightforward matter of transporting a patently mad academic with a personal staff of seemingly Special Forces-educated intelligentsia deep into the unexplored with the expressed intention of breaking every game-preservation law in the international book while sandwiched between two opposing guerrilla armies and, seeing we just happened to be going up a certain river anyway - an amazing coincidence which I hadn't overlooked and fully intended to raise with Trapp at an appropriate moment - searching a human-skeleton-populated jungle hell for some masochistic pseudo-phantom's alleged pirate treasure as a bloody SIDELINE . . . !

Not when Trapp was involved.

Lord, no.

No, there had to be an unorthodox aspect to the voyage as well.

Like the modifications Beedham-Smith requested we made to the *Charon* before we sailed - the intriguing questions raised by *that* particular exercise - allied with, of course, those two quite inexplicable and rather grisly murders we'd had on board already.

And then there was the niggling uncertainty posed by that deck carg . . .

The MURDERS?

Haven't I *mentioned* the murders yet?

Those corpses I'd sort of stumbled on late that same night? Not long after that thoroughly unsavoury business in which Gorbals Wullie and Second Officer Spew got themselves chased back to the ship in a pedal-powered trishaw by berserk Oriental chaps waving knives?

. . . I haven't covered THAT little episode *either*?

NO?

Well, it's not exactly *easy*, dammit: to keep up with the precise chronological order of EVERY single event that took place . . . yet, on the other hand I suppose, considering those incidents, both the chase and its grisly aftermath, *were* to prove of not-inconsiderable significance during the course of our subsequent misadventures – not that I realized they would at the time, mind you – then perhaps I should recount them in some detail. Before venturing to catalogue the *really* bizarre happenings that were to follow.

Just in case you're beginning to question whether my fourth voyage with Trapp was as eventful as his previous disasters. Was shaping to be a relatively straightforward affair?

It all started about ten o'clock that same evening.

I'd been leaning over the bridge front gazing moodily into space as usual. Not speaking to Great White Hunter Trapp slouching beside me. As usual. Professor Beedham-Smith and his three assistants had gone ashore for the night to arrange for further supplies of scientific equipment – whatever *that* meant, having seen the calibre of the kit they'd brought aboard already – and had departed with the strongroom key still pointedly in their possession. In that context I'd been left with the strong impression that if anybody was ill-advised enough to nosey into its contents in the interim, then the culprit wouldn't have enough fingers left unbroken to continue their lock-picking career for some months to come.

I think that anti-social attitude of our co-partners in the fashion industry was as much a cause for my morose preoccupation as anything. That, and the fact I was still mulling over the apparent contradiction posed by shooting a *crocodylus porosus* with an anti-tank missile while at the same time finding enough of it left to *make* a bloody handbag out of, never mind conduct detailed research on . . . I mean, okay – granted the Prof himself had gravely conceded some element of vivisection was scientifically unavoidable. It was just I hadn't anticipated he proposed to do it with two an' a half kilogrammes of linear-shaped high explosive.

Assuming targets of the *poikilothermic* order WERE what he had in mind?

77

However . . .

We'd first heard the disturbance from a long way away. I suppose it was my fault to some extent; I'd been the one to propose, largely in order to get Gorbals Wullie and Second Officer Spew off my back for a few hours, that Trapp might part with enough of Beedham-Smith's up-front passage cash in lieu of the two-years-plus back pay he owed, to allow them to run ashore for a beer.

Well, you wouldn't believe the peripheral melodrama THAT innocent suggestion had caused f'r a start – Trapp glowering and stamping about the deck in a terrible temper and generally behaving like he'd already behaved once that day . . . on that occasion because the Professor had demanded he spend some of the first *tranche* of passage money on buying a couple of LIFEBOATS for the trip . . . !

Anyway, Wullie and Spew got their pocket money eventually, after I'd threatened to set light to Blackbeard's chart, and off they went searching for the nearest booze shanty.

It had been quite rewarding all the same: waving and watching them go off side by side into the sunset clutching five whole Singapore dollars. A bit like saying cheerio to Laurel and Hardy without the music.

Three hours later they returned, marked not so much by solidarity as a fast-approaching glint of chromed wheel spokes trailing a comet's tail of dust.

At first I'd begun to assume we were especially privileged to witness some official Singaporean attempt on the World Pedal-Powered Trishaw Land Speed Record until I recognized the bicycle jockey with head down over the handlebars, cloth cap flat aback and stubby legs a frantic blur as being our very own Gorbals Wullie.

Mister Spew on the other hand, despite his being pinned firmly against the back of the seat by the G-force of Wullie's urgency, appeared to be maintaining his usual thick-as-mince aplomb reclining, as he was, on the cushioned stern thwarts in company with . . . yes – *yes*, Trapp confirmed sourly, it *was* in company with the moving metal's original coolie owner-driver.

I gathered later the trishaw boy had been upgraded willy-nilly

- or in this instance, Wullie-Spewy - to tourist class because, when the clustard did hit the flan back at the lice wine bar and abandon ship suddenly seemed like a good idea, he hadn't managed to pedal anywhere near fast enough - in Wullie's view - to match Wullie's required level of crisis management.

But I'm digressing again . . . Hard in their wake followed what I can only describe as a sinister and thoroughly unattractive band of Oriental thugs. Chinamen all; all forgetting they were supposed to be inscrutable, and all yelling at the tops of their voices . . . about a dozen altogether, straggling back over the course in varying stages of homicidal exhaustion; mostly kitted out with knives as tools of trade but one or two waving the odd iron bar or nail-studded chain.

'I 'opes them two 'asn't dared invite *that* noisy lot back f'r a tour of the ship without even askin' my permission,' Trapp speculated dangerously, breaking his silence for the first time since he'd paid out money.

'No,' I said, thoughtfully assessing the back-up echelon's general demeanour. 'No, from the irritation they're expressing, I don't think Spew or Wullie actually *invited* them. Not socially speaking.'

'See? Di'n't I warn yer, Mister?' he pronounced with morbid relish. 'You can't give my Key Personnel unsupervised access to a whole can o' Tiger beer without expectin' the ship's public relations image to take a dent.'

We watched Gorbals Wullie hurl himself from the saddle as the supersonic trishaw approached the bottom of the accommodation ladder. His little legs hit the ground, still a blur, and Wullie was halfway aboard accompanied by the squeal of burning rubber soles before you could say *cut-throat* while the abruptly pilotless machine continued to steam erratically down the wharf at full emergency revolutions, still transporting its First Class complement south.

As it passed below the bridge wing, Spew's cheerful recognition hung in the air in a manner akin to the doppler effect of an express train thundering non-stop through a suburban railway station.

' . . . 'allo Captin - 'allo MisterMillerssiiiir . . . '

'. . . but then I suppose,' Trapp sighed tolerantly, raising a languid hand in acknowledgement, 'I can't *always* be a mother to 'em, can I? Not keep 'em outer trouble *all* the time.'

'Yes you could,' I countered mildly. 'The most effective way would be for you to pay them off and not take them on any more of your voyages.'

The trishaw reached a point some half a cable's length from the end of the wharf and began to lose momentum, throttling back to around Mach One.

Trapp surveyed the approaching lynch mob with a world-weary eye.

'Bloody interruptions; always bloody interruptions - where's that Choker BLIGH?' he bellowed, looking down at the crew gathered vociferously on deck to cheer our fugitives on . . . or at least *some* of them to cheer our fugitives on; the majority were rooting for the lynch mob - mostly those harbouring black suspicion as to how Wullie, who always somehow contrived to pass round the straws, had won the breakfast raffle four statistically-unlikely days in a row.

'I'm f*$%*&!-well 'ERE! Standin' by with me fire axe an' chain-stopper rarin' to go - thass where I am, Cap'n,' our cuddles of a bosun bawled back hopefully from his slough of malignancy. ''Ow many of 'em, an' in which order does yer want me ter f*$%*&!-well kill?'

'Belay that, it's not like they're from Interpol. Nothin' over the top; just yer usual hands-across-the-sea welcome,' Trapp ordered. 'Ceremonial side party with knuckledusters an' hoses'll do.'

. . . fifty yards from wharf zero!

I estimated the trishaw had decelerated to well below supersonic by then. Its coolie ex-driver didn't appear so sanguine, not the way his shrieks carried so clearly above the howl of the mob - the home team mob: not the *Charon* mob.

Gorbals Wullie arrived purple-faced and puffing on the bridge. 'See me, Captin?' he panted. 'Ah didnae *dare* stop and stand mah ground or ah'd've massacred every last wan o' they Chinee lads wi' mah bare fists an' gone tae jail an' . . . an' *shamed* ye, so ah wid. Mah trouble is ah jist suffer all the time fae the drawback of being a natural-born Tiger . . .'

We all craned over to watch with interest as Mister Spew's pedalo hackney carriage finally shot off the end of the wharf pretending it was a jet catapulted from a carrier flight deck. Mister Spew, still maintaining his man-about town reclining position, described an impeccable parabola in formation with his petrified associate to embrace the foetid waters for the second time since we'd arrived.

'Ohhhh someone getta ROPE an' haul the Second Mate out,' Trapp grumbled. '*After* you've recovered the wheels. Could be worth a handy few bob, that trishaw. As a marine salvage claim.'

I returned to the by-then deserted bridge deck an hour later to search for my cigarettes. I'd given up smoking some weeks before, on the stern advice of the doctor in Djibouti, but had started again that morning soon as I heard about the crocodiles. It seemed to me if any noxious substance should've been stamped with a health warning, it was Trapp.

Chief Bucalosie's harbour generator was still blown up following Bosun Bligh's enthusiastic rout of the Yellow Horde, largely because Choker had been a bit liberal at interpreting Trapp's caution. It seemed he'd wired our steel accommodation ladder to the ship's main power supply then hung a *Welcome* sign in Chinese characters at the top; the result of which action not only added a whole new dimension to the concept of crispy fried carry-out but also - once the short circuit flashes and the glow of white hot knife blades had died away - an element of near pitch darkness to the already eerie ambience cast by restless cloud obscuring the moon that night.

Fortunately I knew every rust-sick rivet in the ship intimately and had fumbled my way up the starboard ladder with little difficulty, even remembering to avoid the third and fourth treads which were missing. No one else was around by then, the crew having either gone to doss down in the foc'sle or form a committee to debate the best way of emptying half the Singapore Straits out of Second Officer Spew soon as they finally managed to winch his sodden deadweight inboard.

Sod*den*. Not . . . ?

I hesitated, thinking I detected a sound above me: a sort of moan . . . well, more of a gurgle really. Yet the Spew Crisis Management team were still preoccupied down aft; I could hear them arguing from a distance, so it wasn't the Second Mate pumping bilges . . . I listened uncertainly - there it was *again*, dammit. That unsettling, almost liquid cadence!

Taking firm hold on my imagination I crept higher; up past the seventh and final tread, which was also missing, to the bridge deck level itself. To starboard stretched the neon-punctuated skyline of the metropolis; ahead rose the skeleton finger of the *Charon's* foremast and the slab-sided lump of her stubby focs'lehead dominated by its silent windlass; above and abaft the bridge towered the silhouette of her currently redundant funnel which must have been craving a re-energizing draught of smoke as much as I did by then.

Narrowing my eyes I peered inboard, through the salt-dulled windows of the deserted wheelhouse - no sign of movement within. Smiling self-deprecatingly at my own immature fear I took three confident steps towards the wheelhouse door - and stubbed something soft and yielding with my foot.

I stopped smiling and frowned. Uneasily. The only soft thing one would normally expect to trip over on the *Charon's* bridge was Blind Spew when he was what Trapp euphemistically described as *keepin' watch* . . .

Screwing my eyes tightly shut - a rather pointless thing to do on reflection - I stooped; extended one tremulous, exploring hand.

JEsus!

I'd touched something sticky; resilient . . . and *warm*?

My hand retracted as if attached by bungee cord: it took a full minute for it to stop trembling long enough to fumble for the Zippo lighter in my breast pocket, and another thirty seconds before I could bring it to thumb the flint wheel.

The dim flame illuminated just enough of a human face to make out its eyes. They were staring up at me, almond-shaped: beginning to glaze in the fixed stoicism of death only moments old. I moved the flickering lighter sideways, across the slack, open mouth; past the still vacantly relaxing chin . . . and caught the glint of blood where one normally expected to find a tie.

82

Frothy, bubbling blood. Still oozing sluggishly from the gaping slash in the victi . . .

Subconsciously I registered harsh breathing approaching from behind and began to swing; my strangled plea for mercy only half-composed – as a skeletal hand grasped my SHOULDER . . . !

The full bridge lighting had come on again by the time the black tide which initially engulfed me had slowly receded . . . that term 'full bridge lighting', by the way, meant the single forty-watt bulb Trapp had left in the bloody wheelhouse since he'd consolidated his assets.

Anyway, I sensed rather than saw the menacing silhouettes of the killers framed against that miserly glimmer and kept my eyes firmly closed, trying partly to persuade them I'd passed out through fear and so milk the compassion they had obviously kept well in reserve, and partly because I couldn't think of anything more ingratiating to do.

The first killer said doubtfully, 'Why did Mister Miller lie doon when I touched him, Captin?'

I eased my left eye a slit.

'Because', I explained ever so carefully, 'having just tripped over that dead body there, I was already taken slightly aback. Then *you* two bumble along doing your famous imitation of Burke and Hare window-shopping in a graveyard an' scare the *rest've* the living shit out of me – THAT'S why!'

'Dead body? WOT dead body?' Trapp's voice jeered.

'*This* dead body', I snapped, jerking my head at the one beside me. 'The one that just happens to have had its throat slit. If you'd left TWO bloody bulbs in the wheelhouse you'd've been able to see for yourself.'

Trapp bent down through the darkness and prodded where I indicated. His tone changed instantly, lost some of its scepticism. 'Slide the wheel'ouse door open: let a bit more light out', he snapped to Wullie.

Wullie gulped. 'What if the – well, if the murderer's still . . . innit?'

'Then you c'n create a diversion by lettin' 'im cut your throat too, while me an' the Mate here legs it – GO ON, dammit!'

'Ah'm *reely* scared,' Wullie announced.

'Good,' I muttered sourly. 'Not surprising, but still good.'

The black paper cut-out which denoted the whereabouts of Tiger Wullie fumble-footed three hesitant steps, windmilling its arms defensively in front of it, then disappeared from sight with a *thud* as it fell over something at deck level.

'Probably found another body,' Trapp growled, still derisive.

'Ohmah*God*it's*anitherBODY . . . !' Wullie screamed.

'Jesus,' Trapp said, finally shaken to the core.

'I'll lend you my Zippo - it's your turn,' I offered.

The second Chinaman - they were both cadavers of Eastern origin - hadn't had his throat cut: he'd been knifed once, most expertly, below the breast bone. The weapon itself was nowhere to be seen. It had, however, obviously been wiped clean on the second victim's faded denim jacket after removal: that deliberate act and the angle of entry, thrust forcibly upwards and into the chest cavity itself, all suggested a highly professional approach to taking out one's fellow men.

Trapp slid the wheelhouse door back with a crash to allow weak yellow light to slant across the corpses. I was glad of that: my Zippo had almost run out of fuel and I was gasping for a smoke. Not, you'll appreciate, that I planned to enter the chartroom myself to track down my misplaced ciggies. I'd figured on sending Wullie in for them - just in case the killer, or killers, were still hanging around and thus likely to prove the warning on the packet correct even quicker than the doctor in Djibouti had anticipated.

'Come over here an' look at this,' Trapp called in a low voice.

Reluctantly I skirted the pool of blood to join him beside ex-Chinaman Number One. He'd lifted the corpse's right arm and turned it to expose the underside of a limp wrist. I frowned at the tattoo revealed thereon. It was of a stereotypical fire-breathing dragon, red in colour, intertwining two Chinese characters surmounting crossed mandarin swords.

'Makes a change from crocodiles,' I said lightly, trying to inject a touch of sterling British humour into a grave situation.

Trapp afforded me an unappreciative glower. 'Not that much

of a change,' he retorted enigmatically. 'Except this one's tattooed *on* a crocodile.'

He let the dead man's arm flop to the deck with scant respect even for him. 'Now take a dekko at the other bloke's wrist,' he said grimly.

'Move your bucket,' I snapped to Gorbals Wullie, hunched in routine response to threat beside the late Number Two boy. The tattoo proved a match: the same colourful serpent conjoining the characters and everything.

'It's identical,' I called.

Trapp's eyes were bleak in the low light.

'Then we got ourselves a problem.'

I lifted a doubtful eyebrow at the corpses. *We'd* got a problem?

'Them tattoos: proves they're members of the Ying Tong tong, Mister,' he muttered hollowly.

Wullie straightened abruptly. 'Oh NO! No' the . . . Ying Tong *tong*?'

'Aye – the Ying *Tong* tong.'

'Och jeeze – the *Ying* Tong tong,' Wullie whispered going even whiter than his previous white, then crossed himself.

'How long has he been religious?' I asked Trapp interestedly.

'Aboot half a minnit.' Wullie's retch echoed hollowly from the bucket.

'One o' the Singapore Triads,' Trapp growled irritably. 'Criminal secret societies: you know the sort – like the Mafia, except, for spaghetti, read rice. The Ying Tong tong's one o' the most vicious. Carve yer up soon as you c'n say *chop suey* if you cross 'em.'

'Why would I want to?'

'Want to what: cross them?'

'No, say *chop su* . . . oh, forget it,' I snapped. 'Even hinting at people getting carved up – you know how much it upsets me. Apart from which it's an academic issue anyway: I mean, why on earth *should* we want to cross them?'

'Slight correction, Mister. *Why* we should want to cross 'em has already become the academic issue – considerin' we already have.'

'Don't be silly,' I complained irritably, thinking *sod the sterling British humour approach*. 'This is far too serious a matter to joke about.'

'All right,' he shrugged mildly.

I frowned for a while over his worrying submission that we were even less fortunate than a couple of already-dead men; waiting for him to retract it. But he didn't.

'Okay, I give up,' I conceded wearily. '*Why* have we already crossed them, Trapp?'

'You're lookin' at the answer, Mister. We've finished up playing host to two of their own sworn brothers. Which would be very commendable except they just happens to have ended up fallen off their perches in our care ... an' the Ying Tong Family's executive action branch ain't goin' to bother over-much about which one of us killed 'em.'

'Oh,' I muttered.

'Oh *Jeeze*!' Wullie endorsed in a muffled plastic undertone.

Trapp stirred, scratched his head plaintively. 'What *I'm* trying to figure is why they were up here on my bridge in the first place?'

'Not to steal anything, *that's* f'r sure,' I snarled resentfully. 'Not unless there's a chronic shortage of forty-watt bloody light bulbs in Chinatown, 'cause you've stolen everything else worth stealing already.'

Okay, so I accept my outburst was an immature response for someone just informed he'd been volunteered for a worse-than-death sentence, but I had to lash out somehow at the catalyst of my continuing misfortune ... which now looked as though it was shaping to go on a while yet seeing that, according to him, half the Singapore bloody underworld were apparently poised to put out a contract on me.

It didn't even have an upbeat side this time. It didn't make sailing with Trapp to Papua New Guinea in company with mad Professors on a coffin ship to wrestle with crocodiles seem one whit more attractive - it just made my ambition to stay in Singapore and *not* go to PNG seem ALMOST as dangerou ...

'Here, youse twa: I've got An Idea,' Gorbals Wullie suddenly announced out of the blue.

We both stared blankly, struggling to come to grips with the concept of Wullie having An Idea. It was an historic moment.

'*You've* got an idea?' Trapp echoed, his train of thought completely derailed.

'It seems tae me that, like Mister Miller said, there wisnae ony *particler* reason . . .'

'Could you ask him to explain it in English so's I can understand as well?' I requested Trapp.

'. . . f'r they deid Chinee lads here tae pick on *this* ship,' Wullie continued, obligingly refining his accent to Celtic unintelligible. 'While you, Captin, reckons the Ying Tong tong'll jist hit the ones in final possession of the bodies, so tae speak . . . am ah right, or am ah wrong?'

'Right f'r once,' Trapp confirmed, looking impressed already.

'So, the way *ah* sees it, all *we* have tae do is move them tae ANITHER ship, and . . .'

I twigged what he was driving at then and, frankly, was appalled.

'That,' I broke in coldly, 'is the most underhand, the most cowardly, the most reprehensible, certainly the most con*temptible* proposal I've ever listened to . . .'

I reconsidered the options.

'Though on the *other* hand . . . ?'

When I finally received and opened my vagrant cigarette packet with still trembling hands, there weren't any in it. Gorbals Wullie persisted in blaming their disappearance on levitation, even citing the current climate of ghostly happenings long after the missing tubes rematerialized from within the greasy recesses of his bonnet following my cruelly twisting his ear until such time as they did.

I inhaled right down to my boots and the world suddenly seemed an almost bearable place again.

Until Trapp went and mused sepulchurally, 'It makes yer think, don't it, Mister? What it'll be like keepin' watch up 'ere, all on yer own in the middle of a black an' windy night . . . ? Knowing there's a bloodthirsty double *murderer* prowling aboard?'

'*That's* bloody IT - get the POLICE,' I rounded on him. 'I want police protection, Trapp. Round the clock! Gangsters? Corpses already . . . ? A Chinese Triad - a particularly *nasty* Chinese Triad even according to you - now apparently about to conclude WE killed two of THEIR members?'

'Why ever would they think a thing like that, Mister?' Trapp frowned.

.I brought up short and blinked at him, flapping my hands vaguely.

'Well . . . I dunno - maybe because there just happens to be BODIES belonging to them lying about everywhere. Probably *that's* why.'

'Bodies?'

'*Those* BODIES, dammit!'

'Wot bodies?'

His expression was utterly cherubic.

'That, Trapp,' I began to explain laboriously, 'is exactly what you said fifteen MINUTES ago . . .'

Of course they'd gone by daylight - the nomadic cadavers. In the glow of the rising sun the bridge deck sparkled with the well-scrubbed look of a hospital operating theatre. I couldn't fail to be impressed. Aboard any of Trapp's commands the breaking-out of a deckwash hose was an event as exceptional as Gorbals Wullie with An Idea.

I didn't ask where they'd gone to. Even if I'd wanted to know, I didn't really want to waste time and temper raising it again with Trapp on account of I could see he'd been impressed by Wullie's Idea - based on the well-known *Now you see it; now you don't* philosophy of sidelining evidential corpses to confuse and delay the enemy - and would be too busy trying to accelerate our departure for Papua New Guinea before the Ying Tong whoevers did finally put two and two together and came up with the *Charon*.

Personally I didn't plan to co-operate any more than I usually did; still tending towards the view that staying put and facing two-legged threats of whatever ilk was marginally preferable to steaming nearly three thousand miles just to hurl ourselves at *four*-legged ones with sixty-odd teeth and coach-built like armoured cars.

But events were to proceed despite my enthusiasm. The Professor and his scientific team arrived back aboard shortly after dawn, presumably having been back to the laboratory to collect a few more items of heavy calibre nature-studying kit, judging by the shapes of the gun cases they were slinging, and by then it was time, as I'd begun to explain earlier before corpses and turbo-charged trishaws and Chinese secret societies intervened, to mull over the reasoning behind certain modifications Beedham-Smith requested we made to the *Charon* before we sailed.

To preoccupy myself with the intriguing questions raised by *that* forthcoming exercise.

Chapter Six

Take the heavy lift derrick on the foremast for instance.

It was perfectly capable of hoisting a crocodile carcase aboard. Well, a small crocodile carcase ... well, sort of a *lizard*-size crocodile carcase. So long as the creature hadn't eaten a substantial meal just beforehand.

Okay: so I'd been the *Charon's* previous skipper and should've ensured the ship's cargo handling gear was properly maintained, like Trapp, who'd never bought a lick of paint or a spit of grease for a ship in his life, so hypocritically implied. But those former Owners of mine, the Djibouti Mafia or whoever – still a lot nicer people to work for than Trapp – I mean, *they* hadn't exactly invested lavishly in her future either, had they? Other than pick up the tab for planting a couple of scuttling charges or so ...

Anyway – the Professor had frowned long and hard at the rusted wire topping lift; crumbled a couple of shackles to dust between his fingers, then stared dubiously up at the corroded length of the *Charon's* heavy lift tube derrick which, notwithstanding, was probably still the most efficient piece of equipment left aboard since Trapp's sales drive.

'Tell me, Chief Officer: what would you consider the maximum working loading for this device in its ... ah, present state?'

I considered the question in depth taking into account complex technical factors like the gear being totally fucked from the heel of the derrick up.

'A good-sized basket of grocerie – ' I began to opine.

'Twenty ton,' Trapp lied shamelessly. 'Renew the old shackles, gins, runners and guy falls – rig a three-fold purchase rove to advantage? Twenty ton at least, Prof!'

'I'm sorry, gentlemen, but that simply won't be enough', our nicotine stained academician sighed.

'Not *enough?*' I echoed, overlooking Trapp's slight departure from any resemblance to the truth in my astonishment. Just what size and type of lift did our charterer have in prospect?

'Not enough, sir.' The Professor's beard sagged despondently. 'I regret, gentlemen, that we may have to review our charter arrangement. That this vessel may not be suitable for our purpose after all.'

'Gosh, *that's* a pity.' I looked utterly crestfallen. 'Twenty ton lift not enough, eh . . . ? Oh well, we'll just have to cancel going to New Guinea and look for something else.'

'*Thirty* ton if we do a bit o' modification, o' course.' Trapp upped his bid quick as a flash. 'Quadruple the lifting purchase an' span – rig preventer backstays; strengthen the deck plating and so on?'

'We'd have to strengthen the mast, derrick an' winches along with the *rest* of the bloody ship to lif – ' The agony of a crushed instep blinded me momentarily.

'Yeah: thirty ton easy', Trapp dismissed, eventually removing his heel. 'Long as you're paying the bills, o' course.'

The Professor heaved an even bigger sigh. 'Still not enough capacity, I fear. Still not enough.'

'Exactly what sort of cargo size and working load DID you have in mind?' I winced through the tears.

The odd light appeared in emeritus Professor Walter Beedham-Smith's compelling eyes again. That burning, fanatical light as if visualizing something . . . I felt what was becoming an all-too familiar prickle at the nape of my neck every time I found myself in his presence. Why *did* the Professor's seemingly recurring vision strike me as being one conjured by sane people only in the kind of nightmare from which they awake screaming and stare-eyed?

Then his gaze cleared: fixed me innocently.

'I estimate some sixteen metres long, Chief Officer – say fifty-odd feet? And weighing in the region of . . . ah, forty to forty-five metric tonnes?'

'What's a *metric* tonne?' Trapp whispered anxiously. 'Is that the same as a proper British ton?'

'It's more - but does it matter?' I hissed back. 'You've made up your mind he's going to pay your way to PNG and that's that. If he asks could we lift the *Titanic* you'll just nod your bloody head and say "yes, so long as we treat the iceberg sepr'ate" anyway'.

Trapp turned, laughed tolerantly.

'Ah, well now, if you'd *said* metric right at the start, Prof', he chastized with great good humour, 'we could've saved ourselves a bit o' confusion. Forty tonnes *metric* we c'n haul aboard easy . . .'

He eyed me warily soon as we were alone.

'Before you say anythin', Mister, all it needs is an extra bit o' seamanlike preparation.'

'Such as?'

'A new rope's end f'r Choker Bligh! You'd be amazed what my lads could lift with Choker spitting blood, guts an' brimstone at the back of 'em.'

I didn't lift my gaze from the departing Professor.

'Hasn't it even occurred to you to wonder, Trapp', I asked uneasily, 'why a naturalist who studies crocodiles should wish to lift the deadweight of a small railway engine from an antediluvian swamp in the first place?'

And then there was the intriguing riddle posed by the Professor's deck cargo.

Okay, okay - so lots of people would argue, 'what's so special about a tramp ship taking on *deck* cargo?'

Nothing.

Usually.

Absorbed with preparing our passage plan in the chartroom, I'd been aware of furious hammering and banging echoing from the after well deck for some time but had resolutely ignored it. As with the Case of the Missing Chinamen, I'd long ago reconciled myself to accepting it didn't pay to be curious where Trapp was concerned, otherwise I invariably found myself qualifying as an accomplice before the fact.

And anyway, trying to reconcile economy-buy charts that had gone out of fashion half a century before with the only copy of vaguely applicable sailing directions I'd been able to obtain from ships' chandler Albert Fuk Yew – whose tally I'd always understood *was* the chap's genuine Chinese birthright until I politely suggested he provide a temporary credit facility against Trapp's account – was proving complex enough without worrying about a bit of routine bedlam from aft.

Believe me, it is not easy to make seamanlike provision for avoiding navigational hazard when you're forced to extract your up-to-date info from a dog-eared broken-spined cocoa-stained *Gulf Of Papua Pilot* which had probably seen service under square rig and which asserted that every bloody lighthouse and buoy from Singapore to bloody Vladivostock was *still* fuelled by bloody PARAFFIN . . . !

. . . but I'm digressing into hysteria again, and shall return to the subject of deck cargoes.

Gorbals Wullie first drew my attention to the fact that something odd was going on when he came sidling conspiratorially through the chartroom door.

'You, er – you don't happen tae know if we've ony . . . ah, ony mint *sauce* aboard dae ye, Mister Miller sir?'

'Mint *sauce*?' I queried blankly.

'Mint sauce,' he confirmed, looking secretive.

'Get a GRIP on yourself, man,' I snapped. In some respects I sympathized. I'd seen survivors rescued after spending weeks adrift hallucinating about vittles: the creak of moving lifeboat timbers inducing fantasies of groaning tables; the foaming crest of a wave engendering delusions of beer by the keg; white napkins conjured by the flap of a canvas sail; silver service in the glint of sun on gunmetal . . . but he'd *had* a banana and half a can of Tiger beer yesterday. Dammit, this wasn't some pampered cruise ship.

I sent him firmly about his business and resumed my study of the chart.

Then thought about mint sauce again, and what it went best with – all juicy and tender with a sprinkling of rosemary . . . succulent, steaming aromatically within its cloak of brown crispy skin or even ready-carved, rising irresistibly from a sea of real *gravy* . . . ?

I whimpered, cramming white-clenched knuckles into my

salivating mouth and biting down unbearably until the pain cleared my head.

Second Officer Spew came lumbering in a few minutes later, pumped out dry as a bone again following his trishaw flight, and all thrilled.

'My *friend's* coming back ter visit me, 'e is, Cap'n.'

'I'm the Mate,' I pointed out gently. 'Captain Trapp's the captain and he doesn't look a bit like me and anyway, he isn't here just now.'

'Oh, *'allo* Mister Miller, sir. Di'n't recognize you,' Spew enthused, offering a handshake to my cap and oilskins which hung on a peg by the door. Then hovered around looking vague.

'You've forgotten why you've come, haven't you? Something about a friend, was it?'

His battered face lit up. 'Thass right - my friend from the *aero*plane. An' this time he's bringing a lot o' his friends wiv 'im.'

'That's nice,' I mused absently, still trying to decide whether it was worth laying off courses to take us as far as the Timor and Arafura Seas, especially now we'd actually got lifeboats, in that, God willing, we'd probably never make it half-way across the Indian Ocean. 'And which friend is that, Mister Spew? The lovable furry one with jaws like a mantrap or the green one from the space ship with the bug eyes and tentacles?'

'Now I comes ter fink about it I 'asn't seen them two for ages . . .' he frowned, feeling for the door.

I couldn't settle after that. Especially once the hammering and other echoes of construction had abated and silence fell over the ship. Briefly. Until a further sound - a distant, intermittent sound but coming ever closer - began to impinge upon my concentration.

I raised my head, frowned: drummed my pencil uncertainly on the table. No . . . no, it couldn't be. Not on a tropical *dockside*? No way. I mean . . . no. No, not even Trapp would entertain carrying a cargo of . . .

'. . . live SHEEP?' I exploded a few minutes later when I caught up with him hanging casually over the after end of the boat deck and watching our latest influx of passengers being shepherded, all hop-skipping and clambering over one another and *baaa*-ing volubly, up a rickety livestock gangway. That flight the *Charons* had made as rejected hostages! Now I knew what Spew had meant when he talked about his airborne friend, except these were still wearing their woolly jerseys.

As *well* as why that devious little turd, Gorbals Wullie, had evinced such sudden enthusiasm for acquiring mint sauce.

'There's only a hundred or so,' Trapp defended. 'An' the pens we knocked together'll stand a China Sea typhoon which, you gotter admit, is more'n this old ship of yours will!'

'Oh, only a *hundred* sheep,' I echoed with withering sarcasm. 'I was worried for a minute in case you had another hundred arriving this afternoon.'

'Don't be SILLY,' he jeered, caustically amused. Then added in a tentative undertone, '. . . the other 'undred don't arrive 'til tomorrow.'

I opened my mouth to scream, then shut it again, diverted by a sudden thought.

'Why?'

'Why what?'

'*Why* are we taking a flock of sheep crocodile hunting? They're rotten shots and most of them lack the killer instinct.'

'Because the Professor says we'll need 'em. It's part of the deal.'

'Why?'

He shuffled uneasily. It was becoming perfectly obvious he'd never thought to ask.

'Why wha - ?'

'Why, Trapp,' I pressed levelly, 'does the Professor need a cargo of live animals aboard when he's supposed to be filling us up with crocodiles for the return voyage?'

'Yeah, well you've answered the question yerself, 'aven't you?' he muttered sullenly. 'A cargo o' crocodiles? They won't half get through some grub before we c'n sell 'em off!'

'True,' I nodded, beginning to feel very, very apprehensive indeed. 'Except they won't EAT too many sheep - certainly not as many as we will be carrying - because *my* understanding of the Professor's intentions is that, by the time they - the crocodiles - *do* get hungry, they . . . the *crocodiles*, Trapp, will be dead as . . .'

'Mutton?' he hazarded contentiously.

'. . . themselves. Largely on account of them being measured up for handbags, skinned, then salted and stowed down in the TWEENdecks.'

'Oh you an' yer constant nit, nit, NIT-pickin' at trivial DETAIL,' he yelled before storming off in one of those childish Trapp-huffs which he invariably resorted to when stuck for an answer.

'All right - so I'm a worrier,' I bawled after him tightly. 'But you jus' ask yourself one THING, Trapp . . . You just ASK yourself what weighs forty-odd tons; measures up to sixty feet *long*; lives in a SWAMP - and needs fed two hundred SHEEP f'r its bloody breakfast . . . ?'

And finally, there was the Mysterious Apparatus.

I think it was the Mysterious Apparatus which appeared on the foc'sle during the closing hours before we sailed that ultimately convinced me the Professor was not disclosing his true intentions.

Or more - the *type* of Mysterious Apparatus.

. . . not that it would have been mysterious in the first place, mind you.

Not if Trapp had had the guts to warn me about it beforehand.

Of course it arrived in the middle of the night. The typical Trapp scenario - some cumbersome object delivered to the wharf by sinister longshoremen on the back of a lorry without lights, and swung aboard by a mobile crane shrouded in tarpaulins.

The cumbersome object being shrouded that was. Not the crane.

All the deck lamps had been extinguished deliberately, which made a change from Bucalosie's harbour generator breaking down or being converted to a super stun-gun by Choker Bligh. I could barely make out the stocky form of my Captain taking charge of the lowering operation, directing the Professor and his personal staff who had, it seemed, at least forsaken their scientific weaponry for clutches of scientific spanners.

'What the hell *is* it?' I muttered, padding up behind Trapp.

He jumped nervously at the sight of me in pyjamas. I felt a twinge of concern in case there was something wrong with them until I realized it was my presence, not my jimjams, causing his discomposure.

'What're YOU doin' here?' he snarled in greeting.

'I'm cargo officer, remember? Cargo officers are supposed to be involved when cargo's being loaded.'

'Not cargo – laboratory equipment. Highly specialized, Mister. Not your part o' ship as Mate, so you c'n go back ter bed,' Trapp muttered, avoiding eye contact in the sort of shifty way guaranteed to galvanize every curiosity cell in my brain. Then further compounded his deceit by fading into the darkness again so's I couldn't press him further.

'It seems an odd place to install a laboratory,' I commented to the space where he'd been. 'Right up in the eyes of the ship where half the bloody time it'll be submerged in bad weather.'

Gradually I became aware of a further nocturnal creature behind me and froze, some vague sixth sense telling me not to react too impulsively. Slowly I turned to discover that (a) at least it wasn't Chinese with a dragon tattoo, which represented the total sum of the good news, because (b) my sense of foreboding *had* still been amply justified nevertheless, when, (c) I learned that not all of our passengers were currently preoccupied with matters of strictly mechanical bent.

The Sturm-Ruger bored for three-fifty calibre Remington Magnum couldn't have been said to have been *deliberately* aimed at my navel but, cradled casually in the crook of the bristle-headed research assistant's arm as it was, that's just about the spot where an accidental discharge would've ended.

'*Gute Nacht, Herr Kaleunt,*' he encouraged flatly.

I recognized him as not being British and ignored him.

' 'Course YOU, Trapp, have to go an' get yourself involved with KRAUT head-bangers as well, don't you?' I yelled into the night, by then totally pissed-off. 'Arrogant bastards the whole LOT of 'em – if there's one bloody race I can't bloody *stand* it's the bloody Germ–'

'Especially bloody Germans who happen to be English-speaking head-*knochenbeltun?*' the Hun with the gun intervened. And smiled a humourless smile. 'As a Kraut with your best interests at heart, I say again – *gute NACHT, Kaleunt!*'

97

I mustered a pretty withering retort before re-registering the glint of that horrendous razor slash dividing the stubble of the fellow's cheek; imagined what rough social circles he must have tended to move in to have come by it in the first place; and came down firmly in favour of European coexistence.

'As you say, *mein Herr* – *guten* night, then.' I inclined my head affably. 'And please, should you require anything at all to make your voyage more comfortable, don't hesitate to call on me.'

I had to conceal myself behind a well-deck winch for nearly an hour before the activity on the foc'sle ceased and the last clump of booted feet faded towards the accommodation.

Considering the very tangible threat posed by the Ying Tong factor until the moment we could depart from Singapore, it was strange how often, during that waiting time, I found myself imagining movement over by the shadows of the quayside mimosas where the Wurstest Pyrate There Ever Wus had so garrulously materialized a few short nights before.

Huddling, trying to keep my pyjamas clear of oil-soaked layers of grime beneath the winch, I simmered without requiring any support from the oppressive humidity. Once we got to sea and clear of land, Trapp really would have to be pinned down to an analytical discussion of how it was that a bizarrely kitted-out Professor of Natural History, who'd just happened by in a sampan, and an even more bizarrely-kitted-out Great-great-whatever-it-was relative of his wot wus 'anged in Sixteen-ninety-whatever-he'd-claimed – who'd just *happened* to pass by in a cloud of ectoplasm . . . how it was they both appeared to be acting in concert to encourage *him* – Trapp – to search for some hell-hole of a river which hadn't even been proved to exist as yet other than on a chart allegedly produced by a ghost or in the mind of a transparently eccentric academic.

Both of which items – chart *and* Professor – I'd become convinced were equally flawed.

Above me on the foc'sle a steel drill began to screech and whine, drowning the faint tinkle of Chinese music carrying from some distant teahouse. Delicate, haunting . . .

. . . *haunt*ing?

98

I scanned sharply, nervously, along the still wharf again. Just to make quite certain that something which incontrovertible logic told me couldn't possibly exist, didn't. Then I shrugged, smiled deprecatingly – froze . . . and sweated all at the same time.

Because the one thing I *hadn't* expected to see was a hagridden spectre actually living on BOARD! The one that suddenly materialized from the darkened midships accommodation before flitting forward in surreptitious, kangaroo-like hops to ground behind the cargo winch next to *mine*.

'Oh, Jesus', I whispered, drawing back in fright. Then frowned. The latest spectre did look remarkably familiar when I came to think about it: hagridden certainly, but nevertheless quite definitely of this world. I crept over and tapped its shoulder. Fastidiously. Using the extreme tip of one finger.

The *Charon's* In-House Apparition squealed and scrabbled astern like a startled rodent. Which it was. It was also a very satisfying reaction: I felt I'd finally squared the account for his surprising *me* on the bridge that night.

'What're YOU doing here?' I demanded of Gorbals Wullie, using the recognition phrase of the night.

'Same as you, Mister Miller, sir', he muttered when his heartbeat had returned to normal sluggish. 'Spying on the Captin.'

'That's a damned outrageous calumny', I snarled.

'Oh aye?' Wullie raised an interested eyebrow. 'Is that the same as spyi-'

'Geddown', I hissed anxiously as feet moved to the rail above us. A glowing cigarette end arced to the water as my Teutonic associate halted idly for a minute, then the footsteps receded again.

'If you're no' spying, Mister Miller, sir', Wullie reasoned, 'then how are you so keen no' tae get caught?'

'For the last time, I am NOT spying', I informed him coldly, 'I am merely observing from a discreet vantage point.'

'The Captin?'

'Among other things.'

'Like to find out why he's trying tae double-cross us this time?'

I eyed him reluctantly. While I hated to even admit it, we always had shared one thing in common – our mutual mistrust of Trapp. Nevertheless I *did* bear a disciplinary burden as Mate to ensure

99

blind loyalty to the master.

'Don't be so bloody impertinent!' I snapped. 'That sort of flagrant criticism of your captain is tantamount to open mutiny.'

I thought about it.

'. . . apart from which I already *know* WHY he's trying to double-cross us. It's just *how* he's trying to double-cross us I'm still trying to figure.'

And I did know why.

Trapp, over the years, had almost certainly begun to recognize there were times when I didn't agree with him. So Trapp, being both a considerate and caring person desperately anxious to avoid fractious confrontation, tended not to . . . well, not to *mention* every little detail of ship's business in case it injected a note of disharmony into our relationship.

Either that or, being a life-time virtuoso of the ultra-devious *fait accompli*, he'd figured that if, just a few hours before we sailed, he could sneak whatever it was under that bloody tarpaulin aboard and bolt it down while I was asleep, then – by the time I'd noticed an extra ton or two of non-ship's gear had been bolted to the *Charon's* already cluttered foc'slehead – we'd be virtually departing the dockside: too late for me to do anything BUT shout about it!

To the inexperienced eye the Mysterious Apparatus might have looked a bit like a naval gun at first sight, all wrapped up and projecting forward over the bow as Beedham-Smith's team had left it.

'Looks like a gun,' Wullie whispered, fascinated.

'Course it's not a *gun*,' I dismissed authoritatively. 'That sticky-out bit you presumably think is a gun barrel's far too short and stubby – and anyway, the whole thing's mounted too low for a gun. You ever seen a gun with a barrel that short, which only stands as high as your waist . . .'

I reconsidered his scraggy, undersized build, and amended the thrust of my argument. '. . . chest?'

Tentatively Wullie unwound the projecting part of the shroud to reveal blued metal with a big hole in the end.

'It's a gun,' he confirmed.

'Of *course* it's a gun,' I jeered. '*Obviously* it's a gun - and wipe that bloody expression off your face!'

Ferreting underneath the tarpaulin concealing the breech I exposed a verdigrised brass plate. It seemed to be engraved in Norwegian or something: Trapp, it appeared, was really heavy into Europe this trip. The only words I recognized were *Svend Foyn* . . .

'Didn't he invent some kind of whaling harpoon gun?' I frowned.

'That wid maybe explain this,' Wullie hazarded, now a dim goblinesque silhouette poking about up in the bow.

'This what?'

'This harpoon.'

I walked up and gazed into the rough, elongated packing case blankly. The iron shaft - it must have approximated the weight of a man - was about one and a half metres long and built like a battleship's keel. Four massively hinged cast-iron barbs lay folded back to facilitate initial entry; obviously designed to expand and lock into the flesh of its target when triggered by the explosive warhead . . .

. . . its TARGET?

'I wis jist thinking, Mister Miller, sir,' Wullie muttered uneasily.

'WHAT?'

'That this is *anither* fine mess the Captin's about tae get us into.'

I just changed straight out of my pyjamas into shoregoing rig soon as I got back to the illusory security of my cabin and stopped shaking. Then did what I should've done right at the start - the moment I'd received that bloody letter from the Jewel of Malaysia Chinese Lestaurant, Accommodation Addless Servlice and Massage Parrour . . .

Trapp met me as I was struggling to ease my carelessly-packed seabag along the musty internal alleyway leading to the deck.

'*Now* where're you goin', Mister?' he greeted sourly.

'I don't know,' I said. 'I don't really care either - cheerio!'

'Why?'

I explained about the harpoon gun.

And my reservations regarding Beedham-Smith's sixty-foot

long, forty-odd-ton lift requirement.

And about the Professor's two hundred oven-fresh sheep, as well as his German scientists with razor scars who poked guns at me aboard my own ship in the middle of the night. And his - TRAPP'S, this time - *his* taking even half seriously the antics of some theatrically-dressed fruitcake claiming to be an ancestor tipping him off to pirate TREASURE f'r Christ's sake - buried, like I've said, uppa nonexistent bloody RIVER . . . an' . . . an' then I just touched, in passing, upon a few of the other things which worried me a bit.

. . . Like the crocodile poaching and the handbag smuggling business, including the possible *quid pro quo* that the saurians might figure to turn some of US into fashion accessories instead, an' . . . and the *murders* we'd had on board before we'd even got STARTED on the really stressful part of the voyage which - apart from the future nightmares they guaranteed through speculating on which jolly shipmate aboard the *Charon* had dunnit in the first place - had already made me a prime target for a Chinese secret bloody society HIT SQUAD!

'Yeah, but wot *I'm* tryin' to get yer to tell me, Mister,' Trapp frowned, trying hard to understand after I'd finally run out of breath, 'is why you're actually *leaving*?'

'It doesn't matter,' I panted, hoisting my bag again with steely resolve. 'Hardly worth mentioning, really. But be sure of one thing - and read my lips, Trapp: read them *very* carefully . . . I am NOT - I repeat, NOT - sailing - with - you AGAIN!'

I turned at the head of the gangway for a last defiant look at the genuinely perplexed millstone I'd finally cast from around my neck.

'No way, Trapp. Never, ever again. No WAY am I spending two weeks on this ship going to Papua New GUINEA!'

Chapter Seven

And I didn't, either.

It took the *Charon* nearly FOUR weeks to get there.

It should have taken less than two. Singapore to the Gulf of Papua . . . ? For any normal, half-decent ship with a normal half-decent crew and a reasonable turn of speed, a simple trip like that *would* have taken less than two weeks. Certainly not a day more than three; not even taking into account all the engine breakdowns and steering gear failures we'd suffered.

Not even allowing for the added time lost through the fire we'd had on board - or not so much the fire even, as the spineless way Chief Engineer Bucalosie had panicked half the crew and one or two of the sheep into abandoning ship within minutes of Choker Bligh's setting it alight as his way of protesting about the quality of the vittling.

Unfortunately they'd been self-centred enough to take the two new lifeboats, of which Trapp was secretly very proud, so he'd been forced to sacrifice a full half day just to recover *them*.

It had taken another thirty minutes for me to persuade him to allow their *occupants* back aboard as well . . .

And then there'd been the hours we'd frittered on retracing our wake to search for Second Officer Spew after he'd fallen over the side yet again just when the sharks were about to give up following us . . . I mean, I ask you: how could ANY navigator be expected to factor *that* sort of operational eccentricity into his presailing speed, time and distance equation?

So the bottom line was *no* - no, it hadn't only been those lunatic diversions that made us spend a month in accomplishing a fortnight's task.

No: the most time-consuming delay had been caused by the fact that the *Charon* finally ended up steaming TWICE as far as any *other* ship would've done to make the same bloody TRIP . . . !

That for MOST of our passage in search of the River Beetel – and for reasons which I shall explain in a moment – we'd steered the kind of zig-zag evasive course I hadn't experienced since serving in convoy escorts during the halcyon days before I'd even heard of Lieutenant-Commander Edward Trapp RN, and when only common-or-garden hazards like U-boats and surface raiders and sea mines and the *Luftwaffe* had tended to interrupt voyages still tedious by comparison.

One might, I suppose, argue that our trans-oceanic meanderings must have had their plus side: would have at least afforded me a little more time to appraise our passengers in the short spells snatched between crises and disasters. To become familiar with their ways.

Unfortunately such a potentially reassuring rapport proved impossible to establish. In the case of Beedham-Smith's so-called research assistants, their 'ways' consisted largely of ignoring everybody aboard INCLUDING me – an attitude I found *particularly* difficult to comprehend – while the Professor himself hardly ever appeared on deck, preferring, it seemed, to spend hours secreted in his cabin poring over . . . well, I never found that out either, because his curtains were always closed when I tried to spy on him. Scientific works, I suppose?

Either way, the familiarity I'd hoped to establish certainly didn't turn out to breed contempt.

More an added dimension of paranoia.

The rationale – if such bizarre behaviour could be described even loosely as rational – for our eventually pursuing the aforementioned dog-leg passage all the way from the Timor Sea to our ultimate destination, had begun with the perfectly innocuous sighting of another masthead light breaking the horizon astern.

Nothing extraordinary in that, of course. One could argue it would have been more unusual in those waters *not* to have raised at least one other ship during a four-hour bridge watch.

I'd noted it first when we were two days out. It had been about five in the morning and pitch dark, during a period of sullen rolling while the *Charon's* main engine had just failed for the second time and was only beginning to establish such frustration as part of our overnight routine.

The light hove into sight; hovered dead astern for maybe fifteen, twenty minutes bisected every so often by our gyrating mainmast, then gradually faded from view. I'd watched it idly and thought nothing of it; still enjoying the feel of the wind on my face, listening avidly to its keening voice in the tattered rigging: relishing being, quite simply, a sailorman again after all the dreadful weeks of strain since Trapp bounced his way back into my life as the harbinger of our current pantomime *noir*.

The light reappeared half an hour later: it loitered awhile, a glimmering yellow speck against a backdrop of velvet, then sank yet again below the horizon.

The engine-room voice-pipe in the wheelhouse squealed and I walked to answer it. No helmsman was on the bridge: there wasn't a lot of point in steering seeing we weren't going anywhere at the time. Chief Engineer Bucalosie's garlic-laden petulance wafted up the tube the moment I unplugged the whistle.

'Okay: I dunna de amazing tings widda da spanners so amma ready to getta de machino started once-a more, Signore - you-a ready to getta de shippa back onna da course?'

'*Of* course!' I snapped, instantly offended.

There was a long silence while he worked that out. Then:

'I tella you, Signore Mate, amma shagged-out. Finito! The main engine: *she* issa finito. The boilers - THEY are-a finito. The goddamma *sheep* - SHE issa finito . . !'

'You'll find the complaints department asleep in the master's cabin, Bucalosie', I informed him tartly, 'but before you commit suicide by disturbing him, kindly shut up, hang up - an' bloody START up!'

The deck began to vibrate again just as Gorbals Wullie arrived to take the wheel, fresh from his spell as forward look-out and still rubbing the sleep from his eyes.

I forgot about the distant light.

Nothing special about a light observed at sea, after all.

*

105

The following night, same scenario: a muffled explosion from the engine room just after eight bells in the middle watch; an eruption of carbon from the ancient funnel which scattered a light coating of volcanic ash over everything, whereupon the *Charon's* bridge deck took on the fuzzed aspect of a Roman galley evacuating during the last days of Pompeii.

A succinct discourse between me up top and Bucalosie down the tubes followed, which covered everything from how best I proposed he deploy his largest spanner to my general opinion of Italian Chief Engineers whose only previous hands-on machino experience had been in the Fiat getaway motor pool of the Naples Chapter of the *Cosa*-soddin'-NOSTRA ... while, as far as his fitness to handle reciprocating compound surface condensing *marine* engines went – boiling an occasional kettle to make-a da espresso forr-a da GODFATHER did NOT qualify him for a soddin' f*$%*&! STEAMship ticket!

Then I crammed the whistle back into the voice pipe; stamped out to the starboard wing in high dudgeon – and immediately observed either. the same, or a remarkably similiar, white masthead light dead astern. It's not easy to differentiate between light bulbs at several miles' distance. Frowning uncertainly I reached for my binoculars in the bridge box but, by the time I'd raised them, the light had gone again: dipped, presumably, below the curvature of the horizon once more.

Scratching my head, I tried to persuade myself that what I was beginning to imagine, couldn't possibly be. That I was merely suffering a relapse into a Trapp-induced paranoia which invested perfectly ordinary everyday events with sinister implications. Or in this case, perfectly ordinary every-night events.

Then I decided I wasn't, because perfectly ordinary every-night events never got time to become a part of Trapp's lurid tapestry of life on account of the emergencies which jostled for attention – and anyway, the whole *point* of paranoia is that it exists only in the imagination whereas, whenever happenings connected with Trapp assume the kind of sinister undertones *I'm* referring to, then they invariably turn out to be precursors of the reality, not mere mental aberrations.

Through the open engine-room skylight I could hear Bucalosie still hitting metallic things down below with clueless malice while screaming Latin imprecations at his hastily co-opted assistant spanner-holder, Lucille Grubb – as Fred the Greaser fondly thought of himself as being at that time, seeing third night out was traditionally a floral print dress-night among Trapp's more unconventional crew members, when it – the light, not Fred – reappeared yet again some forty minutes later.

This time I was prepared and waiting. Having already climbed the vertical ladder to the monkey island, I immediately took a compass bearing of it.

The bearing didn't change. That meant the distant ship wasn't passing across our stern; it was quite specifically steering to overtake on much the same course as we were following. Or would have been following had we been going anywhere at all.

I laid the glasses on it, but gained little by the exercise. It was too far away and still too dark to identify anything other than that single light . . . until the single light was joined by the overtaking ship's second mastlight breaking the black cusp of the horizon, which only helped marginally by confirming that, whatever and whoever she was, she exceeded fifty metres in length.

A few minutes later her red and green sidelights popped up.

It was then that I stiffened, pulled the binoculars closer into my eyes. The masthead lights were separating. Then the green starboard running light vanished, leaving only her red. A moment later that, too, was extinguished to be replaced by a white sternlight as she completed a wide turn to starboard, and began to steam on what could only have been a roughly reciprocal course – back, in other words, whence she had come . . .

. . . until she had gone altogether.

Yet again.

Which was *very* odd indeed.

'Wot d'yer mean, Mister – you think we're bein' *followed*?' Trapp jeered at breakfast.

'Just you wait,' I'd said confidently. 'Soon as Bucalosie's engine breaks down tonight, you'll see.'

He and I repaired to the bridge around three the following morning to put my theory to the test. It was actually Mister Spew's watch, the middle watch, but I didn't mind at all: I never slept while Spew was driving anyway. It's difficult to in a narrow bunk when you're wearing a bulky lifejacket.

About three-thirty Mister Spew fell down the port ladder thinking he was stepping into the wheelhouse, and Trapp took over the watch while Spew, bleeding enthusiastically, was carted off for routine emergency repair and maintenance. The incident proved to me that, despite everything, there still *was* a God – a big Greek cruise ship blaring disco music and lit up like a Christmas tree passed close across our bow from starboard less than half an hour later.

As it had only been twenty thousand tons of juggernauting steel, Second Officer Spew wouldn't even have *seen* it, never mind given way to it as the collision rules required.

'We'll break down any moment now,' I said, turning to gaze astern and handing Trapp my binoculars.

We waited until two bells in the next watch: five a.m. The bloody engine kept turning steady as a steam-powered metronome for the first time since we'd left Singapore.

'Bloody useless bloody Bucalosie,' I muttered. 'How was *I* to know he'd hit it in the right place by accident last night?'

'Might as well get back to me kip,' Trapp grunted irritably. 'I mean, we can't do nothing about checking whether ships is or isn't following us if the *engine* won't break down, can we?'

'I suppose *some* Captins could tell their Chiefs tae stop it on purpose,' Gorbals Wullie remarked to no-one in particular from the steering grating. I looked at Trapp, who deliberately avoided my gaze.

By the time we'd lost all way and had begun to roll in the trough of a freshening sea, Trapp had regained the moral high ground: bawling Wullie out f'r being a sloppy useless *sloth* of an 'elmsman wot would steer a bloody RAILWAY ENGINE crooked onna dead straight bloody LINE!

*

We didn't have to wait long after that. In order to make doubly sure they sailed into my ambush, I switched off all our own lights this time.

'There,' I said tensely. 'Dead astern and just breaking the skyline - a masthead light.'

'So it's a light,' Trapp muttered sourly, firmly entrenched in perverse mode by then. 'A light don't prove nothin'.'

'Wait 'til she comes full over the horizon,' I persisted. 'If I'm right, and she is following us, she'll turn tail and scuttle back down soon as we switch ours back on.'

'Proving what exac'ly?'

'Proving,' Gorbals Wullie's disembodied resentment chipped in from his eavesdropping position behind us, 'we're in even deeper shit than we *thought* you'd got us intae already, Captin.'

When the mystery ship came clear I switched our own lights back on. *'Voila!'* I announced proudly, with the flamboyant theatre of a master puppeteer.

The lights on the horizon parted on cue as our long-range shadower began a wheel-hard-over retreat.

'All right,' Trapp conceded sullenly. 'I suppose there's a *faint* chance 'er Old Man might be followin' us.'

'Ah,' I said understandingly. 'In other words he might have some other reason to turn around in the middle of the ocean and go back the way he just came?'

'He might. He might . . . well, might've *forgotten* somethin'.'

'Aye - like his cargo,' Wullie interjected maliciously.

'Four *times*?' I persisted. 'Five now, counting his current absent-mindedness?'

'All right.' Trapp tried again, looking really clever this time. 'All right, Chief Officer Smarty Pants - so you kindly explain ter me why he NEEDS to lift 'is foretop over the horizon to get a visual on us? Why 'e don't just track us on radar from thirty miles back.'

'Maybe he doesn't have radar. Maybe he's got no choice but to come close enough to Mark One Eyeball us.'

'Everyone's got radar nowadays,' Trapp shook his head in tolerant disbelief. 'Honestly, Mister, I reely don't know what planet you been on these past few years. I mean, what kind of clapped-out Mickey Mouse ship nowadays 'asn't got *radar*?'

'*This* kind of clapped-out Mickey Mouse ship hasn't, for a start.'

'Oh, there you go AGAIN,' he'd shouted, storming off. 'Always the prissy intellectual, ain't you? Always tryin' to win the argymint by nit, nit, NIT-picking at detail.'

He returned ten predictable minutes later, having gained time enough to formulate some face-saving way out of the logical dead-end his mouth had led him into.

'Lissen, Mister: I ain't prepared to argue with you a minnit longer,' he announced firmly. 'Far as I'm concerned it's obvious even to a *blind* man we're bein' followed, an' that's that!'

I made a point of looking suitably chastened while Wullie's eyebrows met in the middle as he tried to reconcile such steely resolve with the general tenor of Trapp's previous attitude. But Wullie never had learned there were more ways than one of skinning a captain.

'Not that it matters,' Trapp supplemented airily. 'They don't know it yet but they took on the Scarlet Pimpernel o' the blockade trade. I'll shake 'em off in no time, you see. Jus' a few subtle course changes an' they won't know whether it's Christmas or Good Friday.'

. . . Three weeks and two-thousand-odd miles of subtlety later – and with the *Charon* having left a wake slightly more circuitous than that of a disoriented sea louse in the interim – that same light was still reappearing over the dark horizon to hover stubbornly astern soon as the engine faltered, choked on its own carbonized bronchial tubes, then coughed into suspended animation until Bucalosie belaboured it again.

It – our ever-present shadow – never came close enough to disclose its flag, its type, or even its size. I tended to dismiss it after the first few days as being almost an irrelevant menace, the origin of which I would occasionally speculate upon but never actually fear.

I mean, why lose sleep over some purely speculative threat several miles remote when I could perfectly easily lie awake, sweating and staring unseeingly at the scabrous deckhead above my bunk for hours and hours simply conjecturing on the perils which were undoubtedly fomenting like some extra-malignant witch's brew WITHIN the confines of the bloody *Charon* herself?

Not the least of which, I didn't take long to persuade myself, were destined to arise from the actions of her own passenger complement.

The Professor didn't take much figuring.

I settled for assuming he was crazy.

I could never quite put my finger on when I finally reached that conclusion. I mean, he didn't foam at the mouth or anything. He didn't suddenly run berserk, or cackle peals of crazed laughter . . . It was more some darkness I sensed within him: particularly when you caught him unawares on those few occasions he appeared on deck, and he turned that laser stare on you from below those great tangled brows of his, and you just knew he hadn't quite caught up; wasn't so much focussing on you, the actuality before him, but was still visualizing – no, *relishing*, dammit – something that I became convinced was inconceivable to the minds of ordinary men.

In a nutshell, I came firmly to the view that, were a good brain man to create some Frankensteinian composite drawing from the really screwball elements of Trapp, Gorbals Wullie, Second Officer Spew and Chief Bucalosie – and *then* incorporate the more eccentric aspects of the psychopathic cesspool that was Bosun Bligh for good measure – he STILL wouldn't have cobbled together a Being half as disadvantageous to the health as emeritus Professor Walter Beedham-Smith.

Not that Trapp would hear of it, of course. Trapp only saw, in our flamboyant charterer, precisely what he wanted to see, and that was a vittles-and-fuel ticket which would bankroll him as far as the alleged location of Blackbeard's treasure hoard, plus affording him access to a nice little earner in two-ton handbags on the side . . .

But I won't allow myself to be sidetracked into *that* particularly contentious area of disagreement between us yet again. No; the point I'M making is that, so far as Trapp was concerned, incipient maniacs in the *Charon's* complement were neither remarkable nor worthy of forward planning: there were simply too many of them. Maniacs who triggered into active homicidal mode, on the other hand, were then upgraded to the general heading of crisis management and, as such, would be allocated at least their place in a usually pretty-pressing queue.

Yet, despite my reservations about crazies, it still wasn't so much Beedham-Smith as Beedham-Smith's assistants who really worried me: all the more so because - paradoxically - I didn't consider *those* three mad at all. In fact I figured them as knowing *exactly* what they were doing.

And in that conclusion lay, perhaps, the greatest enigma of all.

. . . especially when, just prior to our landfall, I was given disturbing cause to question whether *their* interests in reaching the swamps of the River Beetel coincided, even remotely, with those harboured by the Professor.

Bormann - Heinrich Bormann, the German chap's name was; the scar-faced fellow who tended to have the butt of his Sturm-Ruger permanently grafted under his armpit and seemed to be their senior man.

The other two turned out to be non-Aryan, as it happened, but I didn't warm to them any the more for it. How could anyone feel bonded in common cause with a thick-necked Bulgarian called Kolio Despatov who obsessively orchestrated a metronomic love affair between a broad-bladed hunting knife and a whetstone, and a Frenchman named Destremeau whose most intellectual preoccupation appeared to be with continually smashing one leg-of-mutton fist into the palm of his other hand while all the time eyeing me wistfully.

Destremeau, I gathered from a chance remark from Bormann - about the only one he ever made - had been a Sergeant-Major in the *Legion Etranger* prior to his dishonourable discharge: an event unlikely, in my jaundiced opinion, to have been occasioned by his being too soft on the recruits . . .

It had been a particularly windy day as the *Charon* rounded the southern tip of Kepulauan Tanimbar - three times as it happened, on account of Trapp getting more desperate than subtle by then to shake off our masthead tail - and finally set course in the general direction of the Torres Strait.

I'd wandered forward to satisfy myself that, after three weeks, the anchors had neither rusted through and fallen out of the hawse, nor been stolen by certain ferrous scrap *afficionados* among the crew. While returning to the bridge along the forward well deck, I noticed a fluttering scrap of what appeared to be newsprint caught in a locking bar of number two hatch.

Something made me extra cautious - Trapp's commands had never lacked a fifth column of concealed and shifty eyes watching your every move - so I glanced quickly round. The only obvious presence was that of our three aforementioned heavy calibre scientists huddled in earnest debate further aft and engaged in studying something - I could not see what, but they appeared to be either papers or maps - spread on the hatch cover between them.

The moan of the wind was enough to afford them privacy in their muttered deliberations, even if the steady slice of knife on whetstone in company with the fleshy thump of fist in palm hadn't afforded sufficient discouragement to would-be eavesdroppers.

Under the pretence of examining the wedges, I secreted the vagrant scrap in the pocket of my shorts and wandered, looking hyper-casual, up to the bridge. Slipping into the chartroom I smoothed it on the table, and frowned.

It *was* a cutting from a newspaper. Or a part of one; torn, presumably, from the whole. Only a few lines from the original articles were legible on either side. They were in English. The upturned side read:

> . . . IGH SPOT OF
> Darwin Ladies Needlework Circle
> last night was a patchwork com-
> petition based on Funny Bunny
> Rabbit motifs; a hard-fought
> contest finally won by Circle
> President Mrs Viola Henny. The
> competiton judge, the Very
> Reverend Arthur Tweed, was
> accorded a sincere vote of thanks
> by all members. Fortunately it

> proved possible to deliver this
> accolade prior to the Reverend
> Tweed's being taken violently ill
> during the celebratory tea and
> bunfest which follo . . .

I thought about that for a moment, and decided that - if the cutting *had*, as I suspected, been grabbed by the wind from the collection *mein Herr* Bormann's boys had been examining - then I was possibly looking at the wrong side of the newspaper.

I flipped it over. And chewed a thoughtful lip.

> . . . RAFT WHICH
> vanished from Moresby radar
> seven days ago report that an air
> search of the upper reaches of the
> Fly River has now been called off.
> The twin-engined Cessna and its
> two-man crew will never, in this
> correspondent's view, be found.
> That area of Papua New Guinea
> has swallowed whole army groups
> without trace; surely, therefore,
> even the resources of the world's
> largest insurance company must
> prove inadequate for such a
> tas . . .

'Ow could a *raft* disappear from a radar screen?' Trapp's gravelly derision hooted over my shoulder. 'I mean, a RAFT wouldn't hardly show *up* onna radar scree-'

'AIR-c-*raft*!' I corrected wearily without looking up. 'It refers to a lost aircraft. Look, if you have to creep up behind me and spy on my private documents, Trapp, at least read the bloody things properly.'

'It's just a shred o' newspaper,' he defended huffily. ' 'Ow private c'n a shred of newsp-'

I watched his eyes widen predictably - the initial symptom of an affliction known as *Trappus Avaricious Congenitalis* - once he'd scanned enough of the article to hoist in the critical trigger phrase.

'*Insurance* company, it says. Which 'as to mean, presumably, there was something aboard that plane worth a lot of money.'

114

I shrugged. 'So what? The Kruger Gold's never been found; but we're not going to South Africa either.'

'No. But we *are* goin' to the River Beetel, Mister.'

'We are going to a river, Trapp, which will require this ship to be fitted with wheels before it can enter, because it - the river - exists only in the mind of a whiskered lunatic.'

'Stop callin' poor ol' tortured Blackbeard a lunatic.'

'I was *talking* about Beedham-Smith,' I informed him tartly. 'I have already expressed my considered view regarding the sanity - indeed, the entire credibility - of your Great-great-whatever-he-claimed-to-be Grandpa . . . apart from which, Trapp: from what I saw of him, if your ancestor's ghost *was* f'r real, then torturing him must have given some people a great deal of pleasure. I only wish I'd been there to help out.'

'There you go AGAIN - argymintitive-spiteful as ever. AND missing the whole point while you're at it.'

'I didn't know there bloody WAS one.'

'Well there bloody IS, Mister Prissy Smart-arse!' he yelled back. 'And it's that the *Beetel* runs NEXT TO - an' roughly parallel *with* - the FLY . . .'

'The *alleged* Beetel.'

'So ask yerself - iffa *naero*plane wot was supposed to 'ave crashed in the Fly River ackshully went down in the BEETEL . . . ?'

'Hang on a minute,' I said as a thought struck me: one which would have occurred considerably earlier had Trapp not turned up to obfuscate the issue. 'Hang on a minute . . . I suppose there does have to be some practical reason for the Boys From Brazil out there to cart this press cutting around.'

'DON'T keep changin' the SUBJEC'!' he roared.

'I'm not,' I demurred, conscious of a certain disbelief. 'In fact I - well, I think,' I gagged briefly, but pressed on with a rush: '. . . I think I'magreeingwithyou, Trapp.'

'DON'T KEEP *AGREEING* WITH - ' He broke off in mid-tantrum. '. . . beg pardon?' he echoed blankly.

We eyed each other uncertainly. It was a unique moment: neither of us knew quite how to handle it.

'Did I jus' hear you say you . . . *agree* with me, Mister?' Trapp whispered eventually, looking at a complete loss.

I stirred, nodded cautiously as the shock began to wear off.

'I'm saying *maybe* you're right . . . but ONLY in this one instance! That maybe there *is* a case for believing Blackbeard's River Beetel does exist after all.'

'Jesus, 'e *agrees* with me,' Trapp muttered, sitting down abruptly.

I tried desperately to rationalize: to fathom some connection between the press cutting and the situation as we knew it.

'The one thing that strikes me is that Bormann and his mini-panzer division out there certainly aren't the kind of guys to believe in mythical rivers, even if Beedham-Smith seems quite capable of so doing.'

'So?'

I shrugged uncertainly. 'I don't know. It doesn't add up. For some reason I keep asking myself *why* are they really here?'

'As the Prof's assistants,' Trapp frowned. 'He told us that at the start.'

'He told us they were research assistants. Scientific colleagues. Those three couldn't muster a first year diploma in elementary natural history studies, never mind a university degree – and they don't exactly give the impression of academics preparing for a field study of saurian *longevity*. Not packing Sturm-Rugers and anti-tank missiles.'

'So maybe they're just mates of his. Helpin' out.'

'No way. They've hardly spoken two words to him since we sailed.'

Trapp began to wriggle in frustration. 'Then 'e's *payin'* them for the little earner he's got planned on the side. Hired guns just f'r the croc hunting.'

'Then why the subterfuge? Look . . . let's just suppose for a minute that Bormann's crowd *do* have concrete knowledge of the Beetel's existence. Let's *also* suppose, Trapp, that they have good reason to believe the aircraft mentioned in the cutting – and its cargo, which is obviously of considerable value judging by the cutting's reference to insurers – '

'The Prof's heavy LIFT!' Trapp broke in excitedly. 'That explains it, Mister – the Prof an' his boys reckon they know where that aeroplane crashed, and are out to *recover* it!' His expression turned to black affront. '. . . an' they ain't even got the decency to cut ME in on the deal – they tried to con *me* into providing the technological back-up, usin' some thin-as-tissue story a half-brained *bat* woul'n't've fallen for about crocodiles . . .'

'*Tried!*' I couldn't resist observing dryly, then shook my head. 'It still doesn't stack up – or not so far as the Professor's concerned anyway. Beedham-Smith was clearly obsessed with lifting aboard an object sixty feet long and weighing over forty tonnes metric, remember? Far as I know, Cessna don't build aircraft of that size and weight . . .'

The chartroom door curtain rattled aside and Gorbals Wullie wandered in wearing an uncharacteristically beatific smile.

'*Apart* from which,' I forced myself to ignore the unwanted interruption, spurred by a mounting but as yet unidentifiable unease, 'it was the Professor who personally specified the extras we carry – and Cessnas don't need shot with harpoon guns, Trapp. No more than they need fed with two hundred sheep!'

'Twa hundred?' Wullie burped. 'Are you no' mistook about that, Mister Miller sir – ah could've sworn it wis jist a hundred an' ninety-*nine* woollies we took aboard?'

I gave up trying to rationalize anything with Wullie around, especially after turning to catch him dabbing gravy and what looked suspiciously like freshly-dribbled mint sauce from an already bacteriologically lethal shirt front. Ingrained as I was by years of Merchant Service ethics, I simply couldn't dismiss as brazen an implication as that.

'Before you incriminate yourself further, Ordinary Seaman, I must warn you that the theft of *cargo* by a ship's crew is one of the most serious – '

'Yours is in the oven, Mister Miller sir,' he volunteered. 'Ah've saved ye some o' the crispiest bits.'

'Gravy?'

'Lashings o' it. Jist creepin' up tae the edge o' the plate and . . .' he played his ultimate card with tantalizing innocence, 'all floaty wi' they little *fatty* thingies!'

I nodded stiff acquiescence, prepared to overlook the breach of international shipping practice – particularly such a trivial breach: I mean, *one* leg of lamb out of eight *hundred*? - in order to conclude what had been, after all, an extremely important thesis.

'. . . therefore I put it to you, Trapp, that what the *Professor* is seeking in the upper reaches of the River Beetel - the form of which we cannot yet guess - and what the *Bormann* team is after - namely the as-yet-unspecified, but certainly valuable cargo from a crashed aeroplane - would appear, by definition, to be different.'

Trapp could have co-operated with me at that point: tried to apply his own brand of laterally bizarre logic to solving the riddle - but he didn't. Instead he just began to shuffle irritably. I guessed what was displeasing him right away. Apart from possessing the concentration span of a stick of bloody rhubarb, Trapp invariably got jealous resentful when it wasn't him at centre stage.

'That's ridIClous,' he jeered weakly. 'I mean, 'ow *ridiclous* can you get, Mister - the Prof and his mates both 'aving different motives f'r going to the same place?' He shook his head pityingly. 'Next thing you'll be arguin' that ship followin' us is . . . is . . .' he cast around desperately for the most unlikely scenario he could devise: 'is the Ying Tong *tong* out ter murder us an' . . . an . . . to hijack Blackbeard Trapp's TREASURE.'

'Now it's YOU being silly,' I taunted him back. 'Apart from anything else, how could some Chinese secret society in Singapore possibly have *known* about Blackbe- ?'

I broke off and stared at him.

For a very long time.

Putting two and two together.

Until.

'I *told* you that bloody GRANDPA of yours was trouble,' I heard myself yelling. 'Your Blackbeard bloody *Trapp* an' his Mickey Mouse bloody TREASURE chart!'

I regained my composure following yet another display of psychic phenomena in which my current cigarette packet dematerialized from its resting place on the chart table. On that occasion I discovered it had levitated into Wullie's grubby pocket and not under his bonnet as I'd first assumed when I began twisting his starboard ear.

Anthropologically speaking, it was interesting to note that Wullie's desire for an illicit after-dinner drag diminished in direct proportion to the interrogatory agony he suffered before admitting guilt.

I released his ear; lit up ostentatiously, and blew just sufficient smoke in the little bastard's direction to make him whimper, but nowhere near enough to satisfy.

'I know it's hard to credit, but we have to accept that *some* people can lose all sense of proportion at the mention of buried treasure.' I gazed pointedly at Trapp next, who had the grace to shuffle uncomfortably. 'Which would at least explain why a Chinese tong might covet Blackbeard's chart enough to be prepared to go to the extreme lengths of organizing a ship to *steal* it . . . right?'

'I s'ppose so,' he muttered.

'What it does *not* explain, however, is how your Ying Long dong . . .'

'Tong *tong*,' Trapp corrected primly. 'I likes my officers to be accurate.'

'. . . should have come to *learn* of the chart's existence: indeed, even be aware of the fact that it was kept up here in the chartroom in the first place. Because if we accept your first hypothesis - that the ship astern *does* relate to them, and IS trailing us with a view to grabbing the loot once we've recovered it - then we must also assume that Blackbeard's map was the target for our uninvited visitors before we sailed.'

'Visitors?' Trapp obstructed sullenly.

'I refer to the recently passed-away Brothers Ding - Oriental Cadavers Marks One and Two, if you remember? - whom we discovered flaked out there on the bridge wing and separated in death only by Willie's bucket.'

It was at that precise moment in my discourse that the aforementioned bucket proprietor suddenly started in a most guilty manner, frowned in neanderthal recall, then began to sidle surreptitiously towards the exit. I reached out a by-then practised hand and apprehended his previously uninterrogated ear before he, too, could dematerialize like my cigarettes.

'. . . which leads me to return to that memorable night of The Great Trishaw Race, Ordinary Seaman. Tell me – just exactly what *did* occasion that crew of assorted Chinese thugs to escort you and Second Officer Spew back to the ship from whichever sleazy pub the two of you got yourselves dissipated in?'

'Got oorsels dissi-whitever-you-said on the measly five dollars *he* gied us?' Wullie derided, adding an '. . . ouch!' having foolishly jerked his head to indicate Trapp.

A thought came to me. A worrying thought. Because of the quite unneccessary and additional degree of stress I anticipated it was going to cause in the not-too-distant future I ignored the Geneva Convention totally, whereupon Wullie's ear took on the texture of stretched pink plasticine.

'You didn't happen to, ah . . . mention the word *treasure* to Spew when what might well have been half the Ying Tong lower deck were drinking within earshot, did you?'

'I . . . ah, might've done', Wullie conceded, standing on tiptoes.

'And explained to Spew about the map?'

'I . . . might've done.'

'. . . kept in the chartroom?'

'I . . . might've done.'

'. . . supposedly revealing its precise location?'

'I, ah . . . might've done.'

'But of course, when you shot your mouth off to Spew', I gritted, 'about the only thing you *didn't* happen to blab was probably the most critical fact of all . . . that the Captain's so-called treasure legacy is based on a three-hundred-year-old lunatic's MYTH that wouldn't even justify hiring a bloody rowing boat to cross an ornamental bloody POND to find – *DID* you?'

'I . . . might *no'* have – OUCH!'

I allowed Turbo-tongue's ear to snap back into place. It made sense now: the light astern in the night, and everything. Obviously the trishaw pursuit had been occasioned by the Ying Tongs' desire to grill Wullie and Spew for more detail on the treasure's precise location – but I had no doubt they'd hoisted in the basic message. Apart from anything else, the Queen's English as mutilated by Wullie could have rendered it far more intelligible to eavesdropping Chinamen than to an Anglo-Saxon like me.

Either way I didn't need further convincing.

Sandwiched as we appeared to be now, between the interests of a psychopathic mini-army aiming to steal cargo from a crashed aeroplane using *our* ship without so much as a *by your leave*; homicidal oriental gangsters aiming to steal a non-existent ghostly treasure second-hand from US; and a stare-eyed weirdo Professor planning to use *us* to search for something heavy as a railway engine in a prehistoric swamp - something which, I'd long begun to suspect, promised to lead us to a fate far more ghastly than our other two adversaries combined could devise . . . ?

I mean, we were good as DEAD already!

And *I'd* been lying awake nights worrying about meeting a few inoffensive CROCODILES?

Chapter Eight

The inoffensive crocodile glared at me through mud-encased protuberances that not even a hundred and forty million years of evolution had contrived to improve upon. They'd always been eye housings bizarre enough to scare the pants off most other living creatures.

Certainly off *one* particular living creature as of that moment.

In chilling close-up I watched as leathery lids shuttered open; the inner nictitating membranes parting to expose slit-like pupils which, in turn, expanded to circular orbs positively luminescent with evil. Forward of them and right up in the bows of the creature, bony nasal discs surmounted gently bubbling nostril cavities while – just in case a REALLY scary back-up was needed – the fourth teeth to port and starboard of the ossified muzzle curved vertically like eccentric tusks.

Even as I stood rooted to the spot, the crocodile smiled an awful rictus of a smile before angling its monstrous reptilian head to eject twin vapoury sprays of musk while, in the same moment, emitting a rattling bellow.

I found myself staring directly into a maw gaping in salivating welcome. Its lower jaw, still resting in foetid estuarine ooze, now presented the aspect of a scarred and leathery tongue fixed to the base of a buccal cavity wide as a fat man's coffin. All sixty-whatever of its *other* previously concealed teeth had meanwhile prized themselves apart to accommodate me with a malevolence of hungering anticipation . . .

And I'd come three thousand tortuous sodding miles f'r THIS . . . ?

I drew on my every reserve in the face of the Beast.

'Get a grip, Miller: don't let it think you're impressed. So maybe it does weigh a couple of tons more'n you do – it's probably thick as mince an' as scared of you as you are of it. Either way, whatever you do - don't RUN!'

But that was before it began to move. Abruptly lunging to full ahead, sliding down the muddy bank on ventral shields turbo-polished by a lifetime of predation, the leviathan impelled itself straight TOWARDS ME!

Terror caused me to swallow convulsively as I registered foreshortened legs paddling sideways, building to maximum revolutions like webbed and deformed oars; the suddenly elevated and scaly-plated back; the laterally-compressed power ram of the Thing's tail now acting as a rudder, furrowing a pooling wake through the primeval slime . . . those implacable liquid-hate EYES filling an' . . . !

I couldn't *help* myself. I retreated one involuntary step astern - and dropped my bloody binoculars to the full length of their straps! Instantly the crocodile receded to being fifty metres distant, a mere six feet long, and didn't look quite so dangerous.

'Course they has ter be processed a bit first, Mister,' Trapp qualified with an unforgivably Sphinx-like expression. 'Before you c'n put handles under their little tummies an' sell them as fashion accessories!'

I turned my back on him and sagged in private misery over the starboard wing end glowering at the crocodile, by then cruising lazily in company with half a dozen of its mesozoic mates and detectable only as an innocuous pair of eyes, a lumpy nose and the tip of a bony cranium breaking the surface. It was dawn: the sun had barely risen, yet sweat from the intolerable humidity was already forming quickly evaporating pools around each elbow as I lifted my gaze to the slowly passing jungle which had come to represent my immediate future.

To question for the hundredth time whether I *had* any long-term future in the circumstances, as the *Charon* penetrated ever deeper into the green awfulness that had unfolded since our landfall on Papua New Guinea.

Maliciously I executed a cigarette end by flicking it over the rail and into the black water sliding below. Even that was glutinous already: only the steady belch and fizzle of marsh gas

123

released by the pressure wave under our slowly moving keel disturbed the pitch-like surface . . . and this was the free-flowing RIVER, f'r Chrissake – we had another fifty-odd miles to steam before we reached the PROPER stagnant swamps!

On either side of the ship, jungle encroached almost to the water's edge. Mind you, it had been doing *that* around here ever since the bloody world itself began. Sago and nipa palm and breadfruit trees fought for roothold as they became pressured by their expanding colleagues. Mangroves and weird creepers and poison-spined bushes and noxious giant plants all wove and intertwined and throttled each other to create a botanic bedlam. And, behind *that* slimed and dripping green wall a legion of mites and fleas and crawly bugs waited impatiently to infest any warm-blooded creature they touched; to bore and burrow into, and lay their eggs under, any sweating skin. Above a man's unwary head reptiles and scorpions and spiders big as kittens and ants the size of a thumb dangled and jiggled in nightmare ambush while, lurking beneath the stinking, rotting detritus which formed the jungle floor itself, half a million *other* species of awful many-pedes peered and blinked and winked a billion tiny soulless eyes in squirming appreciation of our coming.

And then there were the leeches which clung and sucked and grew undulating fat on human blood, and the malaria-carrying mosquitos. And those little snails, and wriggly wormy things which take up residence in the intestine and . . . and parasites which overwhelm what's left of of the human condition with the threads of impetigo and scabies and yaws and tinea and ulcers . . . and then there were the three thousand bloody varieties of bloody *fungi* . . . an' the . . .

Trapp, still wearing his blanket-quality double-breasted reefer jacket with the equanimity of a polar explorer, ambled to lean beside me and cast an appreciative eye over an environment which had gone stark, staring, homicidal mad.

'Go on then, Mister: admit it,' he enthused, inhaling the rotting equatorial miasma with unconcealed gusto. 'It reely does yer *good* to get this close ter Mother Nature.'

The Beetel did exist, of course. You'll have gathered that already.

Maybe, in these days of satellite imaging and aerial surveys and stuff, even the British Admiralty chart-makers will at last be prepared to concede their three-hundred-year oversight of missing a whole river . . . or maybe they won't. Maybe they still work on the presumption that, until a warship can actually penetrate it for real, physically survey it, *and* get back out again with enough crewmen left sane enough to be believed, then it doesn't exist *per se*.

Or maybe I'm maligning the Royal Navy unfairly. Maybe they *have* done their exploration thing in the intervening period since Albert Fuk Yew's 1938 chart became officially suicidal, and since the sailing directions Trapp's economies had forced me to work with had been revised enough to remove at least those references to trimming candlewicks, tar barrel distress signals and navigation aids based on bonfire beacons . . . I mean, from what little *I'd* seen of the Beetel already I wouldn't blame them one bit if they HAD checked it out, decided it was such a bloody awful surface drain on the face of Papua New Guinea that no-one would ever want to sail up it anyway, and just hadn't bothered to add it to subsequent reprints.

In that case, ironically, they'd unwittingly missed a potential major market. Everyone seemed to be heading for the Beetel. They could've sold at least TWO copies straight off – one to the *Charon* for a start – *I'd*'ve been happy to have chipped in out of my own pocket rather than rely on Trapp's usual bull-in-a-chinashop approach to navigating in narrow waters – and one to that still-unidentified ship following us; the Ying Tong charter job or whatever. Now her Old Man would, I'm sure, have been happy to subscribe. Three thousand miles of leech-like togetherness had made it very obvious that whither Trapp went, he intended to goest as well. I was forcibly reminded of his malign presence even in the last few turns of the screw when, before turning to stare hypnotically at the nightmare ahead, the very last thing I'd observed breaking the dawn horizon astern of us was that bloody LIGHT!

Trapp, naturally, still persisted in maintaining it was sheer coincidence.

Anyway, returning to our landfall on the River Beetel . . . he,

Trapp, eventually pinpointed the entrance as he always did: by interpreting the colour of the water and smelling the offshore wind, all supported by a criminally misplaced trust in his Grandpa's ectoplasmic approach plan: those courses and soundings and leading marks scrawled laboriously - and then probably only as an afterthought, I considered sourly - between the real nitty-gritty of skeletal human remains, ink blots and ridiculously overgrown reptilia which preoccupied the bulk of Blackbeard's so-called chart.

Okay, so I freely admit I hadn't expected it. Oh, not Trapp's success in taking the *Charon* into a river which wasn't there - that I philosophically accepted. If you keep tilting at the logically impossible for long enough, as he'd persisted in so doing all his life, then you have to get lucky eventually. Enough monkeys with enough typewriters will achieve much the same result.

No, what really impressed *me* was the incredible coincidence of a stage prop pirate chart having reflected the features of the Beetel so closely. It must've represented a chance in a billion that some forger in Singapore could have sat down, penned off a phoney seventeenth-century parchment to order, yet managed to come up with a virtual overlay of what would eventually prove the geophysical reality.

I won't dwell on the more technical aspects of the *Charon's* actual entry into the Beetel, largely because I was too terrified to look myself most of the time.

Basically Trapp's pilotage *modus operandi* hung on handcuffing our hysterically protesting Chief Engineer Bucalosie to his control platform far below water level with the assurance that, 'If yer don't get 'er to run astern in time an' we hit somethin', Popeye, you'll be the first ter know . . . !', then charging the south coast of Papua New Guinea full ahead while, as I've said, relying implicitly on the word of a masochistic lunatic wot had sworn with an equally straight face that 'e'd been *'anged* in 1692!

Oh, sure, I'd studied Blackbeard's chart in advance myself: I knew precisely what to expect . . . but theory and practice tend to diverge at twelve knots: especially when the weather's a bit bumpy and the ship broaching wildly before a following sea as it was that morning.

Suffice to say that, from little more than a heaving line's throw off, I *still* hadn't been able to detect a crack in the LAND, never mind a river entrance. Just sheer battlements of jungle towering ever-higher from a rocky base against which frustrated seas crashed and rumbled in the kind of liquid, flesh-and-bone-pulverizing malice that positively guarantees common-or-garden shipwrecked sailors an upgrade to being totally drowned sailors.

. . . Only at the last second – when I was beginning to believe my throw-away remark about ships needing wheels really *had* triggered a self-fulfilling prophecy this time f'r sure – did Trapp issue a super-confident 'St'board ten the wheel. St'bd fifteen . . . 'ARD to ST'b'd . . . !' to a stare-eyed Gorbals Wullie who, in turn, was still trying with fear-fumbling fingers to tie his lifejacket tapes, apologize tae Goad fur no' having contacted Him recently, an' steer the bloody ship all at the same time.

And lo and behold, even as the *Charon* lay over in the tightest, corkscrewing turn she'd ever made, thus causing Bucalosie's already unbridled shrieks of Neapolitan alarm to issue even louder from the engineroom fiddley, a previously unsuspected and overlapping finger of land did open and we virtually broadsided through a cloud of scattering, squawking seabirds and into a waterway sheltered and calm.

. . . only to discover that – dead ahead – loomed yet ANOTHER apparently impenetrable wall offering high speed concertina potential!

It was about that point I'd become painfully aware of my fingers trying very hard to squeeze sap from the fifty-year-old teak bridge rail.

'Now we're comin' to the tricky bit, Mister,' Trapp offered cheerfully. 'Ol' Grandpa Blackbeard 'ad a real sense o' humour 'ere – refers to it as *The Drownded Corpse Chicane* . . . 'ARD to PORT!'

'I didn't know they went in for motor racing in 1692?' I said. And closed my eyes.

*

As things transpired, that somewhat unorthodox arrival in Papua New Guinea was actually to prove the high spot of my fourth voyage with Trapp. From then on, my morale began to deteriorate.

For five days we followed the Beetel's tortuous meanderings as prescribed by the legacy of a ghost: slowly feeling our way further and yet further into a foetid tropical interior which became ever more claustrophobic, ever more alien, particularly to deep sea men. The crew sensed it: I sensed it. Trapp, being Trapp, displayed no sensitivity whatsoever.

At nightfall we anchored, not even he daring to anticipate what sub-liquid hazards waited, then doubly anonymous, behind the tar-paper shroud which blinded the *Charon* following the burnished dying of the sun. Every dawn we resumed our cautious passage, with Choker Bligh casting the lead and constantly calling soundings from the chains in a gravelly snarl, and Trapp again sniffing the rancid air like a pointer seadog when he wasn't relying, with that blind faith of his, on the holy writ of Blackbeard's chart.

Not that he was the only one aboard who'd developed an obsession with checking our progress. Every so often the Professor – having spent most of the outward voyage hibernating behind a firmly locked door, as I've told you – suddenly began to scuttle from his cabin like a hermit crab evacuating its shell, to check the curve of a bend against his own notes; peer forward through the wreathing miasmas which parted only with humid reluctance before the rusted ram of our bow, then nod with secret satisfaction before withdrawing into brooding academia once more.

And then there were his scientific assistants – Bormann's tri-national high-velocity club. *They* still hadn't done anything really worth relating either since they'd misplaced that scrap of newspaper which had given Trapp and me such furious cause to think winged, rather than scaly objectives. All in all they'd kept a reassuringly low profile and hadn't cut a single throat in the cause of science: not even beaten anybody up as part of an *en route* research project . . . yet it became very evident that, once we entered the Beetel, *they'd* suddenly started taking a bayonet-whetting, Sturm-Ruger-fondling interest in the speed of our progress, too.

It was all quite thought-provoking. Suddenly everybody was a navigator in a hurry – except, possibly, Mister Spew who was still working through Lesson Plan Number One of his correspondence course: *Learning-to-sharpen-the Chart Pencil* ... However, the point I'm trying to make is that, despite our having ostensibly been chartered to gather reptilian species, we must have passed a thousand potential saurian donors ranging from handbag to full Gucci-travel-set size – all suddenly brightening, incidentally, before plunging from the banks into bug-eyed cruise mode in the fond hope Trapp might just contrive to sink us at the spot where *they* ate ... yet not one of them – our crocodile hunters, that was: not the resident gastronomes – ever requested we stop, even briefly, to acquire so much as a wallet.

So you'll appreciate why, after five days of fly-infested inaction, I was becoming convinced that sinister events were not only inevitable but ever-more imminent: particularly as we chugged closer and closer to the swamps which formed not only the headwaters of the Beetel but also, by definition, the end of the line.

Oh, I'll admit my binocular-assisted musings which I've previously described – on the overall disadvantages offered by touring in close company with mesozoic killing machines and impenetrable jungles and blood-gorging creepies and unspeakable diseases – I freely admit *they* may have helped stimulate my growing apprehension.

Though mostly it reached its peak when, just after dawn on the sixth morning, I witnessed proof positive that Professor Beedham-Smith's mental pressure cooker was finally about to blow.

I registered the incantations as I turned the corner of the forr'ad accommodation. The sun had already begun to beat like a copper furnace; the river glistened slug-black under its scattering of poisoned gas. There on the heat-shimmering foredeck stood the Professor. Or not so much stood, as expounded – a straggle-bearded, lonely figure leaning perilously out from the bulwark to address the narrowing waters ahead.

'I am *coming*, oh Mighty One,' he was intoning. 'Once more I am COMING, thou ultimate of Creation . . .'

I drew back uncertainly, wondering who he was talking to.

'. . . together we will rise through TIME: cast spears of contempt upon the FOOL'S deceit of ignorance . . .'

'Er - excuse me?' I queried.

'. . . I offer you my absolute VENERATION, most awesome and perfect of thecodontian species . . .'

Thecodontian?

'I APPLAUD your grea . . . !'

He became aware of my watching him then, and broke off hastily: swung to confront me. The eyes locked on, wild, staring - then blinked; cleared to innocent recognition.

'Ahhh, Chief OFFICER,' he offered most amiably. 'Dear boy. How NICE to see you.'

'Um,' I muttered dubiously, trying to peer around him to whoever or, from what I'd heard so far, *what* ever it was he'd been chatting with.

He gestured deprecatingly: encompassed the slime-noxious banks. 'You must forgive my thespian flight of fancy, sir. A sincere if amateurish monologue, you'll understand? In deference to my departed friends of the Kiwari tribe whose tribal lands we are now approaching?'

'*Kiwari?*' I frowned. 'Thought I heard you referring to a theco-something-or-other?'

'To the Kiwari, Chief Officer. Only to the Kiwari.'

I mulled over that for a moment. Certainly I was encouraged by the prospect of people - locals: a civil infrastructure, albeit maybe a little backward - being around. I didn't feel quite so comfortable with the hint of their having *departed*, though . . . or with Beedham-Smith's blatant lie.

'You imply they've all left: these Kiwari?' I kept it light to draw him further. 'Or are you going to tell me the crocodiles ate them all, Professor?'

He didn't smile back. In fact it would be true to say that the phrase *deadly* serious sprang immediately to mind.

'Oh no, to a river native *crocodylus porosus* is benign; a

harmonious cohabitee. No, the Spirits drove them away, Chief Officer.'

I eyed him suspiciously. No, he definitely wasn't smiling.

'Spirits, huh?'

'This *is* Papua New Guinea, sir. Still a land where sorcery and paganism are rife: where primitive tribes pallisaded within almost insurmountable geographic barriers still revere local deities; worship local totems, local *kabu* – the spirits of the dead. We Western interlopers have no concept of the supernatural forces which abound outside the so-called-civilized centres of population: particularly in close proximity to the Fly River and to here, the Beetel . . . Tell me – have you ever heard of the *Origoruso*! Chief Officer?'

I shook my head warily, suspecting I was about to.

'It lives underground, you know', he assured me solemnly. 'Like a giant trap-door spider . . . until an unwary man passes. And *then* it will scuttle out; seize, and DRAG him screaming back into its subterranean lair.'

I felt my glance drawn hypnotically to the passing jungle which, until that moment, had only presented the aspect of an ordinary flesh-creeping nightmare.

'Oh, gosh golly . . . is THAT the time?' I exclaimed, suddenly deciding to make a dignified retreat. 'Look, I'd *love* to stay and hear more bu . . .'

'Or the *Poo-poo* creature?' Beedham-Smith persisted. 'A Papuan deity of shapeless, purulent appearance, Chief Officer, which possesses tusks and can spit deadly poison with the accuracy of a – '

' – a harpoon gun?' I retaliated impulsively. Then reflected again upon *Origorusos* and *Poo-poos* and the still-unresolved question of why we were mounting such a hunting device. And then factored the Professor's increasingly odd behaviour into the equation – and began to wish to God I hadn't embarked upon that particular train of logic.

'Or the *Puk-puk* monster?'

I registered his eyes then: those bloody terrifying eyes, and saw them beginning to dilate with . . . I swear it was with conviction.

'A veritable devil in the guise of a crocodile, my boy. Which crawls from the Beetel Swamps at night to sleep with women and suck the life from MEN . . .'

'Then it's gonna have a *helluva* gender problem if it ever meets up with Grubby the GREASER,' I heard myself snap, panic and revulsion overwhelming me in equal measure. 'Cause it's not gonna know WHICH way to jump!'

But I was reacting only against myself. By then it had become clear that emeritus Professor Walter Beedham-Smith had departed the *Charon*'s forr'ad well-deck for another planet.

' . . Or the dreaded *Tchnial Thing*?' his monotone pursued me as I withdrew, desperately seeking the reassuring company of well-balanced people like Trapp, Spew and Gorbals Wullie. 'With matted fibrous hair and long *fingernails*, Chief Officer? Which spears its human prey with unfailing ACCURACY . . .'

Even when I was clear and steaming full ahead for the bridge I couldn't shake off the vexed questions raised by our bizarre confrontation. Just what DID the Professor imagine was awaiting us, lurking in the Beetel Swamps?

Come to that - what form of Thing, precisely, had Beedham-Smith been *addressing* when I'd first surprised him?

Had it been some grotesque product of his own disordered mind - this Thecodon-whatever he'd called it? Or merely another figment of primitive Papuan lore, like the *Puk-puks* and the *Origoruso* and the . . ?

Or could it possibly entail some more tangible, some more fleshly quarry?

I ground to an abrupt halt.

. . . because IF it did - then what dimension of herpetological nightmare *could* be held to represent a crocodile afficionado's most awesome and perfect of species?

I shook my head doggedly. Almost pleadingly. No! No, such a prospect was quite impossible . . . !

And totally illogical. Surely? To conclude - merely because Beedham-Smith had personally insisted the *Charon* be fitted out with enough heavy gear to customize a whaling factory ship prior to sailing - that some species so gross, so utterly grotesque might actually exist for REAL?

A reptile longer than the wingspan of a light aircraft?

132

Weighing forty-odd tonnes?

And which - it must be assumed were ANY part of my hypothesis to be proved correct - our resident Mad Professor actually anticipated capturing *alive* on account of his also considering it likely to eat two hundr - correction: one hundred and ninety-NINE - *sheep* on the voyage home?

Jesus, but I was bloody upset by the time I finally ran Trapp to earth in the chartroom. Foul-tempered, resentful and, by then, scared half to death of the present, never mind the future.

He helped me come to terms with my anxieties, of course. Showed a degree of understanding which was heart-warmingly typical of the man.

'DON'T you come *bargin'* in 'ere sobbing hysterical–fanciful about silly swamp-monsters an' dripping sweat all over me Grandpa's CHART, Mister,' he understood at the top of his voice. 'It's all right f'r *you* ter be irresponsible: lay about in the sun all day social chit-chattin' to passengers. You're jus' the Mate: a junior officer. *You* ain't GOT nothin' to worry abou . . . !'

'Look, *I'll* help you sew the buttons back on your reefer jacket,' I assured a very huffy and even-more-than-usually dishevelled Trapp five minutes later, soon as the finger marks around his neck had faded to a hardly noticeable bluish-black. 'Let's just forget being petulant for now and concentrate on working out whether it'll be the Professor's lunacy; Bormann's Boys; the Chinamen; Blackbeard's treasure location or a sixty-foot-long walking handbag that's most likely to try an' kill us first?'

'Wot Chinamen?' he muttered, still determined to be residual awkward while retrieving his cap from where I'd hurled it out on the wing. 'There's fifteen 'undred bloody million of 'em – which partic'ler ones did you 'ave in mind?'

Mister Spew felt his way through the door just then and forestalled a murder.

''Scuse me, Captin,' he said.

Firmly I swivelled him to face Trapp.

'Hexcuse me, Captin,' he kick-started again, '. . . but Mister German the Bormann . . .'

133

'Bormann the German?' I rearranged helpfully.

'. . . wants me ter . . .'

'See wot I *mean*?' Trapp yelled at me, vindicated. 'NO one thinks to act off their own bat, do they? Take responsibility? It's all down ter ME – I'M the only one aboard this ship's expected to make decisions; use me brain . . .'

He grabbed the seat of a bemused Spew's trousers and rushed him out of the chartroom shouting 'YOU'RE Second Mate aincha – supposed ter be the Officer of the Watch? YOU bloody see to whatever daft frippery it is the passengers want now!'

'I don't think you should have done that,' I demurred uneasily when he returned. 'Given Spew a responsibility.'

'I'm not exac'ly *stupid*, you know,' he retorted witheringly. '*Obviously* I detailed someone a bit brighter ter keep an eye on 'im.'

'That's all right, then,' I nodded, relieved.

'Yeah – Gorbals Wullie's gone with 'im to see what Bormann wants.'

Five minutes after that, the telegraph clanged from the wheelhouse.

A few seconds later the vibrations in the deck died away.

I looked up from Blackbeard's chart nervously. 'Spew's stopped the engine. I'd better go and find out . . .'

'Belay that, Mister. The Second Officer's in charge,' Trapp countermanded primly. ''E'll call when 'e needs advice.'

I knew instantly what was wrong. Trapp had dug another hole with his mouth and now he'd see us all buried in it rather than admit he'd acted hastily.

'The Second *Officer*,' I reminded him tightly, 'needs advice on how to tie his shoe laces.'

'Spew always wears seaboots,' Trapp retorted cleverly. 'Seaboots don't need laces.'

'THAT,' I said, 'is why he *wears* seaboots!'

A few more minutes passed, during which I stared unseeingly at the baleful, sickly-green crocodile on Blackbeard's chart, awaiting the alarm for fire, foundering or explosion at least.

Then came the sound of boots - a *lot* of pairs of boots - clumping aft, towards the boat deck.

Followed by the unmistakable squeal of rusted pulley blocks.

'Oh Jesus,' I panicked. 'Now it sounds like he's . . . ? I'll HAVE to go an' . . .'

'Mister Spew's in charge,' Trapp muttered, dogged, if neccessary, unto death - *every*body's death. 'Like I said, Mister, I 'ave . . .' he swallowed, took a deep breath, '. . . *absolute* confidence in me officers.'

'So much so you insisted on Spew's being supervised by an intelligent chaperone?'

'. . . yes!'

'As intelligent as Gorbals *Wullie*?'

'YES, DAMMIT!'

'I rest my case,' I said.

Five minutes more passed. The sounds of urgent activity from aft gradually diminished until - even more disconcertingly - all was peaceful again.

I tried a different approach: the last, albeit the most desperate measure I could think of.

Reason.

'Look, we've simply GOT to go and find out what's happened,' I proposed with enormous tact. 'You see, it *may* just be that Second Officer Spew ISN'T infallible. It *may* just be that Gorbals WULLIE could've offered some slightly foolish advice - it may *even* be that the Professor and Mister Bormann and their other two scientific associates aren't quite as *trust*worthy as you keep insisting they are . . .'

'Ahhh, but you're forgetting - I got a *Charter* Agreement with 'em,' Trapp retorted cleverly. He put on his pompous look, then: his smug expression. 'There's ethics involved 'ere, Mister: business principles that a commershully illiterate seaman like you coul'n't be expected to understand. A *Charter* Agreement's what counts, see? It's clearly stated in Clause Fourteen: sub-para bracket 'C' end bracket - that PASSengers can't do *nothing* to interfere with the operashunal running of the ship outside of what's written in the *Charter* agreement.'

I gaped at him for a moment, waiting for his expression to change; to become less earnest . . . to signal me he was joking. But it didn't. Because he bloody WASN'T!

I discarded reason, and fell back on panic.

'But they could be creeping uponnusNOW - this very MINNIT! They could be . . . be planning to - to *murder* us as we SPEAK, TRAPP! To . . . to HIJACK US!'

'Oh, now you *are* being silly,' he chuckled tolerantly. "Ijacking? I mean, now you ARE goin' a bit over the top paranoia-wise, ain't you, Mister? Lissen: there's thirty-odd men tough as a collision fender aboard this old *Charon*; all dedicated ter servin' yours truly . . . right? All the cream o' the bunch - right? Every las' one able ter handle hisself in a crisis - *right?*'

I reflected upon Chief Bucalosie, and the way he seemed to scream so piercingly each time Trapp administered a routine disciplinary Indian burn; and upon Fred/Lucille Grubb who could get so high-pitched hysterical if his/her dress ever got a bit wet . . . and frowned dubiously.

'Well, I mean,' Trapp continued tolerantly. 'I mean, there's only FOUR blokes *altogether* in the Professor's mob, ain't there? So you explain ter me, Mister, how only FOUR blokes could possibly manage to overpower THIRTY-ODD, eh?'

I thought about that for a little while.

Unusually for him, he *had* argued the case with a certain, albeit slightly questionable, logic.

*Had*n't he . . ?

'Okay,' I muttered eventually to Trapp, who'd certainly talked *himself* into a state of criminal complacency by that time. 'But, before you go back to burying your megalomaniac head in the sand again during this particularly suicidal ego trip of yours . . . perhaps you would be kind enough to pass me my lifejacket?'

A *further* fifteen of the longest minutes I've ever been prevailed upon to endure, inched by.

Not a single sound had been heard for the last five of them.

Then Second Officer Spew, looking all flushed with pride, finally bumbled in to break the by-then stifling tension of the chartroom.

We both whirled in apprehensive unison. Despite my own misgivings I confess to having gained at least some small satisfaction from catching Trapp gnawing at tension-white knuckles rather than reveal unseemly anxiety.

'I dunnit *all* meself, Captin. Jus' like you said,' Spew proclaimed, obviously thrilled to bits.

'Done *what* - done WHAT?' Trapp croaked.

'Taken responsibility. Just as you ordered him to,' I reminded him unsympathetically; then couldn't resist twisting the knife a little further: '. . . guided, of course, through his decision-making process by the super-brain of Ordinary Seaman Wullie.'

'What've yer *done* with me *SHIP*, DAMMIT?' Trapp bawled, his cool finally disintegrating along with the skin on his knuckles.

'Only made sure you di'n't 'ave to go ter *prison* because of it, Captin,' Spew assured him considerately, incorporating just the slightest tinge of good-natured censure. 'Regulashuns IS Regulashuns all said an' done.'

'Regulations?'

'Yus - regulashuns,' Mister Spew confirmed gravely. 'So when an *inspector* from the Intynat . . . Intranish . . . the IMO-somethin' wus it?'

'He can't possibly mean the International Maritime Organization?' I interpreted dubiously.

'*That's* the one, Mister Miller sir. Well, when he wants ter see a drill . . .'

'Wot's he TALKIN' about?' Trapp pleaded. 'IMO . . . ? Regulations . . . ? *Drill* . . . ? This is the middle of the Papuan bloody JUNGLE, not Southampton docks. An' anyway - WHAT inspector?'

'Mister Inspector Ger . . .'

'Bor . . .?'

'. . . mann,' Spew completed lugubriously. He patted the back of Trapp's hand reassuringly. 'It's all right though, Captin. He promised me 'e 'ad *every* authority. To order a snap boat drill any time 'e - '

'BOAT DRILL?' we both screamed together.

'Oh, I'll KILL 'im,' Trapp bawled as he bulleted between us, heading for the sunwashed starboard wing. 'I'll *kill* that bloody Gorbals WULLIE!'

I followed Trapp at the run through the wheelhouse to stop aghast - as he was actively engaged in so doing - at the sight which met us.

For a start, we discovered that the river had opened into a wider stretch of rancid water since we were last on deck, and that the *Charon* now lay in the middle of a poison-black lagoon.

Secondly, that she now appeared lifeless: seemingly deserted by the thirty-odd bodyguards all tough as fenders and dedicated to protecting Trapp.

And, thirdly, that Trapp's only slightly-used lifeboats drifted half a cable off our starboard side, both packed to the gunn'les with his aforementioned ex-Praetorian Guard: not-so-much tough now as pasty-faced, panting, and collapsed already over oars still dripping treacle slime.

Mind you, I do have to say that, despite Spew's still-somewhat obscure motivation for actually abandoning the ship, I was nevertheless impressed by our Second Officer's previously unsuspected facility for command.

To have enjoined two boatloads of professional layabouts to pull even that short distance from the falls - roughly the equivalent of ordering chimpanzees to row a hundred yards through wet cement - must've called for disciplinary qualities of the highest order.

I also felt a distinct lack of sympathy for those who had inexplicably chosen to exchange our rusted sanctuary for adventure on the high swamps. Apart from it being the first hard work most of 'em had done since their last stretches of hard labour, I'd also begun to form the very firm impression I should reserve as much compassion as I had to spare for myself.

Until I registered the convoy of protuberant eye housings and ossified nostril cavities cutting the marble surface, at least: already beginning to close hopefully on the *Charon*'s ramshackle complement - noted further scaly saurian shapes launching optimistically from the surrounding shores to join their fellow crocodilians in appraising the menu - whereupon I did experience a flush of concern after all.

Ohhh, come ON - I'm not *utterly* callous. Observing a potentially grisly situation like that developing, I could hardly help but commiserate with those poor innocents out there . . . I mean, no unwary crocodile with a black-marketable skin had a hope in hell of keeping it - not once it allowed itself to get within a boathook's distance of Bosun BLIGH f'r a start!

'Awwww, isn't that *nice*, Captin?' Mister Spew remarked tenderly as he followed up behind us. 'All them sweet lickle crocklediles: wanting ter play wiv our friends.'

'Where's friend Wullie?' Trapp grated ominously. 'I'm gonna let *'im* play with the lickle crocklediles, too. In fact I'm gonna drop-*kick* the little turd clear over the bloody RAIL when I find 'im!'

'Perhaps we shouldn't worry so much about *who* should carry the can for leaving this ship as deserted as the *Marie Celeste*,' I suggested, glancing over my shoulder uneasily, 'as concentrate on WHY they elected to leave it in the first place?'

'Ask that bloody Professor pal o' yours,' Trapp snarled. 'I knew 'e was trouble soon as you invited 'im aboard, Mister.'

'I wouldn't be too sure,' I mused doubtfully. 'Spew here reckoned it was Bormann set this up; not the - '

'Oh look, 'ERE'S Wullie now - come to tell yer all about it 'imself, Captin,' Spew interrupted pleasurably. *"Allo*, Wullie.'

"Allo, Spew,' Gorbals Wullie whispered, uncharacteristically meek as he crested the head of the starboard ladder.

'Guten tag - EVERYbody!' Chief Assistant Scientist Bormann smiled thinly as HE arrived one much more confident step behind our Key Personnel.

A greeting which neither Trapp nor myself reciprocated. In fact, neither of us said anything at all for quite a long time.

Largely - for my part anyway - because the Sturm-Ruger hunting rifle pressed cruelly between Wullie's shoulder blades had just resolved one of the most disquieting of all the uncertainties to plague me since we'd sailed.

. . . Precisely *which* of the multifarious lethal entities that Trapp's avarice had contrived to accumulate during THIS trip - either ahead of, astern, or actually aboard the *Charon* already - was going to prove most likely to jump the queue to kill us FIRST?

Chapter Nine

Bormann offered a sardonic bow. It didn't cause his three-fifty-calibre umbilical link with Wullie to waver even fractionally.

'*Kapitän . . . Herr Kaleunt?*'

'Oh, so they di'n't teach yer to click your heels as *well*, then – when you wus in the Hitler Youth?' Trapp managed to growl eventually with his invariably injudicious disregard for sense of place.

Personally, and while not wishing to devalue Trapp's interest in how the *kleine* Bormann had occupied his formative years, I felt there were rather more fundamental questions which might properly have claimed his priority – questions like how the Professor's crowd had *really* managed to persuade our semi-catatonic crew to clear the ship so expeditiously in the first place: logic insisting I should discount Spew's help as a significant factor.

Even more pertinently – did the gun in Bormann's hands mean we'd now reached the end of the line expedition-wise, and, if so, *did* our stopping have any connection with reasons implied in that press cutting, which – depending how you read it – suggested we were either about to be urged at Sturm-Ruger-point to recover a crashed aeroplane, or to rendezvous any minute now with the Darwin Ladies bloody NEEDLEwork Circle!

And then there were those other niggling uncertainties which, had I been Trapp, I would have wished to clarify before I died from a surfeit of immature insults. Like HAD it been them, the academics, who'd vivisected the Ying Tong duo on our bridge that night? Or even, having once broached the subject of bizarre goings-on prior to our sailing from Singapore – *which* particular egghead set up the Blackbeard pantomime which had acted as the precursor to this current lunacy in the FIRST place?

. . . but Trapp, of course, never thought to pose any of those crucial questions, did he? Oh, no. No, *he* was far too preoccupied with helping Gorbals Wullie, Blind Spew an' me commit *suicide* by bloody associATION!

Happily, passenger Bormann merely permitted a further thin-lipped smile in response to Trapp's opening salvo.

Less happily, I noticed, the smile didn't extend as far as his eyes.

'The *Führer* was before my time, *Kapitän*. He was also a loser – which I am not. Now: to business.'

'Far as I'm concerned the Prof's your team's business mouth.' Trapp folded his arms loftily at that point to indicate the interview was terminated. 'So just sod off an' tell 'im to get hisself up here, Bormann. I don't talk to no monkeys when the organ grinder's around.'

It was about then that the German's lips stopped smiling as well. The Sturm-Ruger decided to deviate very firmly towards Trapp, which at least permitted Wullie to relax. So much so in fact, he promptly collapsed on the deck.

'*Herr* Professor Beedham-Smith is . . . indisposed,' our on-board highw . . . *sea*wayman? . . . growled across the conveniently vacated space.

'You mean he's actually begun to foam at the mouth?' I interpreted waspishly.

Bormann eyed me with – I like to think – a certain respect.

'The man is crazy,' he shrugged dismissively. 'But then, Beedham-Smith has never been of any consequence. We have ensured he will not interfere.'

I blinked. Their own team LEADER? The motive force behind the bizarre modifications to the *Charon* – the catalyst, for that matter, for our voyaging here to the Beetel in the FIRST place . . ? Yet the Professor, according to Bormann, had never been of *consequence*?

I saw Trapp had been taken aback, too. Suddenly we were being confronted by yet another twist in the *Charon*'s tale: this one shaping, it seemed, to present the greatest enigma of all.

'But it's *his* expedition, dammit,' I found myself pleading. 'He introduced you as his research associates.'

Bormann's mouth imitated a smile again. Sardonic this time.

'He imagined it was his expedition - that we were working for him . . . until a few minutes ago. But then, the Professor imagines many strange things. As you yourself have obviously observed, Miller, the man is crazy. Possessed of a . . !'

The ice-chip eyes clouded briefly, and for one fleeting moment I thought I detected an uneasy . . . wonderment, was it? Or even a trace of discomfort?

'Possessed of a *what*, Bormann?' I prompted tensely.

'A terrible . . . madness, *Kaleunt*,' he muttered, unexpectedly sombre.

'What kind of madness?' I persisted, beginning to feel the hair prickling at the back of my neck. 'You obviously know him. He sees monsters, doesn't he? What *kind* of monsters does he see in his mind, Bormann?'

He looked at me enigmatically.

'You think they are *only* in his mind, Miller?'

I swallowed. What the hell did THAT mean?

The German stirred.

'So! But now things have changed, eh? I am a hijacker as you may already have concluded - and you have been hijacked. Beedham-Smith - his crazy scientific field expedition - is no longer of concern to you.' He smiled again then: this time mockingly. 'Maybe you should even consider yourselves fortunate to have been stopped here, *ja*? Had you penetrated only a little further up river, into the actual interior of the Beetel Swamps as he intended, then you would *indeed* have learned . . !'

I'd nodded encouragingly, desperate to elicit what promised to be our captor's most crucial disclosure of all, when Trapp - who'd been hovering in sullen rancour because (a) he wasn't interested in swamp monsters, them only being hysterical-fanciful an' not real like ghosts, and (b) it hadn't been him doing the talking for the last three minutes anyway - finally found irate voice.

'Whaddyer MEAN, Bormann - NO concern? The Prof's still my contracted charterer, ain't he? *My* passenger - MY responsibility while 'e's aboard the *Charon* - an' *that* makes me BLOODY concerned f'r 'im!'

Trapp's bellicose attitude changed abruptly then as a further thought occurred to him. Deteriorated from ordinary black umbrage to sheer choleric affront.

'. . . worse'n THAT, *Gruppenführer* - HE still owes me *MONEY*!'

'Oh, thank you very *much*, Trapp,' I surrendered resignedly. 'Thank you EVER so much for your incredibly helpful, incredibly informative bloody SELF-restraint!'

Personally, had I been Bormann I'd've shot Trapp dead there and then, and with unqualified gratification.

No, I wouldn't.

No - if *I'd* been Bormann I'd have only fatally wounded him. Left him to mull awhile over the lost advantages of keeping his mouth shut before he finally shuffled off this mortal coil in excruciating agony.

But Bormann didn't. Either he was a decent chap at heart, or he needed Trapp alive.

'Then restrain your concern, *Kapitän* - that way you may survive. Poor, admittedly; but at least healthy. I will, however, offer you the small consolation that your trust in Beedham-Smith was misplaced from the start. Take it from me, Trapp - he did *not* sail with this ship for the reasons he gave.'

'Whereas *you* did, o' course,' Trapp retorted ungratefully, totally demolishing any faint prospect I'd still cherished of establishing a less contentious relationship. '. . . You, along with your intellecshul mates - that palm-fisting Frog, Destrymoo, an' Fred Flintstone the Bulgarian knifeman?'

'Oh dear,' Mister Spew chipped in, albeit a little tardily. 'So does that mean the poor ol' Professor won't be able ter study the lickle grocklediles after all?'

'It means, leaving aside the fancy excuses, that Bormann 'ere's doublecrossed 'im as well,' Trapp jeered.

'. . . over the downed aircraft, he means,' I qualified hastily, glaring at Trapp. 'Not that *we* resent being double-crossed, Bormann: in fact we're quite used to it.'

Dammit if the Sturm-Ruger didn't change its mind at that, and appraise ME instead. 'So much for *my* trying to be courteous,' I thought petulantly. 'Soften the thrust of Trapp's ascerbic dialogue.'

143

'You know about the aircraft, Miller?'

'Naturally we read the papers - but don't take that as undue interest. We know all about the attempted murder of a vicar by the Darwin Ladies Needlework Circle, too.'

'What wus the plane carrying, anyway?' Trapp, mercurial as ever, asked with interest. 'Platignum, wus it? Diamonds . . . ? Uranium?'

I sighed wearily. Not only was the gun pointing at me now, but *he*, it seemed, had decided to compromise on talking to monkeys. But then, unmitigated greed rather than outraged dignity always had represented Trapp's true Achilles heel.

'Gold,' Bormann confirmed after a momentary hesitation.

'Only *gold*?' Trapp echoed, a little disappointed.

'Well, it *is* a bit old hat, Bormann. A bit mundane,' I muttered lamely. 'Gold's not very exotic nowadays.'

'Ten million dollars' worth is,' Bormann returned stiffly, finding himself being pushed further and further on the defensive which was not, I don't think, quite the way he'd visualized his hijacking as going.

'Ten . . . million . . . *dollars*-worth?' Trapp whispered, and promptly went into turbo-ecstasy.

'Ten *million* dollars-wor . . . ?' another disembodied voice echoed.

I frowned suspiciously down at the deck. Gorbals Wullie's supposedly comatose lips had definitely moved.

'Get UP and stop cringing, man,' I snapped, mortified by the way his lack of fortitude kept embarrassing us.

'Och, well: please yourself . . .' Wullie clambered resignedly to his feet. 'But ah hope you realize your last chance of surprising *him*'s jist gone doon the tubes. A sleeping Tiger, ah wis - jist waiting tae strike an' disarm him.'

'You still CAN. No one's bloody stoppin' you,' Trapp encouraged balefully, annoyed at being diverted from his megabuck-inspired fantasy.

For some reason the internecine squabbling appeared to annoy our erstwhile passenger.

'*Was ist los* - you all IGNORE me?' Bormann shouted swinging the gun. 'Are you *all* like the Professor? All crazymen that you wish so much to DIE?'

'. . . an' YOU c'n keep *OUT'VE* IT, Adolph – it's got NOTHIN' ter do with YOU!' Trapp bawled forgetfully.

Coldly, deliberately, Bormann squeezed the trigger.

The high-velocity round passed between myself, Spew and Wullie; removed the last button from Trapp's sleeve; *spanged* off a steel awning bracket; went ricocheting off into Papua New Guinea . . . and suddenly the black comedy had ended.

'ENOUGH . . ! *Verstehen SIE?*'

Trapp had turned then. Ever so slowly indeed. To gaze deep into the eyes of the man who – although he wouldn't be aware until it happened – had just determined the violent curtailment of his own natural span.

'They're my family, Bormann. All I got', he said quietly. 'I love them three . . . an' *you* just shot at them.'

The Sturm-Ruger vectored angrily; laid on the centre of Trapp's forehead.

'So?'

'So . . .'

'So *leave* it, Trapp. Keep your MOUTH shut!' I shouted, suddenly terribly afraid for him.

'Negative, Mister. He daren't kill us. Because this one's just wind in the rigging – 'im an' his tin-pot hoods an' 'is empty threats. I dunno what's between 'im an' Beedham-Smith yet, but I do know they needs us to rig that 'eavy-lift gear – take this ship back out – more'n we needs them . . . So, Bormann: hear me loud an' clear – I *ain't* goin' ter co-operate in salvagin' NO crashed airplanes or whatever ELSE it is you got planned, an' that's FINAL, see?'

Trapp thought about that a minute, and decided there had to be some economic ceiling, even to Principles.

'Or not 'til you've agreed to an extra-services clause bein' written into our Charter Party, anyroad. Not even . . .' He frowned ferociously then, dredging deep: struggling to conclude his ultimatum with some *utterly* devastating scenario.

'Not even,' he came up with triumphantly, 'not *even* Bormann, if yer chains me out in the burning SUN all day to . . . to *me* own BRIDGE!'

*

145

By noon it was getting uncomfortably hot.

'Oh well - at least that's *another* of Life's Great Mysteries solved, just in case you're interested,' I remarked eventually to Trapp, who was handcuffed to the wheelhouse door beside me. 'Apart, of course, from why YOU never seem to learn from bitter experience. Just keep on failing to grasp nettles even when you've been battered over the head with 'em: make the same ingenuous miscalculations about people time and bloody time again.'

'Wot great mystery?' Trapp muttered, too preoccupied with devising totally impractical counter-*coups* since Bormann had left us anchored there to rise to the bait.

'Spew's unexpected aptitude for commanding men! Now at least we know how he managed to persuade your crew of living dead to row their lungs out so willingly.' I jerked my head towards the foc'slehead. 'It seems he was supported by the force of argument.'

The piece of laboratory equipment we'd first observed in a cargo sling in Singapore - the bit which had borne a remarkable resemblance to an anti-tank missile launcher even then - still sat very professionally and lined precisely on our boats, on the hulking shoulder of former *Sergeant-chef* Destremeau. I'd watched it resting there undeviatingly, under the blazing sun, all morning. Destremeau must've had the constitution of a desert lizard.

And, judging by his permanent scowl, much the same sense of fun as one.

Beside the ex-Legionnaire at the starboard rail - having obviously provided further incentive for our away-day complement to achieve Olympic standard rowing skills, while now encouraging them to remain surrounded by the crocodiles - straddled the seemingly-equally resilient Bulgarian, Despatov: former obsessive knife-sharpener and current presenter of a scientifically deployed submachine gun.

'Uzi,' Trapp growled.

'*Course* I SEE! I've had all bloody MORNING to see,' I snarled, fed up with being parboiled-philosophical if he was determined to act bloody-minded obscure.

'I meant U-*zee* - Uzi sub*machine* gun.'

'I really don't care,' I retorted, deciding going back to being terrified was more fulfilling. 'I really don't care what kind of machine gun it is.'

'Israeli job. Nine-millimetre Parabellum. Grip safety. Foldin' metal sto-'

'Shut *up*, Trapp.'

'. . . six-fifty rounds a minnit! Process your spine inter bone meal inna . . .'

'SHUTTUP, TRAPP!'

'Your trouble, Mister,' he declared huffily, 'is, soon as things run a little off course you get short-tempered and irritable. Even with people that's only tryin' to cheer you up with a bit o' light conversation.'

It began to get boring by two o'clock.

Nothing had changed. The sun still beat down with furnace-like intensity. The jungle all around still chittered and chattered and echoed with the sounds of hidden Awful Things. Our crew still slumped with hardly a plaintive whimper emanating from them by now; enduring the tortures of the damned in those cramped and open boats still drifting sluggishly on the black lagoon. Their crocodilian admirers still surrounded them in hopeful camaraderie, working on their appetites. Destremeau and the anti-social Despatov *still* lounged on guard, seemingly impervious to the furnace sky, ensuring the hellish *status quo* would be maintained.

Trapp still fumed in beetle-browed resentment. *Equally* determined it bloody would not be!

I stirred painfully as a flock of jabiru birds splattered hysterically into preflight take-off from the mud flats on the other side, flogging the saturated air to gain height. A distant sago tree exploded in vicious squabbling – which reminded me of Wullie again; who, along with Spew, had been spirited away at gunpoint some considerable time before – as a few hundred flying foxes gouged and clawed at each other in a bout of temporary insanity . . . the Bosuns Bligh of the Beetel.

I watched in revulsion as the appalling leathery-winged creatures slashed and gouged at each other with crippling thumb hooks in swinging, upsidedown pursuit through the fouled branches. More of them were homing in on the colony, squirting sprays of filth like mini-crop-dusters, skimming recklessly above my Slough of Despond with lower jaws hanging open, fractionally brushing the oily surface to drink . . .

Lord but how I wished, right then, that *I* was a flying fox.

Bormann finally returned to the bridge a leisurely hour later, sipping an ice cold Tiger beer. I knew it was ice cold because dewy moisture still clung like diamond crystals all round the tin.

He carried two more tins: one stuffed into each breast pocket. They were ice cold, too. I could see the nectar patches of condensation dark against the khaki of his shirt.

'You would, perhaps, appreciate a drink, *Kapitän*? These tropical days: they can dehydrate a man in hours, *ja*? Especially a . . . stubborn man?'

'Sod OFF, Bormann - I'm busy!' Trapp shouted, and shrugged his still-buttonless reefer closer around him in case it suddenly got chilly.

'*Kaleunt*?'

'Yes please', I croaked.

'TRAITOR!' Trapp bawled.

'Realist', I whispered back with difficulty. 'One who is disinclined to die of thirst just to bolster *your* ego.'

'What've you done with Wullie and Spew, Bormann?' Trapp growled.

'Your Second Officer is confused: he still imagines you are in charge . . . I have locked him in the paint store forward to reconsider his loyalties.'

'You 'aven't mentioned Wullie', Trapp frowned, suddenly anxious for the first time since we'd been hijacked. 'What've you done with Wullie?'

'The *kleine Schott*?' Bormann smiled. 'I am happy to inform you that your miniature friend is relaxing in the air-conditioned saloon, *Kapitan*. Handcuffed also, I regret, but nevertheless eating good food and drinking many beers.'

'The devious little *turd*', I rasped.

'Don't fall for 'is psychological games, Mister', Trapp jeered.

'Kraut propaganda: lies – I heard it all before. Jus' a last despairing effort ter undermine our solidarity as a crew.'

'True, he does show a commendable loyalty to you, *Kapitän*,' Bormann conceded gravely. 'In fact he only agreed to eat, drink, attempt a crossword puzzle and listen to the radio in order, he insisted, that he might build his strength to overcome myself and my comrad– '

'The DEVIOUS little TURD!' Trapp roared, as black-faced apoplectic as any idealist could be when shafted by the ring of truth.

'Perhaps we could have those beers now?' I prompted.

Grateful that another of Trapp's fantasies – the myth of solidarity – had been firmly laid to rest.

The Cessna's tailplane projected from the muddy water, maybe a hundred metres inshore from the *Charon*'s port side where it had previously been shielded from our view.

Almost certainly Spew hadn't seen it either, when he stopped the ship.

But then *Spew* wouldn't have seen it if it'd been a Boeing 7 4-bloody-7! And, even if he *had*, he'd've probably thought it was just a bigger lickle grockledile than average.

. . . which latter reflection led me to think yet again and increasingly uneasily of emeritus Professor Beedham-Smith and his *Puk-puks* and his *Origorusos,* by then currently engaged – according to the, admittedly not entirely impartial, assurances of Bormann – in munching through the foam-flecked carpet of his locked cabin.

Or had that simply been a German mis-translation of *'lying on it'* . . . ? In other words, had Beedham-Smith already become an ex-professor? Making up a matching set by now with Ying Tongs One and Two?

While, without wishing to harp on the Prof's part in all this, I couldn't help but brood over just precisely what Bormann HAD been insinuating earlier, when he'd suggested we looked upon our hijacking as a blessing in disguise: that we were fortunate the *Charon*'s voyage to the Beetel Swamps with Beedham-Smith *had* been forcibly curtailed here . . . ?

'Wonder whit happened to the flight crew, Mister Miller sir,' Gorbals Wullie speculated, indicating the semi-submerged aircraft and chirpy as ever since Trapp had tired of hitting him.

I cast a sombre eye towards the saurian humps still patiently escorting our protein-packed boats and sighed, envious of Wullie's inability to draw even elementary conclusions.

'Nasty,' Trapp grunted.

'*I* told you that ages ago,' I grumbled peevishly. 'But you still insisted on signing them on.'

'I mean the Cessna crew,' Trapp retorted, 'not me *Charon* crew. If the crash didn't get 'em, sure as hell them crocs out there would have.'

'Ah *wondered* why they'd got they funny wee smiles on their faces,' Wullie debated a little less chirpily.

'Well, she didn't go straight in,' I muttered, anxious to get away from the subject of people being eaten by crocodiles. 'That tailplane's relatively undamaged. She must've glided in dead stick and pancaked on the water. The weight of the engines pulled her forr'ad section and cockpit under, then . . .'

I frowned: the wreck's tail was still too far away to make out details but there did seem to be splashes of orange - a sort of day-glo orange - around the point where the surface swallowed the fuselage. I reached for my ubiquitous binoculars.

'Good lord,' I said. 'There seems to be . . .'

'What . . . WHAT? Lemmee see - lemmee SEE . . . !' Trapp snatched the glasses childishly, betraying a deeper anxiety beneath his outwardly morose exterior. 'Where, *where?*'

'Buoys,' I mused from the brief glimpse I'd been permitted through my own bloody property. 'Orange flotation buoys. Holding the tail section above water.'

'Dan buoys, Mister,' Trapp frowned. 'Like the deep sea trawlermen use to locate their nets - or croc hunters use to mark their baits? They must've been placed there to hold 'er up just after she - '

He broke off then, and looked at me.

'Exactly! *Just* after she crashed, Trapp.' Suddenly I began to feel cold again. 'Within minutes of her coming to rest, in fact. Otherwise she'd've gone to the bottom entirely once the trapped

150

air was expelled, and never been seen again. So . . . ?'

'So 'oo *did* place 'em there, Mister?' Trapp muttered. 'Who might've been here on this same cesspool a few months ago, maybe researchin': maybe just poaching skins, when it 'appened - *watching* her crash? Close enough . . . ?'

'. . . quick enough . . . ?'

'. . . and - assuming the impact didn't kill the pilots outright which, if she just made a controlled belly flop on water, seems unlikely . . .'

'. . . *callous* enough . . . ?'

'. . . to be more preoccupied with keepin' 'er afloat until, say, they could return here equipped with proper salvage gear . . .'

'. . . rather than save her *crew* from . . .'

'. . . the CROCKLEdiles!' Wullie completed in a sepulchral whisper; eyes protruding by then on mesmerized stalks.

Slowly, ever so slowly, we all swivelled as one.

'As you say - sheer chance, gentlemen,' Bormann confirmed sardonically from the wheelhouse. 'That Destremeau, Despatov and myself just happened to be laying out croc baits from our skiffs when she flew in. Chance - that later proved our amply-justified intuition that her cargo may have afforded some residual value . . . and a question of priorities.'

'*Priorities*, Bormann?' I muttered, nausea by then acrid in my gullet.

'In the all-too-short time it takes an aircraft to sink, one cannot be all things to all men - not lifesavers *and* salvors, *Herr Kaleunt*.'

The German shrugged then, with a chilling matter-of-factness.

'. . . while, as you yourselves will undoubtedly discover: the Law of the Jungle reigns supreme here. There are few Good Samaritans in the Beetel Swamps.'

The proposal was to sling a padded wire beneath the wreck's projecting tail, then hoist the fuselage just enough to drain her and allow access into the cargo space roughly amidships.

Bormann didn't specify at that point just *who* was expected to be stupid enough to enter an already-fatigued aluminium coffin delicately suspended above a swamp filled with crocodiles by a dicky derrick, and I didn't ask. I simply felt encouraged that he'd released Second Officer Spew back into our care, which must have indicated *some* kind of forward planning on Bormann's part.

Bormann also came to a working arrangement with us about his Sturm-Ruger. A slightly unilateral one certainly, seeing we weren't given any choice, but, basically, he offered to forgo pointing it at us so long as we took the *Charon* alongside the aircraft wreck, then prepared her for the lift without any further argument.

He went further.

Even if we did attempt anything devious – 'we' essentially being directed at Trapp, of course: me being too gentlemanly; Spew being too thick; and Wullie being Wullie and almost certainly scheduled for a convenient migraine when it came time to risk brave action anyway – even if we DID try some such unsporting and less-than-British ploy – then he *still* wouldn't point it at us.

'Perish even the *thought!*' Trapp's wide-eyed innocence had protested at that implied calumny.

'I don't think I believe you, so I'll demonstrate the proposed alternative anyway,' Bormann's cynical expression had nevertheless indicated.

He'd walked to the bridge front at that stage of the negotiations, and raised a hand. Destremeau, still on the foc'slehead, had immediately triggered the rocket launcher which, in turn, induced a supersonic lick of flame to jet from its after end . . . whereupon one of the largest of all the crocodiles – one which had, until then, merely been cruising amiably between the *Charon*'s boats – exploded in a ghastly crimson fountain.

Even while ragged gouts of saurian flesh, flails of whisping skin and a hazing spray of explosive-tinged gore were still hissing across our shocked complement, Bormann had flicked the Sturm-Ruger to *safety* before slinging it nonchalantly over his shoulder.

'Please understand, *Kapitän*: we are not so callous as you may have assumed. Should you choose to prove reckless to the point of sacrificing the lives of others, even then we would not wish

152

to appear vindictive . . . *Sergeant-chef* Destremeau will take out only one boat – only half your crew – before allowing you time to reconsider.'

"Ow *much* time?' Trapp probed keenly; struggling to weigh the commercial odds against principled revolt – the financial disadvantages of losing half a very cost-effective crew, cut-throat cheap to run on account of their need to keep on the move aboard the *Charon* at any price to evade the arrest warrants pursuing them around the world.

Bormann gave the enquiry careful consideration.

'About, say . . . thirty seconds?'

Trapp swallowed. Got blacker and blacker.

'Oh, aye: hardball, is it? Then if that's the way you're aiming to play it, I only got *one* thing ter say back to YOU, Bormann . . .'

Bormann shrugged carelessly: half-turned to signal Destremeau again.

'. . . if it *does* come ter the pinch – could yer possibly take out the boat with Choker Bligh innit first?'

Trapp gritted.

I suppose, to maintain the strict chronology of those increasingly harrowing hours, I should report that Trapp didn't even win *that* one.

Choker Bligh was forced back aboard, kicking and spitting in berserk protest less than five minutes later, largely because the rest of the crew presented Trapp with yet *another* unilateral option – either he accepted the will of the majority gracefully, or they'd feed 'is fucking Bosun, already cut up in bite-sized pieces, ter the crocklediles afore 'e gottem ALL killed!

The trouble was that Choker had actually *liked* it out there. Felt he'd at last found his natural element – cast adrift in the middle of a primeval slough. He'd thoroughly appreciated those few hours of being surrounded by killing machines almost as dedicated as him. He'd seen it as offering a sort of opportunity to . . . well, demonstrate his true personality for once. A challenge: a means of establishing a *rapport* between Man and Mesozoic Beast.

Which would've been okay with the others – already terrified into mute acceptance of nearly everything else including being anti-tanked - except that every time Choker lunged over the gunn'le to try to grab an overly venturesome croc so's he could strangle the bastid wiv'is bare f*$%*&! 'ands, he violently rocked the boat which, coincidentally, presented *their* only chance of survival.

. . . unless of course, *everyone* strangled a crocodile once Choker's antics had inevitably capsized them.

Chief Bucalosie was given special dispensation to return aboard at the same time: Trapp argued he needed him at the engine controls again to help manoeuvre alongside the aircraft. It was the first time I'd ever seen Bucalosie kiss the *Charon's* deck: usually it was the nearest dry land each time we docked.

Who said the tattooist was only being uncharitable when he'd abbreviated Popeye's nickname on account of the Chief's untimely cash flow deficency?

P . . . O . . . P . . . E . . . ?

I *still* wasn't happy about the state of that bloody jumbo derrick.

But as you know, I'd been telling Trapp that right from the start; even before we'd cleared Singapore.

I went to the bridge and told him again after Spew and I had topped it in preparation for the lift: shackled on the massive chain span then eased the masthead tackle and led the runners to the winches to prepare the cumbersome spar for swinging outboard.

Frankly, it had worried me - the way strands of wire forming the highly critical foremast preventer stays kept breaking off and crumbling in my gloved hands even though Albert Fuk Yew had sworn *blind* they were 'le-conditioned good ass new, sair, and only extla cheap like Tlapp expec's beclause I do him speshial Janually Sale offer.'

But Trapp rejoined in - well . . . fairly *colour*ful dialogue that HE was more concerned right at that moment with the depth of water Choker Bligh was sounding under our f*$%*&! keel - taking us so close in to the jungle banks like he, Trapp, was being forced to; and broadly hinted I should go away and stop bothering him with trivial domestic detail.

I conceded the point as I limped back down the ladder to the boat deck. Long before he'd finished manoeuvring the *Charon* gingerly alongside the downed aircraft's tailplane I could see her screw already stirring up great whorls of mud which hadn't seen the light of day since the world was born. It suggested, even at that stage, that her keel was distanced from the bottom only by a wafer-thin envelope of foetid marsh gas – and we weren't even positioned yet.

'You know, the *really* exquisite irony of this situation, Miller,' I gloomed to myself as I waited for the bump, 'is that a few inches less water and you'll stay in Papua New Guinea for ever. At that point Bormann will inevitably assume that the *Charon's* taking up permanent residence as a grounded hulk in the River Beetel is simply a Machiavellian Trapp ploy designed to aggravate, whereupon he will blow away the very lifeboats that we will then have to rely on to get any of us back down to the sea.'

And the thought of spending the rest of what must inevitably end as a disease-, bullet-, or crocodile-foreshortened life in the sole company of raving neuropaths like them was enough to make me gag . . . Even worse – *apart* from Trapp, Spew and Gorbals Wullie, I'd have to put up with Beedham-Smith and Bormann's Boys as WELL!

Which, talking of dotty professors . . . ?

I sneaked a surreptitious glance around the deserted decks. Bormann was safely shielded from view by the wheelhouse: Destremeau and Despatov were still hidden from sight down on the foc'slehead . . . tiptoeing to the door of Beedham-Smith's cabin, I hesitated nervously.

Then shrugged, totally pissed off by more or less everything and careless now. So what the hell – one more lunatic loose aboard the *Charon*? The Prof would have to do something pretty spectacular even to stand out from the crowd, and anyway, if he *was* going to show homicidal antipathy to anybody, then it was odds-on Bormann was top of his hit list, which could only be to our benefit.

I knocked dubiously.

No answer.

I knocked again, more resolutely.

Still no answer.

I kicked the bloody door hard as I could.

'*Lissen* - d'ya WANT fuckin' rescued or NOT?' I yelled forgetfully and with an element of pique.

. . . The door creaked from the top, loomed towards me . . . and fell flat on the deck with a *crash*!

It took a full two minutes for my heart to slow to ordinary double-beats, as well as to realize that someone had drawn the door's internal hinge pins, eroded by half a century of use and already practically dropping out by themselves.

. . . and I *didn't* need a university degree to tell me which most recent occupant had been crazy-cunning enough to do *that*.

I now had three options. Either I could continue down to join Spew and ignore the fact that a possibly-homicidal lunatic was now free to prowl the ship; or I could run away, lock myself in my *own* cabin and hide in my wardrobe until the potential slaughter had resolved itself; or - lastly - succumb to my own shameless curiosity concerning anything or anyone remotely connected with Trapp.

I selected Option Three.

Being nosey.

Well . . . surely *everyone's* entitled to one tiny Achilles heel?

Tremulously I entered that dark and curtained space, sliding with my back against the mildewed bulkhead.

Of course the moment I embarked upon my exploration I wished I'd picked Option Two, conjuring as I did, with every faltering step, ghastly images of a Nightmare called *Origoruso* - a Thing like a giant trap-door spider which lived in other people's cabins - until an unwary Chief *Officer* who couldn't learn to mind his own bloody business happened by: whereupon it would scuttle forth, *seize* . . . and drag him SCREAMING back into its subterranean lair.

'An', BOY, will I scream,' I promised the *Origoruso* savagely. 'No kidding, pal - I'll scream so *bloody* LOU - '

. . . But the cabin of Beedham-Smith proved to be deserted. No Professor: no dreaded Monster: not even a dribble of blood on the carpet - no nothing. Just piles of textbooks and reams of papers

156

scattered across every inch of deck.

Shakily I mopped my brow, gazing curiously at the mostly weighty scientific tomes spread before me. Some bore English titles – *Tetrapod Reptiles: a Treatise* . . . *Papua – Beasts, Myths and Cults* . . . *Living Fossils* . . . *The Outlines of Palaeontology* . . . *Dinosaurs and Prehisto* . . . ? I frowned a bit at that one – *Dinosaurs and Prehistoric SEA Monsters* . . . ?

I flipped through one or two. Tongue-twisters like *Erythrochampsa* and *Protosuchia* and *Mystriosaurus* and *Bernissartia fagesi* tripped ponderously off the pages. I hastily moved on.

Many of those erudite publications were of foreign origin. *Les Bêtes Sauvages de Préhistoire* . . . Prehist . . . ? Of course – pre*historic*! Bloody silly language, French: almost as bad as Latin . . . then there was another entitled *Herpetologische Ergebnisse einer Forschungsreise Papua* . . . a further, no-doubt riveting German number entitled *Putzerfische saeubern Krokodi* . . . !

My eye fell upon a red-bound volume laid aside from the rest. Something made me reach for it. The hand-embossed cover read:

Report on the Proceedings of the
49th United States Herpetological Convention
New York 1978

I opened it, squinting in the dim light.

The very first paper I selected at random gave me cause to blink. It had, apparently, been delivered by a speaker called – I tensed . . . *Smith*? Then I looked a little more closely, and my immediate suspicion proved unfounded. A Professor *William* Smith, it had been . . . not Walter. And certainly not a Beedham-hyphenated-Smith.

Oxford Fellowship, eh? Durban University . . . Harvard *research* grant . . . ? Unquestionably Plain Smith must've been, at least a few years ago, a herpetologist without peer; an absolute authority on every species which ever slithered, wriggled or craw –

I frowned. Why did my thoughts keep reverting to the *past* tense? To history . . . pre-history . . . *préhistoire* as the Frogs would say . . .

157

I shrugged; grinned weakly at the crazy tricks a chap's mind could play: flipped the page . . .

. . . and started back in shock!

For there before me, in the form of a coloured artist's plate, was the answer to something which had niggled at me for some time now. Something I'd heard the Professor mention earlier – during his rave session with the *Puk-puks* and the *Poo-poos* an' other mystic Papuan fauna, remember? Down on the foredeck?

The legend said *Phobosuchus – Phobosuchus hatcheri* . . . largest of the THECODONTIANS!

But it wasn't even coming across THAT which upset me so much – the discovery that the Professor had been holding an earnest conversation, not only with myths and legends ghastly enough to make your eyes water, but also, according to the book-plate notation, with a once very *real* Creature which had seemingly become extinct around the end of the Upper Cretaceous period.

Had, in other words, ceased to exist sixty-five *million* YEARS ago?

But no; as I've said, it wasn't simply that artist's reconstruction of a mega-saurian that gave me such a start. Not even though it had, I learned from briefly scanning the text, been the largest crocodile ever to lumber across this planet Earth; deploying the girth of a full grown elephant, the height of a battle tank, the striking speed of a praying mantis and the compulsive killer instinct of a giant bloody SQUID . . .

No, I didn't mind any of that. After all, I have done four trips with Trapp remember, on various *Charons*? I'm not entirely unfamiliar with the two latter characteristics anyway.

No: what *really* chilled my blood – compelled me to stare with mounting horror in that madman's bibliotheca – was that the long extinct prehistoric monster presented by a certain Professor W. Plain-Smith as a subject for serious scientific discussion by an International Herpetological Conference as recently as 1978, bore . . .

Dammit, I STILL don't believe it!

. . . bore an unmistakable resemblance to . . . No – was the very *same* animal in fact! – as the ludicrously detailed crocodile which always stared so balefully at me from Blackbeard Trapp's ectoplasmic TREASURE chart!

I must have stood transfixed for ages, trying to conceive of some rational explanation.

But I couldn't.

I simply couldn't escape the conclusion that Plain Smith's *Phobosuchus* - the largest crocodile there ever wus - and the baleful giant recorded by Edward Teach Trapp, the Wurstest *Pyrate* There Ever Wus, wus . . . *was*, dammit! - one and the same.

And wurster . . . *worser* . . . WORSE, even! Not only had Trapp's late ancestor claimed to have been HERE, where we lay now, up this same virtually unexplored river, but - if the already proven accuracy of his chart was anything to go by - then it followed he *must* have drawn that ghastly animal from LIFE shortly before someone with an impeccable sense of public service had 'anged 'im so 'orrible!

Yet Great-great-whatever Grandpa Trapp had only swung off this mortal coil - purple-faced an' with his mouth kept firmly SHUT f'r once, I hoped vindictively - a mere three centuries ago.

Not even a spit in evolutionary time.

Not compared with *Phobosuchus hatcheri*'s sixty-five million years of SUPPOSED extinction?

Chapter Ten

I didn't mention any part of my discovery to Trapp, of course. Not even to conjecture together upon the intriguing questions raised if one associated, say, a distinguished Professor Plain-Smith of a 1978 natural history conference, with a currently demented Professor Beedham-*hyphen*-Smith at present prowling the nether-decks of our good ship *Charon* – both sharing an academic passion, it seemed, for exceedingly large field samples.

Well, would *you* have tried to? Knowing such disclosure would inevitably have led to your being baited into telling him everything *else* you'd concluded from the Prof's reading habits . . . ? INCLUDING your newly formed theory that we might just be sharing the same jungle as a forty-ton living *fossil*?

I didn't want to talk about it. Jesus – *I* didn't even want to share the same PLANET with it!

I'd have much preferred not to have had to share the same planet with *Trapp* either, come to that. However . . .

On the brighter side, the *Phobosuchus* theory did at least help to rationalize – well, maybe not so much *rationalize* as afford some psychiatric understanding of, the Professor's pre-sailing requirement for two hundr . . . one-ninety-*eight* sheep now, seeing Wullie had produced more mint sauce a few days ago – as well as his, the Prof's, deployment of a *Svend Foyn* whaling harpoon gun backed by the tactical support of half a dozen anti-tank missiles.

Admittedly it still didn't quite explain how Beedham-Smith had managed to talk three mercenary crocodile hunters as cynical as Bormann into *helping* him capture a walking battleship alive: especially in view of the qualification that the aforesaid quarry had been scientifically presumed DEAD for sixty-odd million years . . . though, on the other hand, maybe it did act as a pointer to why they finally did decide to join forces? Presumably Bormann and Co had, in turn, been scouring the Orient in search of someone who could finance *their* aeroplane-fishing expedition back to the Beetel.

Maybe even someone prepared to finance it without even being aware of the Cessna's existence? Some academic obsessed with an entirely different vision, perhaps?

But one thing WAS clear, now. Both of them - both Bormann *and* the Professor - had certainly been on the lookout, by the time they got to Singapore, for a third party who not only captained a portable heavy lift kit, but was also gullible enough and stupid enough to believe the first lie offered with money behind it, without asking any one of at least three hundred searching bloody *questions*!

. . . which brought me full circle back to TRAPP again.

But I'd stopped worrying about all that by the time I'd returned to the foredeck and its attendant shaky derrick problem. Many years ago I'd found myself developing a subconscious defence mechanism: rising above the mental stresses caused by those run-of-the-mill *Charon* problems which always had tended to embrace elements like hijackers and prehistoric monsters and mad Professors and the ever-imminent threat of liquidation as a matter of course.

Positive mind control, I like to pride myself - my ability to force any current anxiety to fade into relative obscurity.

. . . I'd just learned to concentrate on worrying about all the OTHER perils Trapp and Gorbals Wullie invariably provoked into homicidal pursuit of us INSTEAD!

Take the ocean-going Chinese Triad they'd accidentally started a blood feud with, for instance - by now THEY'D almost certainly be organizing some fiendish Oriental ambush down-river f'r a start! Patiently awaiting our return carrying Ye Bountiful Pyrate Treassures of Blackbeard Trapp . . . ?

I hadn't found a spare moment to get paranoid about *them* for ages!

We were finally positioned and ready for the lift shortly before dark.

I'd put Gorbals Wullie in the saddle of the port winch where he perched, spitting on his hands Humphrey Bogart-style and looking toughly competent. That concerned me right away: Wullie Super-confident was usually a Wullie who didn't know what he was doing.

On top of that I'd felt it advisable to handcuff Choker Bligh to the starboard one in case he had an attack of swamp nostalgia halfway through the lift and tried to get back to decimating crocodiles while leaving a forty ton water-filled Cessna hung up to dry.

I was given cause for further anxiety when I discovered my key winchmen were only visible – could only observe *my* critical hand signals, come to that – through infrequent gaps left by the clouds of steam constantly escaping from Bucalosie's faulty packing glands, but it was a bit late to buy a new ship. Or better still, hire a new Chief Engineer after having butchered the old one.

Trapp was pacing the bridge in black-impatient displeasure as usual, bawling orders that everybody ignored. As usual. Bormann stood with him looking tense for the first time: it was significant to note that he'd unslung the Sturm-Ruger, which didn't say a lot for either the German's confidence in our joint agreement, or for his preparedness to overlook perfectly legitimate snags in the lifting operation, even to hold a reasoned post mortem into what had gone wrong if – or, in my jaundiced view – *when* it did.

Incidentally, it occurs to me as I write that I might fruitfully have thought in less evocative terms than of 'post mortems' at the time. However . . .

Even Destremeau and Despatov had begun to look a bit touchy by then, after standing out under that sun all day – *that* didn't encourage me to think optimistic either: knowing that people holding rocket launchers and machine guns immediately adjacent to me were verging on the irritable.

The hulking ex-Legionnaire still straddled, steady as a desert rock, covering our boats. The Bulgarian, on the other hand, while still porting his Israeli Uzi was, by then, summoning himself to scramble precariously out onto the Cessna's tailplane as soon as the derrick strop already passed around it took the strain – he, along with Mister Spew who'd happily volunteered, just like I'd hoped, to scramble inside and haul out the gold as soon as my winch team got their act together.

Well – maybe not 'volunteered' so much as . . .

Beg pardon?

. . . taking *advantage* of the Second Officer just because he possessed all the native caution of a sacrifical anode supported by a lemming-like faith in the goodness of Man?

Me?

Lissen – it wasn't ME promised Spew he could keep any lickle grockledile 'e found inside the grockledile trap f'r a PET, *wus it*? Just so long as the cost of its on-board keep wus deducted from 'is *wagis* . . . ?

And I'm damned if I'm going to hint more broadly than THAT at who it was actually said it – other than to point out that Trapp just happened to be working on a vested interest as well: in getting that gold cargo out before the plane finally sank.

Not that *Bormann* knew it at the time, fortunately.

No more than *I* bloody DID!

'Heave away – and EASY now f'r God's sake,' I called tensely to Wullie.

The winch began to chug and chatter and grind and squeal on worn and rusted gearings as Humphrey Bogart spat on his hands one last time – then engaged the clutch like a Formula One driver making a grid start.

Twenty seconds later and I'd completely lost sight of our Key winch Personnel in the squirting, swirling fog of Bucalosie's inadequacy. Ordinarily I'd have been grateful: a welcome obliteration; but I was worrying right then as the massive cargo hook took the strain on the strop – the strop took the strain on the plane . . . an' finally the wire itself slammed taut as a bowstring before beginning to vibrate with a thrumming resonance.

'It's stuck – avast HEAVIN', Mister!' Trapp's totally unnecessary roar came from the bridge.

'Ah cannae STOPPIT, Mister Miller SIIIIR,' Humphrey Bogart's suddenly terror-stricken appeal reached out from somewhere within that super-heated miasma.

'Ohhhh JESUS, EVERYTHIN'LL CARRY AWAY!' I panicked, diving into the swirling fog and pummelling frantically at the vaguely-seen form in the winch saddle.

'Stoppit, stoppit, STOPPIT . . . !'

'You f*$%*&!-well HIT me again - 'ooever yer IS - an' I'll f*$%*&!-well RIP yer TRIPES OUT, pal!' Choker Bligh's berserk fury protested.

'Sorry - wrong *winch*!' I screamed.

'Oh, *thass* orl right then,' Choker rattled magnanimously. 'You'll find that Wullie over there on the port side.'

I blinked, oblivious to mere mechanical pandemonium in the face of such a quite extraordinary event.

'You . . . you didn't use a single profanity then, Bligh,' I whispered disbelievingly. 'In all these *years* of cordial antipathy towards each other I've NEVER - *ever* - heard you not use a swear wor . . .'

'Ohhh if there's one thing I f*$%*&' 'ATES more than Chief Ossifers,' Choker fulminated, reassuring me his relapse was only temporary and that my whole world hadn't gone entirely mad, '. . . it's Chief f*$%*&! *Ossifers* wot can't speak ENGLISH proper and 'as to resort ter DOUBLE *NEGATIVES*!'

'Well, in *my* professional opinion, that aircraft's nose is stuck firmly in the mud, and we've got more chance of ripping its tail off than recovering it the way YOU want us to,' I said firmly to Bormann who'd stamped down from the bridge to threaten us all with death a few minutes later. 'It's not just a cork in a bloody *schnapps* bottle, you know!'

He eyed me dangerously. I could see he was tired: tense with strain - and *he* was the one who'd had it all HIS way so far!

'You have a better idea?'

'No.'

'Then you will try AGAIN, *JA*? *Sich beeilen*. Miller - *Raus*!'

'AN' *YOU* JUST GO . . .'

There was a thin sheen of gun oil around the muzzle of Bormann's Sturm-Ruger. I could see that very clearly because it deliberately rose to a point only a few inches in front of my eyes.

164

'. . . back up to join Trapp on the bridge so's you won't get hurt if the wire carries away,' I recommended, concerned for him.

'Heave AWAYYYY, winchman – give it all you've GOT!' I roared the next time, simmering.

'You sure youse is speakin' tae *me*?' the cloud of steam asked uncertainly.

'Bloody *right* I am – HIT IT!'

'Gie it a' ye've got the first time – an' HE starts tae *thump* ye,' the Steam muttered. 'Take it *slow* the second time . . . an' whit happens? – HE starts tae . . .'

'JUS' GETTONWITHTHEBLOODY*LIFT*AN'SHUTTUP-DAMMIT!'

'Och well,' the Steam shrugged philosophically, then kicked off the friction brake; engaged the clutch, and spun every pressure valve it could find wide open . . .

. . . *chugga-rattle*-SCREECH . . . CHUGGA-*rattle*-SCREE . . .

The wire slammed taut. Steel bar taut. Almost immediately I felt my previous black resentment tempered by dubiety. Uneasily I watched as the nylon strop stretched like a piece of elastic. The tailplane jerked violently; creaked . . . bits of kiln-dried mud flaked and fell into the black water below as rivets began to pop and explode.

Then the *Charon* herself lurched: started to list hugely to port, drawn by the mechanical advantage afforded to the outswung derrick.

'Keep increasing the pull and we c'n look forward to three options,' I debated morosely. 'Either the aircraft comes clear; we pull the tail off it – or we capsize the bloody *ship*!'

From the corner of my eye I noticed the distant scaly humps keeping vigil by our boats – what must, by then, have represented a bulk catering consortium of two-hundred-odd crocodiles – begin to swivel as one to glare in our direction, suddenly absorbed by the way the *Charon* had begun to heel so invitingly.

Ten degrees . . . *Twenty*. Twenty-FIVE . . . !

'It's *not* gonna MOVE – Dammit, I TOLD you it wasn't gonna BUDGE!' I yelled up at the bridge, surrendering to outright panic again.

A panic due mainly, I should add, to my ingrained familiarity with phenomena of particular concern to any young ship's officer harbouring ambitions to become an *old* ship's officer - particularly those physical laws variously described in maritime text books under headings like: *Leverage - Parallel Forces and Principle of Moments: Centre of Gravity of a System of Weights: The Heeling Experiment* and, most succinctly - *Ship Stability*!

. . . apart from which: keep the *Charon* lying over like she was for very much longer and the crocodiles, who'd already begun to head in line astern formation for us, wouldn't NEED to wait for her to capsize completely - they'd be able to clamber aboard over our already-nearly-submerged bulwarks and eat in the bloody saloon!

'STOP *LIFTIN'*, DAMMIT,' Trapp bawled from the remorselessly angling bridge, hanging on grimly.

'You *stop* and Destremeau will take out the FIRST boat, Miller!' Bormann countered, already lifting a hand in preparation.

'Ohhhh, *bugger* it . . . KEEP *ON* LIFTIN' THEN!' Trapp corrected furiously. 'But so 'elp me: if yer DOES rip that tail off, Mister . . .'

'Then Destremeau will take out BOTH boats, Miller. At the same time as Despatov takes *YOU* out!'

'Look - *YOU* TWO read the bloody BOOK f'r a change!' I screamed back above the creaks and the clatters and the humming of wire coming under ever more intolerable strain. 'YOU read the bloody book as *well*, RIGHT? Cause I'M getting bloody *sick* of the way you people in command can't make up your bloody MINDS . . . ! '

The first indication that something was about to go catastrophically wrong was when the steam parted to allow Gorbals Wullie egress at about sixty miles an hour and still accelerating.

I immediately began to worry. As a seaman Wullie was useless. As a human BEING Wullie was useless. As a local early warning system, Trapp could've exploited him for millions.

Indication Number Two was an explosive *crack* from somewhere above and forward of where I stood. At first I thought it was Destremeau triggering the holocaust, but apparently it wasn't because, when I whirled nervously, HE was doing much the same thing. Whirling nervously.

And staring up at the *sky* with shock-eyed disbelief.

. . . it struck me then I'd overlooked a fourth alternative in our options for cataclysm.

The possibility of our ten-ton FOREMAST snapping like a carrot.

It was then that the Domino Effect – that typically Trapp phenomenon which I have previously described – took charge once again.

Meaning on this occasion that, because the recently re-rigged foremast which supported our heavy lift derrick had begun to topple – on account, I later discovered, of the good-as-new wire preventer stays supplied by one, Albert Fuk Yew, marine chandler and rip-off artist of Singapore, being more riddled with rust than the Titanic and starting to part like threads under a stoker's armpit . . . triggered by that fundamental structural failure, everything ELSE aboard the fucking ship began to go pear-shaped.

First, the strain abruptly came off the wreck's tailplane, which in turn sagged sharply, which in turn unbalanced *Despatov* who'd just that moment scrambled onto it unthinkingly to cover SPEW with his submachine-gun in case the Second Mate decided to forgo the chance of picking up a lickle grockledile f'r a pet and scarper instead . . . though where to and why, in the middle of a swamp in the middle of a bloody *jungle* only God and – presumably – Despatov could imagine.

Mind you – with it *being* Spew . . . ? Though, having said that, ever since observing his previous unhealthy absorption with knife and whetstone, I'd suspected that Despatov wasn't no Einstein himself: in less contentious circumstances, I thought wryly, each might well have discovered in the other his intellectual peer, and got on splendidly, chatting in different languages without either realizing it.

Anyway: Despatov uttered a despairing grunt and began to totter precariously, because you can't hold a machine gun in both hands *and* leave one free to cling for balance – whereupon *that* event marked the point where I MYSELF began to lose concentration . . .

. . . but perhaps I should explain at this juncture that, if there's one recollection I've cherished ever since I was a child - one which may even help account for my continuing fascination with, yet simultaneous revulsion for, the creatures - it is of that scene in *Peter Pan*: remember? The bit when Cap'n Hook got swallowed by the *tick-tock* crocodile?

I simply *had* to spare at least a brief glance over the bulwark.

And there I noted, not without a certain malicious satisfaction, that one of the biggest reptilians I'd ever seen had positioned itself - jaws already on stand-by: wide and welcoming - directly BENEATH the teetering Despatov . . .

Regrettably I was denied the opportunity of experiencing the conclusion of that, my darkest fantasy, because the rest of the dominoes hadn't so much begun to teeter by then as go into FREE-fall.

As had - it turned out - everything *else* above deck level!

I'd only become vaguely aware of the *Charon* beginning to recover - to right herself monstrously amid a cacophony of flailing, buzzing wire cables and snapping chain topping lifts an' runaway winches and jetting pressure as the *rest of* Bucalosie's bloody steam lines gave up the ghost - before Gorbals Wullie arrived at full throttle to distract me further: hurling into his standard hedgehog ball under my feet like he did: grubby hands clasping his ears, and squealing he wis sorry Mister God sir aboot kicking off yon brake an' hadnae MEANT tae sink the ship . . .

I wasn't at all persuaded of his conversion. What possible good he hoped such long-overdue penitence might've done him I *really* couldn't imagine, considering the die was already cast and the gear *en route* downwards.

I realized that because, when I finally did drag my eyes from the overbalancing Bulgarian to gaze uncertainly aloft, I suddenly discovered there wasn't anything left up there to GAZE at. Most of it - topmast, derrick, blocks, several tons of tackle - appeared about to land on ex-*Sergeant-chef* DESTREMEAU: a realization which not only made *me* feel eternally grateful, but also said something for Gorbals Wullie's power of prayer.

Destremeau, in the meantime, had obviously arrived at much the same conclusion himself because HE also began to scream in a manner which proved, sunstroke-impervious or no, that the chap had still been human after all.

I closed my eyes and turned away just before Destremeau's terror was abruptly cut short by a thunderous roar; thus proving that everything the book had said about *Leverage – Parallel Forces and Principle of Moments* had been absolutely correct . . .

Ever so cautiously I eased an eyelid open after the last snaking wire – the last practical demonstration of what happened to those who trusted Fuk Yew then abused the force of gravity – had clattered to the wreckage-strewn deck.

To be followed by a dumbfounded silence.

Choker Bligh's shaven head still protruded from the twisted detritus which now littered his winch. An ecstatic beam creased his already pugilistic features. Only part of his scalp and half of one ear had been ripped away this time: no injuries to speak of: not by Choker's standards. Not even comparable with the state he usually came back in following an ordinary run ashore.

And anyway – cast adrift among crocklediles inna swamp? Followed by screw-ups, disaster and absolute *carnage* . . .? This just *'ad* ter be the very BEST day of Choker Bligh's whole f*$%*&! LIFE!

I looked shakily at Wullie: still strangely subdued, it seemed, for a man who'd avoided being squished because of a last-second religious conversion.

'Well, at least that's two down,' I muttered, searching for the bright side. 'Now we've only got to worry about Bormann.'

I frowned. Wullie had begun to jerk his head convulsively . . . brain damage? No, couldn't be *brain* damage.

The NEXT time he jerked his head I gathered he was trying to direct my attention outboard. I followed the hint just in time to observe Second Officer *Spew* helping what *I* had assumed was our EX-Bulgarian tormentor scramble *back* over the bulwark with caring concern.

'Now you allus remember the seaman's golden rule from now

on, Mister Despytoff,' Spew chastised gently. 'One hand f'r the ship – or in your case, f'r the *aeroplane*, eh? heh, heh . . . an' *one* hand f'r yerself. Otherwise NEX' time yer might not 'ave *me* handy ter stop you gettin' ate by the grocklediles.'

'Spew?' I called faintly. 'Spew, what the HELL are you *doi* . . . ?'

'Oh – an' yer nearly dropped THIS too, silly.'

Mister Spew finished.

Solicitously handing Despatov back his sub-machine gun.

I swung to stare wildly up at the bridge in search of support.

Only to find that Trapp, who'd been hanging over the extreme port wing countermanding his own orders last time I'd looked, wasn't likely to prove of much help on this occasion either: not backing slowly, truculently, as he now was, towards the wheelhouse door with his hands in the air and grimly eyeing Bormann who, in turn, prodded him with the Sturm-Ruger.

Worse. As I turned resignedly back to face my own continuing Nemesis, courtesy of Mister Spew, I suddenly froze – blinked at the ten-million-dollar tailplane still projecting from the lagoon behind Despatov.

Something was, well . . . happening to IT now!

Something which, I predicted with a fair degree of gloomy certainty, wasn't destined to please *either* of our two surviving hijackers a lot.

I was proved right again. Even as I stood aghast the Cessna tail gave a last tortured shudder: air began to screech in moisture-laden sprays from eviscerated rivet-holes. More rivets began to pop as the internal water pressure increased . . . and slowly, inevitably, the only justification for Bormann's keeping us alive began to disappear below the muddied grue.

Until there was only a treacle swirl, a useless nylon strop; a few orange dan buoys and a very large and very disappointed crocodile left to mark where a king's ransom in gold now lay on the bottom.

'Oh dear: now YOU'VE dunnit, Mister Miller sir,' Gorbals Wullie accused pointedly from the deck, obviously hoping Despatov would register, and be sympathetic to, the subtle implication. Appreciate his, Wullie's, non-involvement.

'Ten *million* dollars, that wus!' Trapp's disappointment

bellowed from the bridge; taking precedence over any concern for Bormann. 'Ten million bloody DOLLARS, Mister – an' YOU went an' *DROPPED* IT!'

I stared back speechlessly. Incredulously. For that brief moment. Until . . .

'That's IT! Ohhh, that's bloody IT!' I screamed back. 'EVERBODY always blaming ME f'r *EVERY*thing . . . !' I began to jump up and down with frustration. 'LISSEN – I'm just as fed up with bein' hijacked as YOU are, Trapp! An' on top of all THAT – *I'm* fed up with YOU an' your bad temper . . !'

'Bad temper – ME?' Trapp's utterly genuine bewilderment echoed.

'. . . an' I'm fed UP with . . . with always bein' stuck with *THIS* scrofulous, useless, snivelling, pusillanimous little pain-in-the-*ass* down HERE . . !'

'Doon here?' Gorbals Wullie frowned around him interestedly. 'Er – wid that be Choker *Bligh* or Spew you're referring to, Mister Miller sir?' he eventually enquired with – I swear – equally genuine mystification.

'. . . an' what's MORE, Trapp – I'm fed *up* with your bloody CONTRACTS an' your bloody SHIP an' your bloody *CREW* an' your blood . . . !'

'*WATCH* IT, MISTER,' Trapp bellowed sharply.

I stamped childishly, furiously: outraged. 'Don't you DARE tell *ME* to *WATCH* IT . . . !'

. . . just before I heard the *click* of the Uzi's safety catch being released.

Even as I was whirling, the fear suddenly a claw in my belly, I heard Bormann's rage – far colder; far more constrained than mine – carry clearly from the bridge.

'Kill them all, Despatov.'

The next few moments dissolved in a bedlam of confusion.

I don't just mean ordinary confusion: the kind one might reasonably expect from a situation in which people were trying to stop themselves getting shot. Good lord, no. No – *confusion*, in the context of the *Charon*, had been refined to an exercise in manic divarication over the years. Add the well-documented

Domino Effect; sheer ineptitude; Trapp's overbearing conviction of his personal immortality *and* Gorbals Wullie who invariably provided just the right catalystic measure of hysteria, and you had the sort of lethal cocktail which had been known to confuse whole armies and navies: never mind one solitary German and a non-too-bright Bulgarian.

'REMEMBER yer CAP!' Trapp began first, pointing inexplicably at his own head and roaring to Wullie. '. . . TAKE yer *CAP* off!'

Despatov had already begun to swing the colandered barrel of his submachine-gun towards ME, dammit! Why always *me* . . .?

'Cap?' Wullie stared white-faced-vaguely up at me for clarification; concentrated more upon his coming demise rather than any formality Trapp apparently felt should be attached to it. 'Whit's he goin' *on* aboot mah CAP fur?'

'*I* dunno DO I . . .?' I bawled, already fully preoccupied with debating whether to pick him off the deck and hold him in front of my vital parts, or take my chances over the side with the crocodile.

'Yer BONNET! That thing on yer *'EAD*, STUPID.'

'Ohhh - *youse* means mah BUNNET, Captin?' Wullie finally cottoned on.

Instantly the little seaman's expression changed: became strangely cunning. Despatov must have seen it, because he hesitated uncertainly: faltered in his control of the Uzi and, slow-witted or no, I couldn't honestly say I blamed him.

I mean, have *you* ever seen the eyes of a cornered rat? Glittering with malice - evil incarnate? Wullie's eyes had become like that: gimlet-menacing and unrecognizable as those of the snivelling little coward who'd scrabbled to avoid Despatov a moment before.

I understood, then: appreciated the thrust of Trapp's sartorial concern, and felt encouraged. Wullie had more in common with a rodent than just the way he looked. I'd seen him in action before when really driven into that corner, and discovered why they called him Gorbals Wullie. Years of being the underdog, the runt of the Merchant Service packs, had taught Trapp's unsavoury little shadow that, if feigning passive resistance - keeping yer heid doon when the bullets an' bottles wis flying - didn't get you out of trouble, then pre-emptive violence offered a sound tactical alternative . . . especially if combined with the tricks of the old Glasgow street fighters: the hard men fae the Gorbals of years ago, who'd tutored Wullie in the true art of self-survival at the expense of others; wid happily take on the polis, the bar staff and and a' the customers doon the Mocambo Ballroom at the same time, jist so long as they wisnae expectin' naebody tae stick tae the Queensbury Rules.

. . . so when Wullie reached *behind* his head – not above his brow to grip the peak as would most people when intending to remove a hat – and snatched the oil-contaminated cloth cap from the back of his skull to hold it dangling loosely, almost casually in one filthy hand, I knew precisely what to expect, and felt just the slightest twinge of sympathy for Despatov.

I only prayed that Wullie hadn't left Emergncy Plan 'B' too LATE.

Despatov made up his mind. He diverted the Uzi to take Gorbals Wullie out first, just to make sure.

'*Despatov!*' I called sharply: urgently.

The big man blinked, hesitated again.

'Bugger Bulgaria,' I said.

. . . just as he was swinging back to gun me down an' the *hell* with it, Gorbals Wullie finally catapulted from the deck, his arm already a blur of motion: the cloth cap arc-ing and fluttering towards Despatov's head with the fear-induced energy of desperation.

Despatov let out an utterly shocked grunt and staggered back, bright red blood already spattering from his slashed cheek. Wullie stroked him ever so gently on the backhand with the peak of his innocuous cap again, and a second hideous wound exploded against the rough stubble: causing the submachine-gun to fire wildly in the air.

Wullie stepped away; crouched: began to circle Despatov crab-like, with the cap loosely poised.

'C'mon, ye big poofter,' he grinned evilly; super-confidently; blackgapped teeth bared in the quintessential Glasgae hard-man snarl. 'C'mon an' see whit a TIGER c'n dae tae ye, pal. Ah'll cut ye wide OPEN so ah wull. Chop ye intae . . .'

'You're not in a bar brawl NOW – he *has* got a MACHINEGUN . . . !' I roared anxiously, launching myself at Despatov while knowing, even as I did so, I'd be far too LATE!

173

Wullie broke off abruptly, stared nervously down at his cap. The line of razor blades sewn so viciously into it were ideal for close quarter disputes. Trouble was with him having opened the distance between them, and with his opponent holding an Uzi firing six hundred and fifty rounds a minute, they suddenly left something to be desired - while Despatov was tough: a street fighter himself. Already he was dragging the weapon down: lining it on Wullie; teeth bared in the Plovdiv equivalent of a Mocambo Ballroom snarl.

'Ohhhh shit!' Wullie muttered, frantically trying to remember what Plan 'C' was.

'Ohhhh SHIT!' I heard myself bawling as I heard the Uzi explode into staccato life again above my lowered head.

'You reely can't do *that* sort o' fing wivout permission from the Captin, Mister Despytoff: not even as a *passenger*,' Mister Spew's concern carried through the reek of cordite.

I opened a cautious eye again just in time to watch our hulking Second Officer encircle the almost-equally hulking Bulgarian in a giant bear hug and lift him kicking, bleeding and raging impotently, with the Uzi still firing in astonished bursts at the sky.

'Sorry, but yer'll just 'ave ter leave the ship 'til you learns to behave yerself proper!'

Mister Spew said firmly.

Before dropping Despatov clean over the side.

I only heard Despatov's extremely realistic impersonation of Cap'n Hook meeting *his* crocodile - that, and the splashing and the threshing and the roaring before Despatov was finally dragged below the swirling black grume to join the flight crew of the Cessna. Once again I couldn't spare time to look, to satisfy my morbid childhood curiosity to the full; which was, perhaps, just as well, because I don't think it would have done very much to help purge my revulsion for crocodiles.

But as Bormann had pointed out, in the Beetel Swamps it was invariably a question of responding to priorities. I was acutely conscious that we were totally exposed on an open deck, and, even though the score was now *Charons* two - *Hijackers* nil, there was still one Sturm-Ruger to go.

174

'Ah reely AM a *Tiger*, so ah am, Mister Miller sir,' Wullie claimed with slowly dawning surprise, puffing out his chest and starting to show off.

'I'd keep that quiet if I were you,' I snarled over my shoulder, taking off for the bridge in a desperate race against time. 'Or YOUR skin'll be hung on Bormann's trophy wall alongside TRAPP'S!'

The oddest thoughts passed through my mind as I raced helter-skelter up the ladders from the foredeck before shots rang out that would mark the end of Trapp.

First, I realized I didn't want Trapp to die. Yeah, okay – so *that* came as something of a surprise to *me*, too.

Secondly, I was actually grateful for the company of Gorbals Wullie who was pacing me neck and scrawny neck – not, I suspected cynically, because he was prepared to do or die to save his Captain so much as that, buoyed by euphoria and cocky as hell now, he'd probably clean forgotten Bormann was on the bridge too, and falsely assumed we were both running *away* from the next threat.

But, as I say, I was grateful for his close support. I hadn't overlooked the fact that a patently insane Professor who conversed with prehistoric monsters was still prowling the *Charon's* decks; maybe waiting in ambush around the next corner of deckhousing; maybe drooling and lurking – maybe even along with an *Origoruso* and a couple of *Poo-poos* – down the next alleyway . . . so, the way *I* figured it: if TWO of us happened to be passing, then there was a fifty-fifty chance he – they'd – leap on Wullie instead've me.

And boy – would *he* show 'em what screaming REALLY sounded like!

Then there was the quite extraordinary direction in which my growing resentment was subconsciously being channelled – not against Bormann or the Professor as one might have expected, for having lied to us; nor even against Trapp for having believed them. No – no, the one *I* was bloody furious with right then was BLACKBEARD. That over-exaggerated, over-weening, over-stuffed, over-dressed Great-whatever-he-claimed *Grandpa* of Trapp's!

175

'The wurstest Pyrate there ever WUS,' he'd had the absolute *gall* to boast.

'The most diabolickle; the mos' cruellest cut-throat ever ter sail the 'igh *seas!*' he'd asserted.

'The mos' FEARSOMEST; the mos' buccaneerin'; the most terrible of ALL,' he'd solemnly assured us.

'Bound me 'andsome body tight in *chains*, they did – then set me 'ead inna metal cage so's the bones of me skull would stay in place when me TISSUES rotted', he'd positively SWORN with a straight face.

'An' *then* the 'ot sun slowly dried me flesh-like crusty BREAD . . . '

He'd said.

The lying, hypocritical, garrulous old TURD!

If they'd done all *that* to Blackbeard three hundred bloody years ago, then why was he so loathe to rematerialize NOW, eh? I mean, there was hellish little left a Sturm-RUGER round could do to *him* – WAS there? So why couldn't *he* peg-leg it up to the bridge to save his Great-whatever grandson and heir, an' save *ME* from rushing to meet the highly likely prospect of getting myself blown away?

Funny, like I said: the way I was building such resentment against a ghost. Particularly when I didn't even accept that ghosts existed.

But then, I was also giving every corner and alleyway a wide berth, wasn't I?

And I didn't believe in *Origorusos* or *Poo-poo* Creatures either.

If there was one dynastic trait Trapp had inherited from a cloud of ancestorial ectoplasm, it had to be the Trapp Family Mouth. He was *still* managing to keep Bormann talking instead of shooting when I arrived breathless at the bottom of the starboard bridge ladder.

Not entirely accurate: it was Gorbals *Wullie* actually arrived one step ahead of me before skidding to an abrupt halt; frowning in that ratty, devious way he had – then politely, if totally unexpectedly, standing aside in favour of my right of passage as Mate.

About bloody TIME he learned his place: gave way to senior officers ... I reflected sourly, clambering past him to face Bormann first.

Trapp was standing, his back to me and hands raised, in the wheelhouse itself. The Sturm-Ruger with a German on the end of it still hovered out on the far port wing, facing us both now. Its blued muzzle gestured bleakly as I breasted the head of the ladder, indicating I should move into the wheelhouse beside Trapp.

The shakes had got to Bormann. I knew then, beyond any doubt, he was going to kill us: if not immediately, then very shortly when the last of his bravado disintegrated. Trapp sensed it, too. When I glanced sideways at him he had that bland, expressionless look. If I'd been Bormann, and had been able to interpret that look with the benefit of hindsight - like those who'd already died on our previous voyages, shortly after observing it - I'd've squeezed the trigger there and then. Stacked the odds as high as I could on my side.

'YOU took yer time comin', didn't yer, Mister?' Trapp still growled though, appreciative as ever for my loyal support. 'So where's that bloody Wullie, then?'

'He's here behin . . .' my voice trailed off as I turned to view an empty space.

'You were foolish to come, Miller,' Bormann broke in harshly. '*Mein Kamerad* Destremeau has died because of your ineptitude.'

'Fuk Yew!' I snapped, needled by the slur on my professional competence. Then saw his finger whitening on the trigger and added hastily, '. . . Albert, that is - *Albert* Fuk Yew? The guy who supplied us with the duff gear back in Singapore?'

'You also killed Despatov,' he countered. 'You and your damned seamen.'

'It was the *crocodile* killed Despatov,' I pointed out as reasonably as I could, still hoping to find a compromise. 'We can hardly be held responsible for the actions of every crocodile on the River Beet- '

'SILENCE!' Bormann screamed.

'He's *very* nervy,' Trapp excused. 'I been explainin' to 'im how, if 'e blows us all away in a fit of pique jus' 'cos *you* lost 'is aeroplane, he's good as up a certain creek without a paddle . . . or

177

in his case – wi'out a navigator. 'E'll never get back down to the sea on his own.'

I ignored what was becoming somewhat repetitive carping anyway: over-exaggerating the signifance of my part in the day's misadventures, mainly because I was still smarting over the failure of a certain Tiger to back me up.

'He can shoot Wullie as a consolation,' I offered acidly. 'Always supposing, that is, he c'n bloody well FIND him.'

It was then that Trapp wandered off at another of his unpredictable and seemingly anomalous tangents.

'*Start walkin' backwards, Mister,*' he hissed in a throaty stage whisper, keeping his eyes fixed innocently on Bormann and talking without moving his lips: a bit like a ventriloquist.

'Pardon?'

'*ShuTTUP – don't let 'im . . .*' Trapp rolled his eyes meaningfully in Bormann's direction, '*. . . don't let 'im HEAR us!*'

'*Why NOT?*' I whispered back, utterly fascinated, half expecting him to have a try at *gottle o' geer* next.

'*Cause I got the elephant . . . !*'

He broke off abruptly. Bormann's eyes had narrowed suspiciously; become hooded. Dying Time was rapidly approaching – the man was as near breaking point as anyone in an impossible situation could be, which, under normal circumstances might have led me into a further analogy with cornered rats being the most dangerous rats of all . . . only it didn't.

No – *I* was left hanging in mid-air, still trying to figure out what *Trapp* was on about.

Why, in the few very precious seconds left before we departed to join the choir invisible, he seemed so intent on informing me that *he* now, apparently, owned an ELEPHANT?

Of course I should have remembered that, even given all the time in the world to explain anything, Trapp still inclined towards cryptic obscurity as a matter of ill-tempered course.

But I didn't, owing to the stress I was suffering at the time. So I was almost as taken aback as Bormann when Trapp – hands already raised – suddenly lunged even further towards the dark space between the door frame and the deckhead just above the starboard door and yelled: '... elephant GUN ABOVE THE DOOR, MISTER ...'

While reaching for it in one smooth, well-rehearsed motion!

Dammit, I knew *precisely* why Trapp had harped on about elephants then – he'd been referring to his elephant GUN!

The one he'd always kept secreted in that same location aboard every ship he'd owned until he'd accidentally sunk it. The ultimate tie breaker, Trapp insisted it was; when differences of contrac'shul interpretation caught up with him, and his current business associates finally decided he was bad news either ethically or commercially.

Or just a plain bloody liability by then, of course. On account of Trapp's shortsighted parsimony invariably having been the cause of screwing up every meticulously-planned ambition to get rich they'd ever harboured.

Personally I considered the elephant gun a typical example of Trapp's inclination towards intemperance. Once he'd been backed into producing *that* double-barrelled shot-filled nineteenth-century gunpowder machine at the negotiating table like he was doing now, it didn't merely invoke Para 64, Clause B of his standard *Charon* Charter Party – *Termination In The Event of Fundamental Disagreement Between Principals*... it invariably demolished everything standing within a twenty-foot radius *and* set half the bloody wheelhouse on fire as WELL!

... But by the time I'd figured all THAT out, *he'd* already committed us to our last desperate throw, so – not daring to risk a repetition of the delays incurred through Wullie's earlier foredeck antics – I'd begun to hurl myself low: diving for Bormann's legs to distract him even before Trapp had actually managed to reach into his secret space above the door ...

Only to freeze in mid fumble.

Before turning to view MY already air-launched diversion with an equal measure of black-furious outrage and stunned disbelief.

'Where's me *gun*, Mister?' he snarled accusingly. 'Oo's stole me bloody ELEPHANT GUN?'

I collided with Bormann's legs with a *thud* that knocked the wind out of me.

I wasn't quite sure of what to do after that. In the absence of Trapp's not having blown our adversary into mince before he could regain control of the then wildly swaying Sturm-Ruger, there didn't seem that many options left. Eventually I bit him - *Bormann:* not Trapp - as hard as I could.

Trapp, meanwhile, had begun to advance with nothing more than his bare hands and that terrible expressionless look of his, but I knew there wouldn't be time - not now: not with Bormann agile as a fox and already bringing the gun to bear on Trapp.

'I can't HOLD HIM - you get the hell OUT OF IT!' I bawled, relaxing my bite momentarily.

'Och, all right - ah'll jist go *away* again,' Gorbals Wullie acceded with huge relief, and hastily turned back from whence loyalty - meaning, in Wullie's case, a sitting-on-the-fence prudence in case Bormann *didn't* manage to kill us and Nemesis finally caught up with him, Wullie, in the shape of Trapp's boot - had counselled him to at-least be *seen* to come to our aid.

. . . It was then that I heard the eldritch screech approaching from a distance.

It sounded as if all the Fiends of Hell were scaling the port ladder. A baying, keening wail enough to freeze the marrow in a man's bones; to make him even colder than the ultimate chill brought about by any prospect of death.

Trapp heard it too, and halted, stunned, in his suicidal advance. Even Bormann, now desperately fighting for what he must have known was his own life - even *he* hesitated briefly in his attempt to bring the gun to bear.

Louder it came. And CLOSER - that indescribably bizarre cadence.

'What the *hell*?' I choked.

. . . just as the Apparition BURST upon the bridge from the head of the port ladder, and Trapp bawled a shocked 'JESUS!' and immediately began to hurl himself to the deck beside me while Bormann - who *must* have realized he had embarked upon the formal process of dying in that instant - uttered a last strangled curse: attempted hopelessly to swing the Sturm-Ruger to confront that much more awesome, *much* more terrible target.

'FOOL - UNBE*LIEVER*!' the new arrival ranted. 'YOU could

have been there with your comrades: accepted the ACCOLADES: stood *proud* before those doubting academic CLOWNS . . !'

The first shot sounded not so much like a hand-held weapon as a twenty-five-pounder FIELD gun going off. The Apparition itself recoiled under the monstrous thrust, while *Bormann* simply took off from my suddenly nerveless grasp of his leg to hurl forcibly astern, bringing hard up against the bridge front. An exploded, mutilated starfish of an already-dead man.

Concurrent with that singularly violent event, Gorbals *Wullie* – already happily retreating in accordance, as he claimed with sickening unctuousness later, with MY direct orders – kicked into turbo-thrust and evacuated the bridge for the second time. The wheelhouse windows imploded in a cacophony of twinkling glass shards; and the frame around the door itself began to burn with dehydrated relish, despatching excited armies of little blue flamelets to the deckhead to occupy and start to devour the REST of Trapp's suddenly lopsided command centre.

'. . . the zoological world will *never* forgive you for what your GREED has denied to SCIENCE, BORMAANN!'

Emeritus Professor Walter Beedham-Smith with a hyphen triggered the SECOND barrel of Trapp's elephant gun – which quite unnecessary overkill dramatically underlined both (a) who'd stolen it, and (b) how far past the threshold of logic the Professor had travelled, seeing the initial recoil had already precariously unbalanced him.

Literally, I mean. Mentally, he'd achieved that parlous state long before he pulled the trigger.

This time the butt-kick from the cannon sent *him* flailing haplessly backwards himself, while the now-unrecognizable and bloodied Thing that had been Bormann was blown clean THROUGH the rotted boards and out into humid space to arc hideously, end over bone-and-sinew-protruding end to the wreckage-strewn foredeck forty feet below.

From there Bormann only had one option, knowing Trapp. The crocodiles would receive him too, along with the remains of *Sergeant-chef* Destremeau – which, to be fair, was no more and no less an end than the one they'd so inhumanely afforded the Cessna's flight crew.

181

But, as Bormann himself had said: everything in the Beetel Swamps had to be a question of priorities.

And the freezer space aboard the *Charon* was already full of mutton.

The last image I retained of the *Charon IV*'s steadily diminishing passenger complement was a still-mouthing Beedham-Smith bringing hard against the outboard wing propelled, it seemed, by a hanging cloud of spent gunpowder.

Once again leverage, momentum and the basic principles of stability reacted according to the book.

The small of the Professor's back acted as a perfect pivot against the fulcrum of the scarred teak rail. His yellow-maned head rotated backwards and downwards; his booted legs swung upwards, and - still clutching Trapp's ultimate sanction - he disappeared clear overboard.

The splash marking Beedham-Smith's precipitate disembarkation was followed by a *very* long pause.

Only the spirited crackle of flame; the odd whimper from our virtually forgotten boats' crews, and an occasional plaintive bleat from the one hundred and ninety . . . *eight* passengers still remaining aboard the *Charon* broke the twilight silence.

Eventually Trapp stirred. Lifted a cautious head. Moodily assessed the material damage to his ship then, on finally satisfying himself that *I'd* survived as well, fixed me with a resentful and accusing eye.

'E's taken me *gun*, Mister,' he muttered sourly. 'Wot did yer lettim take me extra-special ELEPHANT GUN for?'

Chapter Eleven

Trapp entered a period of self-imposed *purdah* after that, and retired to his cabin. He tended to, following particularly traumatic events: it was his way of handling sudden bereavement.

Wullie and I eyed each other knowingly as soon as we heard the door close softly instead of slam: the first symptom of his distress. Such sensitivity on Trapp's part had ceased to come as a complete surprise, even though he did only yield to it on infrequent occasions – most notably the time when his goldfish died. You may remember my having mentioned that heart-rending interlude in previous journals? The one he'd kept in a plastic bucket – later appropriated by Wullie for less philanthropic purposes – and everywhere Trapp and the *Charon* went, the goldfish swam too: and usually in much the same manner . . . in bloody circles.

Until, in the middle of one dark and dreadful night in the middle of a force ten gale, the little goldfish capsized and died.

Of seasickness.

Trapp spent a whole week locked in his cabin that time. Poking it morosely as it floated tummy-up in the hope of reviving it – until he finally goaded the little corpse into disintegrating completely to prove, even to *Trapp*, that it never bloody would!

Anyway, the bottom line is that Trapp didn't mess about when it came time to mourn lost loves – so, to Trapp, the shock of watching ten million *dollars*-worth of bullion sink irretrievably to the bottom of a swamp was enough to trigger a quality of deprivation undreamed of by less avaracious mortals.

. . . the fact that the gold had never BELONGED to him in the first place had *nothing* whatsoever to do with the extent of his grief.

I, in the meantime, looked upon Trapp's withdrawal as a blessing without any disguise at all. I felt free – indeed euphoric – for the first time in weeks. Not only was I able to assume temporary command and bully everybody, but we'd also avoided getting ourselves killed; we'd disembarked all but our delightfully edible supernumeraries still penned on the after welldeck, and, most pleasing of all, would be homeward bound the minute Trapp decided to reappear on the bridge.

We couldn't leave the swamp until then because he'd sneaked Blackbeard's chart down to his cabin with him, and only an idiot would've attempted to pilot us back out of the Beetel without it.

But I didn't fancy letting Mister Spew carry *that* much responsibility, official ship's navigator or not.

It was the opportunity I'd been praying for – the chance to answer all the questions which had plagued me; particularly regarding the late Beedham hyphen Smith of whom, incidentally, not one trace had been found when I eventually shut Trapp up from going on about his bloody elephant gun, and found time to look over the side and vertically downwards at the Prof's last dead reckoning position.

My *al fresco* inquest took about five seconds. Ship-to-shore crocodiles provided both suspects and witnesses. I didn't need a coroner's badge to arrive at a verdict of suicide while the balance of his mind was disturbed by a prehistoric monster acting in concert with two blunderbuss cartridges roughly the size of cocoa tins and filled with old-fashioned black powder.

My only quandary arose from how to formally record the Prof's passing in the Ship's Log. *Buried at Sea*, should I enter it as – or *Swallowed at Swamp*?

I left Wullie and Spew to put the various fires out; disinter our still rapturously buried Bosun Bligh; physically drag our by-then slightly agitated Chief Bucalosie from his engineroom where he'd been cowering ever since the mast collapsed and guns had started going off; recover the *Charon's* boats and – last and certainly least – Trapp's heat-, thirst- and fear-distressed bodyguards still in them.

Oh – and to rig a safety line across the void which Bormann's exit had left in the bridge front: largely to pre-empt Second

Officer Spew's spontaneous attraction to any open gap on the principle that it might 'ave a little boy's room on the other side of it.

I myself hastened down to the late Professor's cabin, giving not a fig for *Origoruso* or *Poo-poo* anymore, and almost immediately discovered the handwritten journal I'd suspected had to be there somewhere.

And there, with the sounds of the jungle a fading incursion, I settled down to read what proved a very strange tale indeed.

The account of one man's journey into a Terrible Madness.

Followed, shortly thereafter, by another who loved him . . .

Once upon a time, it began, there were two brothers Smith.

William and . . . Walter.

Even as children they'd loved to play with crawly things. Worms; slugs; eventually graduating to frogs, then on to lizards and things . . . and onwards to university.

Where they both proved brilliant students: absolutely brilliant. In both William's and in Walter's case, as natural historians.

From there they quickly rose to academic eminence - academic *pre*-eminence in fact. For the Brothers Smith during that early period, it was ever up and up the scaly ladder: through Doctorates to Fellowships, to Research Fellowships, to . . . well, they did good; earned a lot of quality letters after their names; became top bananas both of them, particularly in the field of amphibians, and even more particularly, in the field of amphibious reptiles.

It was during the early Seventies that the joint slip-slithery researches of the by-then emeritus Professors W. and W. Smith underwent a major rethink. Herpetology *per se* had, apparently, been okay, but tended to dilute the effort - presented too wide-ranging a discipline in which to make really notable headway.

Which decision, as things turned out, probably also marked the point in time when the distinguished Brothers Smith began to go jointly insane.

It seemed they became convinced that two great brains - *their* two great brains - applied solely to the understanding of one isolated species, would eventually learn everything: might, indeed, discover the very Secret of Life itself.

For that singular study they selected, after deep contemplation, the oldest existing creature on earth - the Order *Thecodontia*; the Sub-Order *Eusuchia*, and, more specifically, the crocodilians!

From the moment of that decision, the Professors Smith literally lived, ate and researched in a scaly, web-footed half-world. All their waking hours became spent on a return voyage through time marked only, within their increasingly strictured brains, by the milestones of the saurian's evolution: *Amphicotylus, Goniopholis, Theriosuchus, Bernissartia* . . . until, one night when the moon was full, Willie and Walter came to what was - to them - not only a soundly reasoned, but quite incontestable scientific conclusion.

That - somewhere in the world - there still exists a real, living fossil.

. . . *apart*, that is, from Second Officer Spew.

But, sadly, *that* conclusion also brought the Brothers Smith into contention for the very first time in their lives - Willie wanted to publish, then to mount an expedition. Walter, on the other hand, wanted to catch it first - *then* advertise.

It must have been a fine-run thing at that point. Which of them was the craziest. However . . .

That was when they decided to split. Part company. Willie *insisted* on going public while Walter started saving to buy a harpoon gun and a very large cage. Walter, in fact, was so mad angry-wise as well by then he even preceded their family name with a *Beedham hyphen*, just to underline his disenchantment with Willie.

And then, in New York in 1978, came the great day of the *49th United States Herpetological Convention*.

And, just as Walter had predicted - Willie blew it!

'. . . a LIVING example of pre-history, gentlemen,' the what-was-then still considered a most eminent Professor William Smith thundered from the podium.

'Not a pale shadow, I emphasize - *not* mere ossified remains such as the *Iguanodons* of Bernissa, or the *Mystriosaurus* of

Wuertemberg's Holzmaden diggings - by GOD, NO! No, I refer, sirs, to a creature first seen on this planet during the Upper Cretaceous period and which - I stake my REPUTATION on - *still* walks the unexplored jungles of Papua New Guinea TODAY.

. . . the greatest crocodile of all *time*, gentlemen. The saurian supreme known to us all as - PHOBOSUCHUS HATCHERI!'

Well . . . that was the moment when the laughter began. It increased from a titter to a guffaw among those academics attending the next annual meeting of The British Zoological Society, while, by the conclusion of that year's International Palaeontological Conference in Moscow, the mockery had exploded into the greatest scientific belly laugh since Piltdown Man.

The Brothers Smith were ruined. Both of them. Both tarred with the same academic brush despite Walter's attempt to insert a hyphen between them - and both *still* disagreeing vehemently about the way ahead.

Prof Willie, foaming-mad embarrassed, wanted to rush out here to PNG *toute suite* - in a motorized canoe if neccessary - and bag *Phobosuchus:* tow all forty-odd tons of crocodile roaring and kicking back to the platform while it was still hot and bawl: 'See it; *touch* it - stick your pig-ignorant HEADS innits bloody JAWS, you supercilious egg-headed BASTARDS . . . !'

Walter, on the other hand - our Walter you'll have concluded by now: lately of the *Charon*? - planned to keep HIS head down for long enough to kit out with the *Svend Foyn* gear and a couple of hundred sheep: find a few croc hunters like Bormann: a mug like Trapp with a coffin ship cheap enough to rent . . . THEN haul *Phobosuchus* back roaring and kicking so's he, Walter, could bawl: 'Stick your HEA - ' - well, you get the rough idea?

Anyway, the bottom line appeared to be, according to Beedham-Smith's journal, that Brother *Willie* - no longer known to the upper crust of the handbag trade as Professor Smith the brilliant researcher, but as *Phobosuchus* Smith, the academic clown - finally worked his way up either the Fly River to the east of where we now lay, or here to the Beetel Swamps themselves.

. . . and then, well - simply disappeared. Without trace! Never to be heard of again.

An' no bloody wonder, I thought knowingly. *NO bloody wonder . . . !*

. . . and that was where the saddest part of Beedham-Smith's journal began. Even the writing ink was blurred at the appropriate references. It was only *then*, you see, that Walter realized how much he'd still loved his brother despite their esoteric differences; and that he, too, should've come out here to help clear the family reputation . . . well, either that, or get eat by crocklediles together as no doubt Wullie wis . . . *Willie* WAS!

I do apologize. It's difficult sometimes. Keeping Characters in character.

. . . or maybe even jumped by an *Origoruso* to his way of thinking, because Walter was really going downhill fantasy-wise by then, what with grief and everything. I mean, if a tiny little *gold*fish could trigger Trapp into a whole week of dewy-eyed finger-poking . . . ?

However, Willie had gone down the tubes – whether saurian or metaphorical will never be known – and all Walter could do after that was gather his team, and sail here to the Beetel with the intention of clearing Willie's good name. Unfortunately, being both obssessed *and* naive, he met up with three European drifters who'd just happened to have seen an aeroplane crash while they were poaching skins last time out: read the papers when they got back, and decided they needed a salvage vessel, too.

One way or another, Bormann and his boys must then have ended up penniless in Singapore where they'd bumped into, and immediately figured Walter for being as gullible as Trapp, although lacking the basic rapacity to consider a straight-up felonious proposition. Instead, they just modified the truth a little; convinced him *they'd* happened to catch sight – not of a downed Cessna full of gold, which wouldn't have interested him – but of a *crocodile* big as a DINOSAUR up the Beetel.

. . . whereupon they'd generously offered to help the Prof out with his specimen collecting. All he'd needed to do was fix the transport, the crane, and the firepower . . .

*

I sat for a very long time in that darkened cabin after I'd finished reading, and unashamedly confess to having shed a tear for the Professors Smith.

Even though I just knew Walter was still holding out on us: albeit from the grave now.

Because never *once* had he made reference, in all those meticulous writings, to his having pulled an even bigger con than Piltdown Man back on that Singapore wharf.

Well, it *had* to have been the Professor, hadn't it . . . ? Sucking Trapp in: focussing his mind and avarice on PNG? Presumably with the contrivance of a very bad one-legged actor hired from some local Tiger tavern.

Ohhhh, come ON . . . *Please!*

I mean - who ELSE could possibly have had reason to stage that phoney Blackbeard charade which had precipitated Trapp into heading here, come hell or high water, in the FIRST place?

But at least that was over and behind us now. Trapp had learned his lesson - never take at face value what you're told by *any*one who turns up unexpectedly and sporting a beard in Singapore.

When he finally stumped back up to the bridge to re-assume command two mornings later, it was as if he'd never been in Morbid Land. He merely threw enough of a pointed glance at the tidied-away stump of our foremast, followed by a purse-lipped survey of the charred area where his elephant gun used to be stashed to let me know he still blamed everyone else apart from himself, then shrugged remarkably philosophically.

'We'll set sail then, I s'ppose. Ready to weigh anchor, Mister - *if* you managed to leave the windlass still workin', that is?'

I swallowed the last of my breakfast lamb sandwich - I'd begun to eat a morsel or two again now we were homeward bound - and nodded enthusiastically.

'Get that Wullie person on the wheel. I ain't telling 'im meself 'cause I don't speak ter useless winch drivers - then whistle the hands ter stand-by. Lemme know when you got the cable up an' down.'

Once I'd seen the hook clear of the ground and felt the engine pulsing on *slow ahead*, with the informal disembarkation area for the *Charon's* late passengers beginning to move steadily astern, I started back for the bridge with an unprecedented spring in my step.

I didn't even mind, as I halted a moment to light a cigarette, catching sight of the lagoon's resident crocodile flotilla propelling themselves lazily, grudgingly from our path as the turgid mud ripple which passed for a bow wave on the Beetel began to spread an oily *vee* across the stagnant surface.

I didn't even care that a billion bug-eyed mini-bogies were still out there; still creepying and crawlying, maliciously resenting our departure. I *certainly* didn't care that the revolting colony of flying foxes was being driven into yet another topsy-turvy hysteria of attempted fratricide by our escape: not even though they were undoubtedly wishing it was *us* and not their best mate they were slashing and biting and gouging at.

Anyway, they were probably watching Trapp's crowd out here aboard the *Charon* squabbling about 'oo 'ad the *very* mos' miserablest time in the boats, and thinking much the same thing.

. . . until I found my attention turning full circle, and got to wondering *which* particular reptilian surrounding us had recently increased its Mesozoic IQ by a hundred and sixty pounds of emeritus Professor. Hastily I decided I wasn't *that* laid back about crocodiles after all: our still being forced to manoeuvre in extremely confined waters a hundred miles inland, with only the rust-fragile hull plates of the *Charon* allied with Trapp's sometimes nerve-racking over-confidence as a pilot to keep them and me apart.

For some indefinable reason my step felt a little less buoyant; my cigarette a little less satisfying, as I re-embarked upon the trail to join Trapp on the bridge.

He was slouched over the rail when I finally arrived.

'YOU took yer time, di'nt you? 'Ow am *I* supposed to give wheel orders to the 'elmsman inna tricky navigashun situashun if *you* ain't 'ere to pass 'em on?'

'You could try calling them out in a crisp, clear and commanding voice like a normal ship's captain?' I suggested, still determinedly cheerful.

'Except I'm not *speaking* to the 'elmsman, am I?' Trapp argued with, you have to concede, incontrovertible logic. 'I told you that already.'

'Then relieve Wullie on the wheel. Get a quartermaster you *are* speaking to. Assuming there happens to be such an unlikely paragon aboard at the moment.'

'There ain't. I don't speak to bodyguards 'oo can't guard bodies neither.'

'Then pass them through Mister Spew.' I made one last dogged attempt. 'He possesses *almost* the linguistic ability of a parrot – and he only has to repeat anything you say.'

'Ah, but 'e 'asn't got the *memory* of a parrot, HAS 'e? 'E forgets wot I says soon as I've said it.'

'What was it you wanted the helmsman to do?' I surrendered wearily.

'St'bd twenty the wheel – *hif* you'd be so kind as ter pass it on,' he advised me with heavy irony.

'Starboard TWENTY the wheel, Quartermaster,' I called to Wullie on the grating.

Stubborn silence from the wheelhouse. The *Charon* continued heading remorselessly for a leather-accessorized mud spit which could very aptly have been named *Crocs' Landing.*

'Repeat the ORDER, Quartermaster,' I snapped nervously.

'No way, Mister Miller, sir – because *ah'm* no' speaking tae HIM either,' Wullie announced firmly. 'An' it's still *his* order. So if youse wants tae get it repeated ye'll jist have tae get someone ELSE tae act as a go-between the other wa– !'

I walked back, licking a satisfyingly grazed knuckle, to join Trapp on the wing as we shaved past the point.

'Midships,' Trapp requested.

'*Midships* the wheel.'

'Mah *nose* is bleed . . . MIDSHIPS – Wheel's AMIDSHIPS, honest tae God,' Wullie whistled through his missing tooth.

'Steady . . . steady as she goes, Mister,' Trapp ordered. 'Tell the 'elmsman to steer in between them forty-odd crocs ter port an' that big sago tree ter starboard.'

'Steady as she GOE– ' I halted in mid-proxy. '*What* big sago tree to starboard?'

'That one a couple've cables ahead. The big green job.'

I smiled; shook my head deprecatingly. 'Sorry, Trapp. Hate to correct you but you've made a perfectly understandable mistake - only a hundred and eighty degrees out in your next course! That tree marks the NORTHERN lead: the continuation of the Beetel *in*land - UP country, Trapp!'

He didn't smile back. But then, to have expected a response of that magnanimity would have been to credit him with a sense of humour he'd never had, and certainly never at his own expense. Trouble was, he didn't even look embarrassed or anything at having made such a cardinal error in navigation.

I tried to let him down lightly.

'Our way out - the waterway BACK to the sea, Trapp, is *astern* . . .'

My voice trailed off yet again. While by that time I'd stopped smiling too. In fact I could feel the nervous tic returning to drag the side of my mouth into the semblance of a worried snarl: something which hadn't happened since . . .

'You're not *taking* us back to sea - ARE you, Trapp?' I whispered. 'You *intend* to push further up this God-forsaken river . . . DON'T you?'

'Yus,' he explained in depth.

'You *still* intend to pursue this wild goose chase of yours for The Treasure of The Trapps, Trapp - DON'T YOU?'

'In the cave, Mister,' he said confidently. Then lowered his voice to a sombre confidence. 'In the cave, it is. Twenty-two paces east nor' east o' the Devil's Head Rock by the Bog o' The Bloodsuckin' Leeches . . .'

'BUGGER THE BLOODY SUCKING LEECHES!' I screamed.

'No, no - BOG o' the Blood-*suck*ing Leeches,' he corrected tolerantly. 'B . . . O . . . G, Mister - as in quicksand?'

'I DON'T CARE *HOW* QUI . . . !'

I broke off abruptly. 'How come you suddenly *know* all this extra stuff anyway? Blackbeard *Trapp* never mentioned caves, or bogs of leeches. And they're not shown on his chart - HIS chart's too full of bloody CROCOD . . . !'

'He told me personally - *that's* how, Mister,' Trapp retorted as if it should've been perfectly obvious. He smiled fondly, reminiscently. 'By golly, but he ain't half a card, ole Grandpa Blackbeard. Full o' stories, 'e is, Mister: 'bout the South Sea slavers an' the Spanish galleys an' the King's Navee. A pirate joke a minnit . . .'

'When did he tell you all this, Trapp?' I persisted. 'Just exactly where and when was this . . . ex-relative of yours actually TELLING you these pirate jokes?'

Trapp shook his head in amusement, as if dealing with a particularly retarded child. 'In me *cabin*, o' course, Mister.'

He turned away to study the *Charon's* final approach into the waterway which would funnel us remorselessly to the swamplands where at least two learned, albeit raving mad, academics held to a thesis that prehistoric MONSTERS would be awaiting us.

'I mean - where d'you think I *been* these last couple o' days?' Trapp added over his shoulder. 'If I ain't been chatting to Blackbeard?'

Well . . . !

. . . but no: no, I will *not* describe our following conversation for fear of vulgarizing this journal in its closing chapters. Suffice it to say that I remonstrated with Captain Trapp in a most restrained and courteous manner . . . whereupon *he*, in turn, proposed that if *I* didn't like it, then *I* could f–

Neither am I prepared to risk harrowing you to excess by recounting the more stressful details of that further passage in a fairly large ship up an ever-constricting, totally un-navigable and BLOODY small channel! Though, to touch upon its lighter moments, I would just mention that sometimes the trees got so close that our supernumerary woollies down aft were able to masticate fresh greens straight from the twig, while we ourselves were able to enjoy sago pudding after our lamb curries during the course of one evening; breadfruit and banana fritters on another - everything being picked straight from the boat deck without our even slowing down.

While so many monkeys dropped aboard for a river cruise direct from the overhanging branches that, at one stage, I couldn't tell apes from Trapp's crew.

193

Unless I looked hard for the tell-tale signs of superior intelligence in the eyes.

And the fur.

So far as my recording the horrors endured on our ensuing land expedition through the jungle to reach Blackbeard's alleged treasure cave by the Bog o' The Bloodsuckin' Leeches once Trapp had even run clean out of liquid *mud* to to force the *Charon* through; never MIND water . . .

Well, I certainly don't propose to dwell on that most appalling experience . . . Pardon? You think I'm merely skirting round it because I'm getting fed up *writing* thi- ?

All right, dammit - if you *really* must know, I . . . well, I can't REMEMBER.

Hardly any of it!

. . . OKAY?

Like . . . my mind: my ability for recall? It ceased to *function*, f'r God's sake - don't you understand? Simply ceased to retain anything other than a cobweb fuzzle of stupefied horror after Trapp had confidently led us beneath that very first twenty-foot PYTHON coiled in the branches above . . .

And there's no use *your* looking so knowing and superior, either. Sitting there criticizing ME in your cosy armchair with a drink in your hand and the prospect of a safe bed beckoning, and wondering who else in the family you could persuade to lift that mini-spider out of the bath - *I* was the guy actually on the rotting leaf mould which passes for ground out there, remember? The fish quite literally out of water? *I* don't have to TAKE that kind've . . .

. . . look - I'm sorry. I *do* apologize most sincerely. Honestly. It's just that sometimes Trapp . . . well, even thinking about the way he was in that jungle, his whole gung-ho attitude overstresses me. But I'll be okay: the doctors all agree it should only take a few more months; a fine tuning of the medication . . .

I mean, even Choker *Bligh* couldn't hack it. We only took the Bosun along - me, Trapp and Gorbals Wullie - because Trapp argued that if *anything* was likely to act as a deterrent to the

Repulsive Things that lived in the wretched place, then it would've been Choker.

That was why Trapp had left Second Officer Spew 'in' what he euphemistically called 'charge' of the ship once he'd finally run her aground on the mud; and taken Bligh instead.

We all agreed the Bosun would feel comfortable with the loathsome denizens of the polluted hell-broth we were about to enter: very much at home among the ants and the mosquitoes and the great black flies like helicopter gunships which carried the spores of the yaws which would eat a man's face away completely before he died . . . and the typhus ticks; the hornets big as fighter planes; the dangling shapeless things; the hairy scuttling multi-legs; the undulating caterpillars doing twenty-five knots to meet you an' lookin' like multicoloured lengths of engine-room hose . . .

. . . and so he *did*. Choker simply loved them. Every last one of them.

Or all except *one* particular species.

I was very disappointed with Choker Bligh in the end.

Found the chap completely lacking in moral fibre.

I do remember that, once we'd hacked our way through the barrier of jungle and Wullie and me had frantically batted all the squiggling, wormy grab-a-rides from our sweat-drenched clothes, I'd collapsed feeling faint. Wullie, naturally, had reached ground zero before me, all curled up and whimpering like a terrified puppy, so I at least had him to break my fall.

'Don't lounge about too long, Mister,' Trapp grumbled impatiently. 'No use relaxin' when we've only come the easy bit so far.'

I lifted my haggard eyes to see, stretching before us, a gaseous quagmire from which occasional globules and humps - quite a few with legs - rose to stir the treacherous tangle of floating mangrove roots.

'. . . an' you c'n tell that *Wullie* person what I jus' said, too,' Trapp added with spiteful relish.

It took the rest of the morning to pick our way across that canting, submerging root web with - certainly in mine and

195

Wullie's case – the fear bile thick in our throats and our imaginations stretched to the limit – well, my imagination anyway, seeing Wullie was spared that suffering by definition – at what toothful Things must be waiting under the slime beneath us should we place one faltering step wrongly.

But at last we reached firmer ground: had run, or at least shuffled even *that* awesome gauntlet, and I turned to stare astern, not without a certain pride of achievement.

'Well, thank goodness that's the Bog o' The Bloodsuckin' Leeches behind us, chaps,' I said shakily, conscious of my duty as an officer to maintain morale. 'Though I have to admit, there were times when I never thought we'd make it.'

Trapp looked up from turning Blackbeard's chart this way and that, and eyed me sourly.

'Bog o' The Bloodsuckin' *Leeches* . . . ?' he jeered uproariously. 'Ho, no, Mister: that weren't the Bog o' The Bloodsuckin' *Leeches*. Lordy, no! No, accordin' ter ole Grandpa Blackbeard, the Bog o' The Bloodsuckin' *Leeches* . . !'

He turned then, to indicate a jungle-scabrous mountain some several miles ahead and reaching almost to the clouds.

'. . . is the *other* side of that bit o' hill there.'

It was around that point in our safari that my mind slipped into neutral.

It sorted Choker Bligh out, all the same: that Bog o' the What's-their-names. I can still recollect *that* highlight of my day with not a little vicarious satisfaction.

Without labouring the rest of our journey, we'd finally staggered through, or across, or in spite of that ultimate and most hellish barrier, and were resting with even Trapp looking a bit red in the face by then and with mud all over his safari-style tennis shoes and thick-buttoned reefer, when Choker suddenly frowned: stared down with mystification at an oddly misshapen lump which had appeared beneath his trouser leg – then frantically began hauling it up to reveal an obscene blue-black growth about the size of a cricket ball clinging to his shin.

'Gettem OFF!' Choker began to scream, totally out of character for a man who enjoyed strangling crocodiles and being interred

196

beneath ship's masts. 'Aw, *please* somebody? Gettem *OFF* OF ME!'

We clustered around him to inspect the offending protuberance with detatched interest. It seemed to pulsate, and have several writhing, bloated tails.

'They're only leeches,' Trapp frowned, unable to see what all the fuss was about. 'Jus' a few *leeches*, Choker. Suckin' yer blood: draining yer fluid of Life.'

'GERREM*OFF!*' Choker shrieked with his bullet head turned away and unable to look. '*Pleeeese*, Captin - they gives me the jimjams.'

'We could try the old Comanche trick - a wet cigarette,' Trapp mused after considerable thought. 'Twist a wet cigarette inna handkerchief then allow the nicotine to drip on the little creatures.'

'We don't have any cigarettes,' I said regretfully, lighting my last one.

'Salt,' Wullie suggested. 'Shake salt on them. Like on fish an' chips?'

'Oh, that's a jolly good idea. So if there wus a fish an' *chip* shop 'andy round the corner from the Bog o' The Bloodsuckin' Leeches 'ere,' Trapp retorted scathingly, forgetting he wasn't supposed to be talking to Wullie, 'we could nip in an' bloody GET some.'

'Look, they're getting bigger,' I pointed out, utterly fascinated.

'. . . an' *bigger*,' Wullie updated.

'Awwww why does they DO it?' Choker whimpered. 'Why *does* them 'orrible crawlies DO this to a bloke wot loves all God's lickle creatures?'

'But that's *exac'ly* why,' Trapp explained affectionately. 'Because you DO love 'em so much, Choker - they knows that if they don't eat *you* first . . . then you'll bloody well eat THEM!'

We found Blackbeard's Treasure Cave eventually. Just where he'd told Trapp we'd find it - twenty-two paces east nor' east of the . . .

If you believe in ghosts, that is. To me, there had to be a more rational explanation. For one thing it could have been a fluke: anyone could stumble on to pirate booty in a place like that. The path to it, as you'll have gathered, hadn't exactly been beaten flat by previous droves of fortune seekers, had it?

Not since sixteen ninety-something, anyway.

According to a ghost.

Architecturally the entrance offered the aspect of Gothic crypt strongly influenced by Neanderthal public toilet.

Dimly perceived within its cabbalistic void, hair-tendrilled root-forms twisted and writhed in mortal combat, prepared to join forces only long enough to garrotte anyone *else* who dared venture into that vegetable free-for-all. Long jelly-like stalactites hung in patient ambush; having already waited three hundred years to defecate their pendulous slime-blobs upon the first unwary head to pass below while, from somewhere deep in the otherwise deathly silent space, the *drip, plob, plop* of ooze in eternal freefall could be heard.

As far as the light did manage to filter through, sagging curtains of mildewed spider's webs proudly displayed the eviscerated husks of equally mildewed things caught in them. From the deeper darkness, other tiny pin-points of light defied closer analysis: glistening and glittering and watching us with insect malevolence . . . above, and at either side of the cave mouth, corpse-green boulders clustered and jostled each other for first chance of taking out whoever was stupid enough to defy their tenuous hold on gravity.

. . . for the *second* time that day I wished we'd brought along Mister Spew, and saved ourselves another inevitable argument.

'Go on, then,' I said enjoyably to Trapp, perfectly happy to argue this one out to the end of time if neccessary. 'It's your family seat – *you* go in first.'

'Navy protocol,' Trapp retorted quick as a flash. 'Junior ratings leave the boat first: senior officers last. An' I'm a full three-ring Reserve Commander, Mister: I gotter responsibility not ter break with tradition.'

'It isn't a boat, it's a cave,' I pointed out. 'And we're entering, not leaving.'

'Same thing . . . AFTER you – Lieu*tenant*-Commander.'

Equally incapable of bringing myself to defy Royal Naval protocol, I felt bound to turn to Choker.

'Master's orders, Bligh: lower ratings first. After you – Bosun!'

All three of us turned and stared in pointed concert.

'Whit,' the most Ordinary Seaman of all swallowed apprehensively, 'are *youse* all lookin' at ME fur?'

Trapp had, of course, remembered to bring a couple of empty seabags with him to carry the treasure back to the *Charon*, which, while revealing a trust in the veracity of a phantom which bordered on the immature, equally demonstrated a capacity for tunnel vision bordering on the sheer inept – he'd never once thought to bring an engineroom lantern or something to FIND it with, had he? And that despite having been constantly assured by the self-same spectre that it wus inna CAVE . . .

He had absolutely *no* excuse for such an oversight. And no – I do NOT feel charitable enough to excuse Trapp's lack of forward planning by labelling him so naive as to imagine every pirate cache in the Bog o' The Bloodsucking Leeches had been tourist-upgraded by the Papua New Guinea Electric Light And Power Company . . . though I did, mind you, notice Choker *Bligh* fumbling for something about chest height as we ventured in.

Just inside and to the right of the entrance . . . ?

However . . . unfortunately I hadn't had the sense to lose my ubiquitous Zippo, so we were able to twist what few dry twigs we were able to find under the surrounding trees into elementary firebrands with which to light our – well, light *Wullie's* palsied advance into that fiendish lair.

. . . until eventually, without dwelling in too much detail on the snakes and the black widow spiders we met – and most particularly on the curiously articulated thing with a glistening carapace and about three hundred bloody legs which scuttled clear up Wullie's shirt-front before catching sight of his expression an' getting a bigger bloody fright than HE did – we came upon what a forged chart left by a ham actor on a wharf in Singapore had jokingly described as . . . well – as . . .

Ye Bountiful Treassures
of the mos' admirable Pyrate,
Captain Edward Teach Trapp.

Honestly!

It even said it was.

The tarnished brass plate on the lid – 'Ye *Bountiful* Treassures
of . . !'

The chest itself was traditional pirate issue: wooden bound
with heavy iron bands as you might have expected. Surprisingly
it hadn't crumbled to dust or been eaten by worms and things,
but that was probably because Grandpa Blackbeard had had the
foresight to treat *it* in much the same way as the King's Navee
had treated HIM in the end, God Bless 'Em! Dipped it in hot tar
and rendered it totally inedible.

The last firebrand died and we were left on flickering
Zippo-power.

'Open it, Mister', Trapp encouraged, entranced.

'No, *you* open it', I demurred, still struggling to come to terms
with what had to be the most incredible coincidence. 'The next
one in there might have *four* hundred legs an' teeth to match'.

Trapp didn't even argue: just moved forward meekly and
caressed it with a hitherto unsuspected tenderness.

'Me 'eritage', he whispered, and sniffed a bit: wiped the corner
of a moist eye with the cotton waste ball he'd had in his pocket
since Singapore. 'Me legacy this is, Mister. The Trapp Family
Testament'.

'Oh for *God's* sake . . !' I sighed, feeling slightly nauseated.

'Go *on* then, Captin', Wullie urged hopefully. 'Open it an' let's
see whit we've found'.

'Whaddyer mean – *we*?' Trapp rounded; through the emotional
barrier already. 'Wot's this "*we*" stuff, Ord'nary Seaman – this is
MINE, right? All MINE . . !'

'So far all you've inherited is a badly painted wooden bloody
BOX, Trapp', I snapped, getting anxious. '*Open* the fucking thing
before my Zippo runs out an' we're left *more* in the bloody dark
than we were when we STARTED!'

'Oh all RIGHT!' he yelled, finally diverted from his

sentimental wallow back to normal choleric. 'DO this - DO that! Let's see *this* - let's see THAT! Greed *greed* bloody GREED . . . !

He threw the lid back with a creak and a *crash*.

I caught one breathtaking glimpse of the dull patina of gold; the glint of rubies; diamonds; pearls, emeral–

Just before my Zippo ran dry.

I remember expressing disconcertion at that point in the adventure.

The scuttling and the sinister rustles and the constant dripping from the almost total darkness which abruptly enshrouded me? And I *knew* they were only caused by Trapp, Wullie and Bligh . . . the other denizens of Blackbeard's cave must've been terrified out of their repellent little . . .

Unusually, it was Gorbals Wullie who saved me from, instead of precipitating me into, advanced-grade hysterics as he usually contrived to do.

'Dinnae panic, Mister Miller, sir: ah'll switch the torch on,' he called.

There was a *click* and a shaft of blessed light pierced the Stygian dark.

'For the last time - that *wasn't* me screaming,' I protested resentfully.

' 'Old it over 'ere at the TREASURE, dammit,' Trapp grumbled at his electricity-equipped goblin, still put out. 'And don't waste it neither.'

'How can ye save light wi' a *torch*?' Wullie appealed defensively. 'Either it's switched aff - or it's switched ON. There's nae economy butto- '

'Hang on a minute,' I frowned. 'I thought we didn't bring a torch *with* us.'

'Di'n't I already *say* we didn't?' Trapp yelled in frustration, desperate by then to get started on a bottom-line valuation of his precious heritage. 'Never take a tellin', DO yer, Mister? Nit-nit-NIT PICK at every tiny detail . . .'

I swung urgently to Gorbals Wullie. 'Where did you find it?'

'On tap o' the treasure, Mister Miller sir,' Gorbals Wullie

pointed. 'Jist in between yon ruby-studded gold box an' the leathery bag o' Spanish duckits.'

'Ducats,' Trapp corrected with proprietory discrimination. '*My* ducats.'

'Torch probably b'longed ter yer Grandpa f*$%*&!-ing Blackbeard, Cap'n,' was Bosun Bligh's contribution to solving the mystery.

'Don't be so bloody SILLY, Bosun,' I screamed.

'COURSE it couldn't've,' Wullie sniggered, winking at me ingratiatingly. 'The *batteries* wid have run oot by now – wouldn't they no, Mister Miller, sir?'

'Or possibly someone else arrived before you, and merely left it lying there, gentlemen?' a disembodied voice hazarded.

. . . a disturbingly familiar disembodied voice?

'All right – 'OO said that? 'Oo's taking the piss?' Trapp snarled. 'Which one o' you come up with a *reely* daft suggestion like THAT?'

'I must confess, 'twas I – my dear and most *loyal* Captain Trapp!'

The overspill of torchlight illuminated the cadaverous, bearded features of the *fifth* human occupant of that awful place as he shambled forward from the shadows. The overall impression – the underlighting: the way it caused the deranged eyes to glitter beneath those Satanic eyebrows was bizarre. Terrifying.

Almost as scary, in fact, as the way it highlighted the mobile artillery piece emeritus Professor Smith – Smith, Walter: preceded by a Beedham hyphen, that was – held. That archaic machine of mass-destruction that Trapp euphemistically referred to as 'me Elephant Gun', and which had last been observed propelling our now seemingly-reincarnated academic outward bound.

. . . but with which he now, it appeared, proposed to blow *us* away. Quite literally too, I shouldn't wonder. Having seen what he'd done to Bormann even *before* he'd benefited from that practice in learning to fire it efficiently.

Chapter Twelve

Judging by the extra-dishevelled and mud-stained look of him, Beedham-Smith had survived by the simple expedient of swimming for the beach.

But then, I'd never thought to look over the inboard side – the shore side of the *Charon*, had I? Well, would *you* have done? What with the reception committee you knew were queueing for second helpings below the bridge wing after consuming Despatov and everything . . . ? Naturally I'd assumed the Professor would hardly have had time to get his *shirt* wet before it got swallowed. With him in it.

Trapp was the first to find voice. '*You're* supposed to be DEAD, you are,' he accused with exceedingly bad grace.

'I do apologize.' The Professor looked appropriately chastened. Then waggled the muzzle of the blunderbuss. 'However, most fortunately for science – albeit sadly for yourselves, gentlemen – I fear I am not.'

'What does 'e mean: fortunate f'r science?' Trapp appealed to the cave's residents in general. 'What's *science* gotter do with anythin'?'

I didn't enlighten him. The merits and demerits of the Brothers Smith's *Phobosuchus* debate were hardly pertinent to the current discussion; and anyway, *I* was more concerned with the 'sadly for us' implication.

'P'raps 'e '*as* turned up his f*$%*&!-ing toes. P'raps he's jus' another spook like yer Grandpa, Captin?' Choker Bligh enthused, obviously having quite recovered his four-letter spirit following the episode with the leeches. 'I ain't never metta f*$%*&!-ing ghost afore.'

'The Captain'll introduce you to a few, Bosun,' I offered faintly. 'Very shortly in fact, if the Professor waves that f*$%*&!-ing gun about much more and it goes off.'

'Oh, you shall know when it is about to, I promise, Chief Officer,' Beedham-Smith assured me most seriously. 'I have given the matter some thought: jotted down a few calculations ... next time, you will observe, I shall assume a triangulated stance commensurate with the even distribution of propellant retroforces imposed by the muzzle velocity.'

Still mad, I confirmed, just to dismiss that faint hope once and for all. *Still definitely mad as a hatter.*

'But what about the crocodiles?' I blurted as he retrieved his torch from Wullie's nerveless grasp, having to stoop awkwardly in the process because Wullie had already lain into action at the first whiff of potential powder and shot. 'How did you get past the crocodiles?'

The Professor really smiled at that. But not so much in the spirit of good fellowship as with a predatory amiability. The sort a cat might display while playing with a cornered mouse. Just before it dismembers it.

'But I *talked* to them of course, Chief Officer. Persuaded them to afford me right of passage in view of the nature of my mission ... an accommodating creature, the crocodile. Once you make it understand that you think as it does.'

'You talked to the . . . ?' Trapp eyed Beedham-Smith with an openly derisive expression. 'You hear THAT, Mister? 'Ow can *any*one be simple enough ter believe 'e c'n *talk* to a crocodile?'

I swallowed: shook my head warningly at him. It worried me: his adopting this attitude before a lunatic holding an elephant gun - particularly one who claimed to mirror the thought processes of an amphibian not exactly noted for its live and let live philosophy ... and especially rich coming from someone perfectly happy to chat *ad nauseam* to a GHOST!

But not even Wullie could resist lifting his head in mid-cringe: fascinated by the hypothesis.

'And whit did the *crockle*diles say, Professor sir?'

'RrrrrrrOUGH!' Beedham-Smith roared unexpectedly, then made a hideous strangled sound. It took me a moment to realize he was laughing.

'Bloody hell!' Trapp muttered, even he shaken by that

mercurial change of mood. 'You could've been right all along, Mister - this one *is* nutty as a fruitcake.'

. . . an' you haven't even read his bloody NOTES yet! I reflected savagely before rounding on him. 'Well, thank you *very* much, Trapp. Not only for your acutely sensitive handling of our current fraught situation so far, but *also* for talking ME squarely in the bloody gunsight as usual.'

'Well 'e *is*,' Trapp defended sullenly; resentful of the slightest criticism. 'There's probably *bats* in this cave not half as batty as . . .'

'. . . caves are a valid point, Professor.' I tried urgently to implement damage control measures: stem the flow of Trapp's suicidal mockery. 'How did you know about this one? We've never let on about the treasure. *He* - this sniggering paranoid here's - always kept Blackbeard's supposed chart a dark secret.'

'Not entirely secret, dear boy,' Beedham-Smith demurred. 'In fact, when I took the liberty of peeking in your chartroom some time ago, I discovered considerable interest being evinced in it already - a quite outrageous breach of your privacy which,' he shrugged reminiscently, nostalgically - *very* worryingly, '. . . which I felt bound to remedy on your behalf.'

'The Chinamen? The Ying Tong duo back in Singers - it was you who parted their cables?'

'I would prefer to describe it as having been a cleanly and expertly conducted vivisection.'

More like a bloody declaration of war on the Yellow Hordes, I thought feelingly.

Trapp must have reached the same conclusion for once. 'The Ying Tongs - d'you reckon they're the ones chasin' us in that ship? Or the ones the Mate 'ere *claims* is chasin' us, at least?'

'Ship? What ship, Captain?' the Professor asked, frowning in perfectly genuine bewilderment: both looking and sounding just like Mister Spew standing watch in a busy shipping lane.

'Doesn't matter,' Trapp dismissed airily, then, always the eternal optimist and careful with it, pointed. 'By the way, if that torch come out o' ship's stores you'll 'ave to pay extra f'r it when we get back aboard.'

Somehow I didn't think the Professor intended us to ever to

205

get back aboard the *Charon*. Not when he shook his great mane of yellowed hair suddenly; gazed absently around the cave as if surprised to find himself in such a place. I could see his eyes were beginning to lose even their soul: slipping from the real world – back, I suspected, into pre-history. He still had, I remembered, a specimen to collect.

'An' then, o' course, there's the fire an' blast damage to me bridge . . .' Trapp drifted off in company; enwrapped by then in *his* own psycho-neurotic preoccupation.

But Beedham-Smith ignored him, which revealed, I had to admit, a quite laudable degree of common sense considering he was mad.

'One final task before we . . . ah - part, Chief Officer?' he encouraged, the dead timbre of his voice belying any bonhomie in the request. 'You will please be so kind as to place the treasure in those splendid canvas bags the Captain has brought along.'

Trapp stared speechlessly.

Almost.

'No, please - yer CAN'T! That's mine - me 'eritage . . . all MINE!' he exploded, abruptly dragged from visions of surcharges into confronting *his* real world of cruel disadvantage, unfulfilled avarice and bad Victorian melodrama.

'You've exhausted *that* particularly excruciating vein of dialogue already,' I retorted unsympathetically, hurriedly starting to shovel about fifteen million quid's worth of artefacts into the equivalent of two pillow cases. 'So why don't you just shut UP, Trapp, and let the Professor get about his extremely important scientific business.'

Trapp watched, ashen faced. ' 'Ow can you bring yerself to *help* 'im, Mister? 'OW can yer *be* such a traitor to me; your bes' friend - the Samaritan wot dragged yer from the gutter . . . ?'

'Because there's a chance we won't get SHOT if I do!' I snarled, panicking.

'In that case *ah'll* gie ye 'a hand as well, Mister Miller, sir,' Wullie offered with an alacrity bordering on outright disloyalty.

'Not a very good chance I fear, Chief Officer,' the Professor qualified, obviously trying to be fair.

'Ah'll stay doon here then,' Wullie decided.

206

'Okay: not a very *good* chance, Trapp – but at least *a* CHANCE,' I panicked, cramming in the last piece of seventeenth-century church plate.

'An' I thought you wus a SCIENTIST!' Trapp turned his spleen on Beedham-Smith. 'I thought you 'ad PRINCIPLES! Educashun . . . a . . . a *research* project? An' now you turns out ter be nothin' but a common THIEF!'

'One with his FINGER on the trigger of your bloody *ELEPHANT* GUN!' I screamed. 'So, as far as I'm concerned, Trapp – that means this distinguished gentleman here can be anythin' he bloody-well LIKES!'

'A thief . . . a thief . . . ? I sir, am a GENIUS!' the Professor finally erupted with a modesty that almost exceeded that of Trapp. 'I, sir, am the Messenger of GOD! *I*, sir, intend to rewrite HISTORY – force those scientific DOTARDS to bow their heads in SHAME . . . ! *I*, sir, wield the *Sword* of TRUTH – carry the burden of my BROTHER with me . . .'

'*Brother?*' Trapp shot off on an even more apopletic tangent now the discussion was broaching upon fundamental shipowning principles. 'You tellin' me you got yer BROTHER 'ere as *well* . . .? Lissen, pal: if *you* sneaked yer BROTHER aboard for the trip I got yer DEAD to rights! An extra *brother* shoulda been declared in the CHARTER PARTY – clause thirty two; sub-para THREE . . . "All passengers – *includin'* relatives – 'AS to be *PAID* FOR . . ."'

'BAUBLES!' the Prof ranted, still pursuing his own course and with the elephant gun beginning to wander unsteadily as a bowsprit in a gale. '*I* care NOTHING for your baubles, Captain! Your damned FRIPPERIES . . . !'

'*FRIPPERIES?*' Trapp screamed, purple-faced with mortification.

'Indeed – FRIPPERIES! And furthermore, I *spurn* your assumption: give not a FIG for your accusation. When marketed appropriately, sir, these trumperies will merely provide FUNDS beyond my brother's wildest *dreams* – funds to equip a major scientific EXPEDITION – TWO expeditions ... TEN EXPEDITIONS if neccessary! The greatest – the most comprehensive – the most *significant* field expeditions EVER MOUNTED in . . .'

'ExCUSE me, but would you mind . . . ?' I yelled, watching the gun hypnotically and thinking he could very easily forget to adopt his triangulated anti-recoil early-warning stance in the heat of the moment.

They *both* swung then, as one.

'An' *YOU* c'n bloody-well keep OUT'VE it f'r a *START,* CHIEF OFFICER . . . !' they bellowed in full-lunged concert.

. . . just as the GROUND – the very base of the cave *itself* – shook beneath our feet!

Well, what can I say? Other than that each and every one of us froze rigid: even the Professor.

No – on reflection . . . especially the Professor!

. . . while little blobs of oozing stuff, and fragments of rock, and trickles of primal earth squelched and clattered and tumbled from above, dislodged from their tenuous centuries-old alliance by some slow-paced vibration outwith.

Whereupon even Trapp stopped complaining: stared instead with bulging eyes towards the dimly filtered light from the entrance to our crypt.

Until even *that* most precious link with the outside world became blocked.

. . . as some monstrous, lumbering object moved to tower before it.

I could feel the temperature drop: the chill of macabre and inexplicable horror descend upon that desolate tomb.

There came a further pounding, scuffling vibration and the sound of branches snapping: of vegetation displacing and threshing without.

And then . . .

'*Hatcheri*?' the Professor whispered with the torch suddenly trembling ecstatically: those underlit, death's-head eyes of his glittering with what was, in truth, a terrible madness. 'Is that indeed YOU, great *Phobosuchus* HATCHERIIIII?'

Trapp opened his mouth: frowned *very* quizzically indeed, then swallowed hard and shut it again.

THUD! whatever was blocking our exit transmitted back . . .

THUD . . . *swish*: THUD . . . *swish* - creak? *THUD*!

. . . while, with each colossal impact the cave shuddered and echoed and more bits fell on top of our nerveless heads - well, on top of Trapp's, Wullie's and *my* nerveless head, anyway; while even Choker Bligh wore the bewildered expression of a man coming to terms with the fact, for the second time that run ashore, that he may 'ave been the wurstest Bosun on the 'igh seas: even pretty good wiv grocklediles - but 'e sure as 'ell wusn't no King in THIS jungle.

The Professor raised his arms in supplication, the gun now angled roofwards. Even if we hadn't been paralysed by the fear of what waited OUTSIDE none of us risked leaping to recover it - one fumbled grab and it would've imitated a smart bomb coming through the entrance should it go off as it fell.

Whichever way it happened to be pointing.

'I am COMING, Gargantua,' Beedham-Smith intoned. 'I am *COMING*, most awesome and perfect of thecodontian species . . .'

He picked up the bags containing the Treasure of The Trapps and began to move towards the entrace as if in a dream . . . or rather, a nightmare. A very private Hell.

'Me *'eritage* . . . !' Trapp started forward with still-black countenance and a considerable lack of originality. 'Me LEGAC- '

'*LEAVE* IT, TRAPP!' I snarled urgently. 'Don't follow him - don't go OUT there!'

The darkness began to close around us as the orb of the torch stumbled away; highlighting the sagging, crumbling tunnel: silhouetting the cadaverous and tortured supplicant.

'You and I TOGETHER, *Phobosuchus* . . .' the demented voice called. 'Nay - you, I and Brother *William* shall CONFRONT the doubters: ascend the podium to *spit* at the gross and facile smirk on the face of ACADEMIA . . .'

The light faded completely from the tunnel. Now only the last will and testament of emeritus Professor Walter Beedham-Smith echoed in the otherwise stunned silence.

'Show me thyne beauty for I am HERE . . .' he intoned. 'Open for me thyne *jaws*, Leviathan - reveal to me thyne teeth which art terrible round ABOUT . . .'

I flicked my Zippo with difficulty. The flickering yellow flame lit three pairs of human eyes clustered round me, and maybe a thousand other hesitantly peering orbs less readily identifiable.

And every last one looked a bit shell-shocked.

'I think', I said shakily, 'the Prof's just about to have his wish granted.'

The roar, when it came, reverberated throughout the cave like a thunderclap - a swelling, full-throated bellow which would have drowned the foghorn of an ocean liner.

The first distant explosion from Trapp's elephant gun came roughly ten seconds later. Followed almost immediately by the discharge of a second cocoa tin of black powder.

After a broadside as scientific as that - always assuming the Professor had remembered to adopt his calculated anti-recoil stance, and *if* his target HAD merely been something as diminutive as an elephant - then little more than four jumbo-sized umbrella stands with smoke wisping from them would've been left standing in an astonished rectangle.

So presumably whatever it *was* out there HAD to have been larger than that. Much larger. Quite possibly encased in some form of Mesozoic armour-plating which was proof against anything with less than the hitting power of . . . well - say an anti-tank missile?

. . . because that was the instant when the *Professor* began to scream.

A vindicated falsetto. Carrying high above the cracking and snapping of tree trunks being felled by some power ram of what might well have been a monstrous and scaly tail.

Gorbals Wullie was propelled gob-eyed from the protection of the cave mouth a good half hour after the last sounds had faded.

We kept shoving him back out for several more minutes, then followed.

It looked as though a bulldozer had moved in to clear the immediate area of jungle. Not a single sago tree or Nipa palm had been left standing within, well - within, say . . . a sixty-foot radius?

All we ever found of the Professor was his slouch hat with the reptile skin band; still with a strand or two of tobacco-stained hair clinging to it - and Trapp's elephant gun. Seemingly guillotined cleanly in half.

As well as a single shredded corner ripped from a seabag.

Nothing else. Not a single Spanish duckit.

'Blackbeard's *legacy*. Me herit-' Trapp started to whisper predictably.

Philosophically I turned for the Bog o' The Bloodsuckin' Leeches and the *Charon*. Neither could offer any terrors greater than those I'd already endured.

'Look at it this way, Trapp,' I consoled over my shoulder. 'If you really want to follow that trail of shattered tree stumps there - on your *own*, by the way - an' you DO catch whatever it was ate the Professor . . . it'll be worth roughly fifteen million quid MORE now than it did when it was just priceless!'

Chapter Thirteen

The mysterious ship ceased to be mysterious only after Trapp had bullied, coaxed and bumped the *Charon* nearly all the way back to the open sea.

We didn't come upon her until we were virtually sniffing salt in the freshening wind: had reached a point roughly ten miles from that chicane-like entrance to the River Beetel itself. She - the other vessel - *did* prove to be Chinese, as I'd always suspected and moreover, being Chinese, her Old Man obviously possessed the commendable patience, as well as the tenacity, of the Oriental.

As well, I reflected darkly, as a degree of caution totally lacking in *another* ship's master not a million miles away.

'Why', he'd plobably thlought, 'lisk my ass chasing Tlapp up liver when I can squat here, play mah jong with the Tong . . . and clut hiss stupid thloat onna way back?'

Anyway . . . we came booting round one of those final tortuous bends at full speed ahead, with everybody aboard beginning to smile at everybody else except Trapp - and sharing a sense of *bonhomie* previously unheard of aboard the *Charon* - excluding Trapp - when . . . ?

Trapp . . . ? Oh yeah - well Trapp still hadn't recovered from his *second* bereavement of the voyage, you see. The shock of watching - or more hearing, really - 'is 'eritage going for the deep six down a prehistoric monster's throat . . . if you really want to believe it WAS a prehistoric monster back there in the Beetel Swamps, that is. Personally I considered the late W and W Smiths' contention fundamentally flawed . . . however that's why Trapp was neither euphoric nor amiable with any of us - not all the way back down: no matter *how* nice me and Gorbals Wullie tried to be with him despite the broad grins of malice we couldn't help displaying no matter HOW hard we tried to conceal them.

He was ever the optimist, though – Trapp. I'll give him that. The very first thing he did when we'd finally clawed our way back to the *Charon* had been to dangle half a dozen crated and protesting sheep outboard from an after derrick, then order Beedham-Smith's harpoon gun loaded and readied. Probably the biggest fishing tackle in the world.

. . . just in case we happened to sight fifteen million quid's worth of hungry super-saurian on the way back.

Anyway, I was saying . . . we were rumbling and chugging round that curve in the river when I suddenly stiffened; gripped the rail in horror as I registered ANOTHER bloody *ship* virtually blocking the main channel maybe seven cables ahead . . .

. . . then began to run for the wheelhouse, waving my arms and screaming 'DOUBLE RING TO FULL ASTERN . . . EMERGENCY FULL ASTERN!'

Mister Spew, who was standing the watch with me, frowned with enormous concentration at the brass engine telegraph, trying to read the segments on it.

'*Which* way is it I put the little 'andle to again, Captin? Ter make us go backwards?' he asked uncertainly.

'The one that says FULL ASTERN f'r Chrisssake – an' *I'm* the MATE by the way!' I shrieked, forgetting he'd only covered *slow* and *half ahead* so far in the correspondence course. '. . . awwww *I'LL* DO IT!'

The repeater clanged frenetically down in the bowels of the ship.

Already the distance between us was now down to six cables – not much more than half a mile.

The engine-room voice pipe spluttered into a plaintive whistle and I wrenched at the little brass stopper.

'WHADDYA *WANT*?'

'You ring-a stoppa the sheep,' Bucalosie complained. 'Amma gonna tell you a-straight Mister Mate – I stoppa dis precision machino now, I maybe never getta it started again!'

'You DON'T stoppa the sheep, Bucalosie, an' five thousand tons of head-on bloody steel onna reciprocal COURSE'll stoppit FOR you!'

'Holy Mother the Blessed Mary we're-a gonna DIE,' the Chief started screaming. 'We're-a alla GONNA DIE . . . !'

Five cables separating us.

'YOU will, an' *that's* f'r certain,' I bellowed pithily. 'Cause I promise – if it's the las' thing I DO, Bucalosie, I'm going to send Spew aft *now* to lock your ENGINEROOM fucking *DOOR* . . !'

Trapp arrived on the bridge at a florid run. 'Wot's all the shouting, Mister? You knows I won't 'ave *shoutin'* on me bridge . . !'

I pointed ahead.

'JESUS!' he shouted.

Four cables . . . Gorbals Wullie arrived panting next.

. . . and a *MACHINEGUN* began firing at us from the other ship.

'Wot wus THAT, I wonder?' Trapp asked, disconcerted by what few wheelhouse windows his bloody elephant gun had left us with suddenly converting to a shower of imploding glass shards.

'S'A MACHINEGUN!' I bawled from beside Wullie.

He stared down at us.

'*What* machinegu– ?'

A diagonal line of holes appeared in the smoke-grimed funnel; six feet of ladder rail blew away, and the starboard lifeboat suddenly collapsed as its forr'ad cradle dissolved into wooden splinters.

'That machinegun,' I said. 'An' *before* you start, Trapp, I suspect it's ex-Chinese Army 7.62 millimetre Type Fifty Seven HMG.'

The *Charon's* engine finally stopped in preparation for running astern, and I breathed a little easier. Except for a niggling concern over my either being shot or getting my throat cut.

'Why's the engine stopped?' Trapp demanded in a typically bellicose tone of voice. ' 'OO's stopped me ENGINE, Mister?'

'I did.'

'*You* did?'

'Yes – I fuckin' DID!'

'I *tried* to did, Captin,' Mister Spew chipped in helpfully, 'but I ain't so good at sortin' out the lickle words on the telegra– '

'Full AHEAD!' Trapp roared. 'Get 'er back up to FULL AHEAD, dammit!'

I scrambled to my knees and stared aghast at the ship ahead. It looked roughly the size of Westminster Cathedral, only much more pointed at the end facing us.

. . . THREE cables now: and closing fast. While *her* bow wave had begun to climb halfway up her stern.

'You absolutely *certain* you know what you're doing, Trapp?' I asked.

'Playing 'im at 'is own game - chicken.'

'Far as I'm concerned he's already WON,' I appealed. '*Please* go hard a port; full astern; and order the boats lowered, Trapp.'

'You may be right,' he mused, unexpectedly conceding my point. 'Maybe I *do* 'ave the wrong attitude. Maybe I shoul'n't be so . . .'

He swung.

'YOU, SPEW - an' *you*, Ord'nary Seaman - get down forr'ad an' man the WHALING GUN . . . an YOU, Mister!'

'Who - me?' I muttered faintly.

That *bloody* expressionless expression was back on Trapp's face. I should've known nobody shot at his property and lived long enough to regret it.

'Take the wheel,' Trapp ordered. 'No half measures. 'We're gonna RAM them bastids *outright*!'

TWO cables . . . four hundred yards - and we were closing like two particularly obdurate dinosaurs with their heads down . . .

The Chinaman was old, too. Maybe five thousand tons gross with a funnel almost as stick-like as the *Charon's* own, but with a bluff bow that looked like it had been designed to smash its way clear through to the Pole and save Antarctic explorers the trouble of walking . . . *far* stronger than ours.

We were *dead* already!

Down forr'ad I could see Gorbals Wullie and Second Officer Spew clambering the ladder to our forecastle and the harpoon gun. As soon as Wullie's head lifted above deck level, and he actually *saw* what was ahead, I could hear him shrieking from the wheelhouse. Helpfully Mister Spew reached back, lifted him by his collar, and planked him firmly behind Mister Foyn's breech with a fist the size of a ham shank.

215

One an' a *half* cables . . .

'Steady, Mister,' Trapp called calmly from the starboard wing. 'Steady as she goes.'

'Don't tell ME – tell my *heart*, Trapp!' I snarled, gripping the spokes and beginning to brace for the now-inevitable collision. *God* but I wished the Professor was back with us at that moment. HE would've been able to calculate to three decimal *places* the most scientifically-efficient stance a chap should take to absorb the impact of five thousand tons of juggernauting steel . . .

'By the way: when we hit, Mister,' Trapp remarked conversationally, 'I don't want yer hangin' back. You climb over on to her foc'slehead along with Choker Bligh an' kick seven shades o' living daylight out o' them Ying Tong machine-gunners . . .'

'When we HIT,' I pointed out tightly, 'I won't *have* to climb aboard – I'll bloody BE aboard! That Chinese job's built like a brick SHITHOUSE, Trapp . . . We'll concertina from our bow back to our bloody ENGINEROOM! You'll be able to argue with HER Old Man on *her* bloody bridge without even havin' to MOVE . . .'

I broke off with my mouth hanging slack.

Stared incredulously over to port.

Closed my eyes tightly: opened one, followed very cautiously by the other . . . and stared *again*?

ONE CABLE left . . . !

'Another SHIP . . . !' I bawled. 'Another *SHIP* fine on the PORT BOW, TRAPP – heading to cross IN BE*TWEEN* us!'

It wasn't possible, of course. The channel wasn't wide enough.

You either steamed up the River Beetel – or *down* the River Beetel. You could NOT steam *ACROSS* the River bloody BEETEL.

No way!

There were mud banks, and mangrove trees stretching broad on either side. But no water. None! Not even enough to float a crocodile . . . and I knew that because I could see *them* too: all three thousand of 'em it seemed. PADDLING!

Not that I spent too long on that still-chilling exercise. No. No, *I* was still gazing shock-eyed at the THIRD vessel – the one over to port: the potential meat in the middle of our ten-thousand-ton Anglo-Chinese sandwich – which was steaming blithely to cross right through the fast-narrowing gap between OUR . . . ?

Hang onna minute, Miller, it suddenly occurred to me. *He's not steaming – he's SAILING! Running hard before the wind under a full press of CANVAS . . .*

. . . which was a *very* odd thing indeed. Considering there WASN'T any wind?

No more than there were *that* many ten-cannon BARQUENTINES in the Papua New Guinea jungle . . . ? And certainly not brigantines cleared for ACTION like that one appeared to be? Not with a hundred-plus ragged, kerchiefed sailors standing ready and lining her bulwarks: grappling irons, muskets, sulphurous stink bombs . . . *cutlasses* in hand?

Not with her decks smeared with butter and strewn with dried peas and tenpenny nails so's an enemy would find great difficulty in sustaining a counter-attack . . . ? No more than with her foreyards slung in chains to prevent them being cut away by . . . by a Chinese *machine*gun? As well as with the powder chests readied on forecastle and poop, and her own nine-pounder swivel guns primed, no doubt, with a savaging recipe of partridge and double chain shot . . . ? While . . .

. . . while – rising above all from that eerie barquentine which sailed without wind, sped without wings – came the measured, funereal beat of a *side drum* calculated to put the fear of the Devil into the hearts of all who heard it APPROACH?

Including, I swear to you – me!

Taptitty, taptitty . . . *Tap* . . . TAP . . . TAP! Tapptitty, taptitty . . . *Tap* . . .

'*Look*, Mister,' Trapp called in a strangled voice, even he diverted from our monstrous suicidal joust. 'Look up at 'er foretop.'

I lifted my fevered eyes and saw the most fearful sight a seaman can ever pray to be spared.

. . . the Black Ensign. The crossed white bones . . . the human SKULL.

217

The pirate flag known as *The Jolly Roger*!

They observed that incredible pirate brig almost dead ahead of them too; our onrushing adversary - so it couldn't have just been a simple stress-induced fantasy: a mirage exclusive to Trapp and me.

I mean, it COULD only have been that which caused the Chinamen to panic. I glimpsed her master out on *his* wing rushing towards his wheelhouse screaming some unintelligible order as the machinegunners on her foc'sle scattered; began racing and tumbling and skidding aft, all babbling and shrieking as if the very Dragon Demons from some particularly exquisite Oriental Hell were risen before them . . .

She began to *swing* then, in panic; her wheel as hard to starboard as her sweat-drenched helmsman could spin it, and the high funnel leaning over as she listed under the press of the turn . . . ten degrees . . . twenty . . . the mud-black river gouting and driving hard against her st'b'd bow as she smashed across, rather than into it . . .

Less than *HALF* A CABLE NOWWWW!

'Bring us EASY to starb'd, Mister,' Trapp shouted. 'Just a *whisker* . . . jus' enough ter . . .'

I HEARD it then - the rip-roaring, rollicking laugh from near enough under our bow. And craned to look down in utter fascination - I *couldn't* have forgone that brief temptation: not even had it been the *Queen Mary* bearing down upon us . . .

He stood there on the barquentine's poop with his wooden leg firmly akimbo from 'is proper leg, and his long black beard streaming in the wind which wasn't blowing: all plaited as I'd seen it once before, with ribbons and so abundant that strings of it were carried back and looped above ears already heavy with golden rings . . .

I blinked: swallowed - as I'd *also* done once before - while taking in the wide-brimmed tricorn hat; the powdered wig; the long, silver-embroidered frock coat with Belgian lace cuffs circumnavigated by the broad leather belt a-sag with powder horn and flintlock pistol; boarding axe; silver hafted dagger . . . and, of course - pirate-issue cutlass.

218

'*Grandpa* ..!' Trapp breathed ecstatically. 'It's Grandpa *Blackbeard*, Mister. Come ter *save* us from the Chinee hordes ..!'

. . . who'd begun to pass close alongside but clear of us by that time, incidentally; still swinging diagonally and now uncontrollably across the channel: heading straight for a nest of suddenly very apprehensive crocodiles who only stood up to their *knees* in water . . .

I watched hypnotized as she struck; ran monstrously aground with the forefoot tearing out of her on the antediluvial bedrock below the mud, and with her mast collapsing and crashing forward and the spindle funnel toppling in a massive spurt of rust and smoke: crushing down on her bridge and upon that most tenacious Chinese master mariner who had coped with every devious ploy of Trapp's, but couldn't quite cope with taking on his whole family . . .

It was unlikely the Ying Tong tong would find their way back to Singapore to persist in their vendetta. Compared to the crocodiles of the Beetel, they were amateurs when it came to ganging up on people.

'Good VOYAGIN', Edward lad,' the Apparition bellowed. 'Loverly chats we 'ad. Thoroughly enjoyed it, but I gotter date with a barrel o' tar anna 'ANGman – I'll give yer love ter Great-great-great-great-wotever she is Grandma Emma ..!'

Trapp lifted a reluctant hand. There really *were* tears in his eyes then. Real tears . . . not crocodile tears at all.

'G'bye,' he whispered. 'Goodbye Great-great-great ..!'

'A PARTIN' *BROADSIDE*, lads!' the voice of Blackbeard Trapp hollered for the very last time on this earth. 'Naught but blood an' BRAINS in their scuppers will we leave them Chinee 'eathens wi', me hearties. Drub the dogs: drub 'em within an inch o' their 'eathen lives – then Edward Teach *Trapp*, the wurstest PYRATE there ever wus, will take even *that* last inch an' SWALLOW IT 'OLE . . .

'. . .FIIIIIRE!'

Yet there *was* no sound apart from that terrifying, muffled percussion from the funeral drum. Only a great spurt of silent gunpowder smoke from every cannon and swivel aboard . . .

219

And, when it cleared: when the last drum beat had faded –
Blackbeard Trapp had gone. Dematerialized, I suppose: along
with his pyrate ship and his pyrate crew . . . faded back through
the mists of time.

And the only sound, on the *Charon's* bridge, was the sound
of Edward Trapp Present – *my* Trapp – gently sobbing.

That . . . and the by-then liquid squelch of his ball of cotton
waste.

Epilogue

Of course, Gorbals Wullie nearly screwed everything at the very last minute.

Well, you might have guessed, where Trapp's voyages were concerned, that nothing tended to run smoothly.

Just as the Chinaman had been brought to thunderous rest on the banks of the River Beetel, and *we* were free and clear to continue seawards ... *Wullie* had swung the harpoon gun screaming with excitement, yelling, 'See ME, Captin? They yellow lads is RUBBISH ... Jist wan look at *me* here wi' this weapon an' they panicked - all they Triads is the same, eh? Scared o' a REEL Tiger, so they are!'

'Don't *pull* the TRIGG ... !'

I pleaded.

Wullie *pulled* the bloody trigger.

Mister Svend Foyn's invention exploded with a force reminiscent to, and almost equalling, that of Trapp's own late elephant gun ... whereupon the harpoon described an immaculate trajectory to strike the already vanquished vessel dead centre below her already flattened bridge.

Into which - because of the massive steel barbs - it became firmly and irretrievably interlocked.

Which would've been fine - a little unnecessary and cowardly-spiteful on Wullie's part, maybe ... but excusable in the heat of the action.

Except that WULLIE had *forgotten* there ALSO happened to be a nylon rope attached to it. Strong enough to tow a bloody WHALE!

The rope slammed taut ... began to haul the *Charon's* bow round and off course, what with the speed we'd built up to and everything. TRAPP stopped crying and began ranting again ...

I spun the wheel feverishly, trying to correct the swing towards the mud, pray, and remember where my lifejacket was all at the same time.

. . . until I remembered I wouldn't need it because I'd be able to WALK ashore to meet all the Ying Tongs who'd temporarily survived *their* little bit of bother. So long as the *crocodiles* didn't mind.

The rope finally parted.

Helped a little, I admit, by Trapp, who'd taken off for the foc'slhead at a brisk pace to express his disapproval of Wullie, but missed him with the fire axe and severed the rope instead of *Wullie's* stupid HEAD . . .

We docked in Darwin eventually. Flat broke as usual, and with nobody speaking to anybody.

Especially not to Wullie.

As usual.

After packing my seabag I'd climbed to the bridge for one last nostalgic visit. Trapp was leaning over something on the chartroom table, frowning.

'I'm going, Trapp,' I said.

'Right,' Trapp muttered, preoccupied.

I craned to see what he was doing. It was a drawing; just a preliminary scrawl really, already spattered with ink blots and liberally smeared with mint sauce. It looked like a large wooden barrel bound with metal bands with a porthole to see out of, and two other holes fitted with rubber-armed glove-like things so that a man sealed inside it could reach through to the outside if he wanted to, and . . . I dunno - *lift* something, say?

Trapp had sketched what might have been an air line leading into the top of the barrel. And a basic bellows contraption - for use, presumably, above the surface.

There was also a large lead weight underneath it. Large enough to overcome any residual buoyancy problem . . . ?

I remembered the gold - Bormann's gold - was still in the sunken Cessna in the Beetel Swamps, then shook my head deprecatingly. No - no, not even *Trapp* could be considering going back to THAT hellish place . . . ?

Come to that, *Phobosuchus hatcheri* was still out there somewhere: maybe even guarding *it* now, seeing it had run short of pyrate treasure.

. . . or what some may have *imagined* was *Phobosuchus*, anyway? Probably the same impressionable sort of person who might have persuaded themselves it was a ghost that saved us from collision.

Quite ridiculous, of course. That para-miraculous deliverance had mostly been due to my skills as a helmsman – assisted to some small and inexplicable degree, I must concede, by an Oriental shipmaster's last-moment loss of face . . . but then – don't dreadful spectres dwell in the mind of every man? Only rising to confront him when the strain becomes unbearable?

Then Trapp grunted, ' 'Ow *big* d'you reckon Second Officer Spew is, Mister?'

'About the size of your barrel thing, I'd guess,' I hazarded. 'Or to put it another way – just about the maximum size that would fit into a Cessna aircraft fuselage?'

He was *supposed* to have laughed at that. Or even told me not ter be silly. But he didn't. He just nodded in satisfaction and studied his plan for the Trapp Mark One Swamp Diving Bell again.

'This'll be about right then,' he said.

Very, *very* thoughtfully . . .

He never even lifted his head as I quietly allowed the chartroom curtain to close behind me.

I stood on the wharf and took one last, curiously lingering look at the ancient *Charon*. She had been mine, once. Now she was very firmly Trapp's. She'd even survived a whole voyage with him, which made her kind of unique.

There was no sign of anyone aboard. Most of them were concealed from view down aft, debating how best to recover Mister Spew who'd fallen overboard again; this time because he'd forgotten which side o' the ship the jetty wus.

I sniffed; felt terribly lonely suddenly. Then swung my seabag over my shoulder and began to head with strangely reluctant steps for the dock gate.

223

'*Mister*?'

I whirled . . . Trapp leaned out over the inboard bridge wing looking down at me. Gorbals Wullie was beside him; the sticking plaster on his wizened ratlike face crinkled into a sad expression. More articulate than any well-schooled accent, it was Wullie's way of saying 'farewell'.

'Maybe I'll drop yer a line sometime?' Trapp said.

Then smiled. A really nice, *really* lovable smile.

I shook my head, and called, 'No, Trapp. Never *again* . . . *NO CHANCE!*'

Then quickly walked away before my tears blurred an enduring memory of those two raggle-taggle figures slouched so close together. So *very* close together.

Maybe for ever and ever. Maybe even until the very end of Time itself.

. . . *if* you believe in ghosts?